"The body had been dismantled rather than dismembered. All of the fingers and toes were separated from the limbs, which had in turn been severed from the torso. The head had been removed as well. It stood on a flat rock with its ears, eyeballs, tongue, and teeth laid out neatly in a circle around it. The fingers and toes were arranged around the base of the stone, each one propped up against it to that they pointed to the sky. The torso was intact, sort of; the ribs had been caved in and most were broken. The internal organs had all been pulled out and were drying in the sun and the man's clothing had been shredded. Sharpton and Riley had been forced to approach on foot; their horses would not come near the body."

From "The Incorruptible"

Managansett Press

Don D'Ammassa is the author of:

Horror
Blood Beast
Servant of Chaos
Caverns of Chaos *
Wings over Manhattan
The Gargoyle
That Way Madness LiesΔ
Little EvilsΔ
Passing Death*
Date with the Dark*

Science Fiction
Scarab
Haven
Narcissus
Translation Station
The Sinking IslandΔ

Mysteries
Murder in Silverplate
Dead of Winter
Death at the Art Gallery

Fantasy
The KaleidoscopeΔ
Elaborate Lies*

Nonfiction
The Encyclopedia of Science Fiction
The Encyclopedia of Fantasy and Horror
The Encyclopedia of Adventure Fiction

*forthcoming from Managansett Press
Δpublished by Managansett Press

PASSING
DEATH

Don
D'Ammassa

Managansett Press

"Bad Feelings" first appeared in *Horrors: 365 Scary Stories*, 1998
"The Chindi" first appeared in *Horrors: 365 Scary Stories*, 1998
"Cleansing Agent" first appeared in *Deathport,*, 1993
"Immortal Muse" first appeared in *Horrors: 365 Scary Stories*, 1998
"The Incorruptible" first appeared in *Showdown at Midnight*, 2011
"Military Deferment" first appeared in *Warfear*, 2002
"A Noteworthy Affair" first appeared in *Space & Time*, 1994
"Passing Death" first appeared in *Deathrealm 18*, 1993
"Remnants" first appeared in *Night Terrors*, 1997
"Salt of the Earth" first appeared in *Weird Trails*, 2002
"Scylla and Charybdis" first appeared in *In the Shadow of the Gargoyle,* 1998
"Sneak Thief" first appeared in *Tomorrow*, 1996
All other stories appear for the first time in this volume.

Managansett Press First Edition 2015

PASSING
DEATH

CONTENTS

Passing Death	7
Scylla and Charybdis	26
Bad Feeling	41
Time Trick	43
Remnants	57
The Incorruptible	73
Line Edits	84
Pale Lake	98
The Chindi	121
Cleansing Agent	124
Sneak Thief	136
Raggedy	149
Salt of the Earth	156
A Noteworthy Affair	170
Tainted Lives	184
Immortal Muse	198
Military Deferment	201

PASSING DEATH

"Why do I always get the looney tunes?" Detective Al Sparfa returned to the squad room after ushering out a self alleged serial killer, his third of the week.

"They sense a kindred spirit," suggested Dana Wilcox, the only female officer in the room. Or on the force, for that matter.

Ben Dardenian looked up from his desk, his face a mask of innocence. "Is that why you always end up with the prostitutes?"   Dana replied with a glare.

"It's spooky though," Sparfa spoke to the office at large, although no one except Dana appeared to be listening. "Most of them are obviously just looking for attention, but there've been a few lately who don't fit the pattern. Stable types, solid citizens. We investigate, and there's never a body, a witness, or any physical evidence. The best I can do is to recommend a psychiatric examination or charge them with filing a false police report." He shook his head. "It's almost as though the delusion was contagious."

Dana shrugged. "It's hot. People are bored and uncomfortable. Swarovsky had one just the other day; woman insisted she'd pushed an annoying man in front of a train. No witnesses, no body, no physical evidence. Released to her husband, but she looked really weird going out, like she couldn't believe we were letting her go."

Sparfa nodded. "That's what I mean. Not the right type at all. I've had a goddamned biker who swears he beat someone to death with a wrench, a sweet little old lady who claims to have run down the man who trashed her garden, and now a college professor insisting he went after some redneck with a brick." "And no bodies or any other convincing evidence."

Sparfa slid into his chair and dropped a file folder onto his desk. "One dirty wrench with no bloodstains, big dents on a Volkswagen, a garden pretty well ripped up, and a few loose bricks. No bodies, though. And no witnesses to the actual crimes, if that's what they were, other than a closemouthed bartender who admits that maybe he did see the biker arguing with somebody, but it was a busy night, you know, and people are always arguing about something or another. The usual bullshit."

"Sounds pretty bogus to me."

"That it is. As if we didn't have enough work to do, we have to hold the hands of a bunch of neurotics with delusions of nastiness." He slammed both palms down flat on his desk and levered himself to his feet. "And on that note, I'm going home, and I'll be back in a week."

Dana raised an eyebrow.

"Back vacation. Take it or lose it, the Captain said, so off I go. Won't even watch a frigging cop show while I'm out either."

"We'll save you the juicy cases."

"Up yours, Wilcox."

"Hey, it'll all go away when the heat breaks. It always does."

"Maybe."

The hot spell passed two days later, and continued cool, but when Sparfa returned to work the following week, Dana's eyes were troubled.

"Welcome back to the insane asylum. While you were out, Ben and I ended up dealing with the nut cases. We'll both be happy to hand them back."

Sparfa rolled his eyes dramatically and crossed to the coffee machine, poured himself a cup. "I'd be perfectly willing to share."

"No thanks, but you really do have my sympathy. Captain DiFilippo told us he likes to give the obvious nuts to you because you have a good bedside manner."

"I missed my calling, I guess."

"You were right about things getting really weird lately." Her voice was suddenly more serious. "I had two teenage girls come in Tuesday insisting some man they'd never seen before accosted them inside Swan Point Cemetery. Their story was he didn't touch them, but used abusive language and kept harassing them even when they tried to leave. Supposedly he tripped over a gravestone and they took advantage of the situation to kick him a few times, at first just so they'd have time to run off. When he didn't get up, they just kept on kicking him and by the time they stopped, he wasn't breathing anymore."

"But no body, right?"

Dana nodded. "I'm pretty sure the girls were only in the cemetery to smoke some grass. They claim they were sightseeing, but it was after dark, and they kept contradicting each other. I figure they did run into some lowlife and they probably did kick him a few times while he was down, but that's as far as it went. They really thought they'd killed somebody; one of 'em was shaking so bad, I thought she was going to pass out or throw up right in the interview room."

He nodded. "My sweet little old lady the other day was the same way, and so was the biker, of all people. Had to put his head between his knees to keep from fainting."

"Ben's was even worse."

Al raised an eyebrow. He was surprised to see that Dana was actively uncomfortable, could not maintain eye contact. Her left hand, which now held a coffee cup, was trembling.

"I had to come in and help toward the end. It got pretty intense here yesterday."

She fell silent, as though reluctant to continue, but finally shook her head.   "A young woman, mid-twenties, named Slaughter of all things, comes into the station yesterday just before lunch. Tells the desk sergeant she wants to report a murder; real cool, no hysteria or anything. I'm out of the building getting sandwiches so they give her to Ben right away. They're together when I come back, but I didn't know what was going on until she started screaming."

Dana's voice was uncharacteristically tense.

"She told Ben she was in her house, sorting the laundry, when this guy walks in. Middle aged, good looking, well dressed. She starts to ask him what the hell he's doing there when he pulls this big knife on her and she runs out to the kitchen, looking for something to defend herself with. But he's too fast, catches her, throws her down onto the floor. She's all set to scream when he apologizes and hands her the knife and tells her to stab him. She almost does it too, but then starts to get up instead, figuring she can make it out the door and over to a neighbor in a few seconds."

"But the intruder won't have that. He grabs her arm and says she's either got to kill him or he'll rape her. Mrs. Slaughter weighs maybe a hundred pounds fully clothed, soaking wet, and pregnant, so she's no match physically for the guy. She says she tried to talk him down, but he got impatient, started ripping off her clothes, until she finally struck out with the knife and cut his arm. It gets weirder after that. Read the report if you want all the gory, and I do mean gory, details, but what it amounts to is that no matter how much damage she did to him, he just kept after her so she had to do more. When he finally stopped moving, according to her, the kitchen and adjoining hall were coated with blood, and she was soaked with it from head to foot. She drops the knife next to what's left of the body, goes up to her room, showers, changes clothing, then calls us."

"Let me guess. No body?"

Dana nodded. "There's a nice shiny knife on the kitchen floor, doesn't match anything in her knife rack, but the blade is clean and so is the floor. Mrs. Slaughter is icy calm and insists on being brought down to the station, and she stays calm even when she must have known Ben didn't believe her. But then she opens her purse and pulls out this big wad of clothing that she says are soaked with the man's blood, except they're clean too, and when she sees that, she throws the worse case of hysterics you ever saw."

Al reached out and tapped Dana's knee. "We all get shaken up once in a while on this job, kid. It gets to you no matter how much you try to hold it back."

Dana shook her head. "You don't understand, Al." She bit her lip. "I live two houses away from Karen Slaughter. She's a nice, well balanced, completely down to earth person, not prone to hysterics." She shifted on the seat, but her voice grew suddenly stronger. "Al, I believe what she said. I can't say that to anyone else around here but you. I think she really did kill someone yesterday."

Al Sparfa was very fond of Dana Wilcox. If he had not already been quite happily married when she moved to Providence from Boston, his entire life might have gone off in a very different direction. The fact that he had accepted her as an equal even before she had proven herself a capable investigator had been the first link in a strong but relaxed friendship that had continued ever since.

It bothered him greatly to think that she might be on the verge of some sort of nervous collapse.

Out of a sense of loyalty, he surreptitiously examined Dardenian's report on the Slaughter woman. He'd been thorough. Despite the fact that there was no real evidence that a crime had been committed, he had a team of technicians go over the kitchen and hall in detail, searching for traces of blood. He'd checked with neighbors and attempted to trace the knife, which bore the fingerprints of Karen Slaughter and no one else. The clothing she'd bundled into her purse was indeed torn in several places, but there were no traces of blood there either.

Karen Slaughter was a divorcee, so they'd released her into the custody of her parents, who lived just outside the city, after they promised to seek medical help for their daughter. As far as the department was concerned, the case was closed; indeed, it had never really been a case in the first place.

There was one thing in Dardenian's report that struck a familiar chord, however. Buried in the transcription of Slaughter's tape recorded "confession" was a description of the man who had attacked her, and whom she had in turn "killed". He was a fairly nondescript man in his late thirties, average build, dark hair but with a receding hairline, less than six feet tall, fair skin, wearing grey slacks and a white pin-striped shirt.

Sparfa pulled his own files on the three similar cases he'd handled personally. The biker described his victim as a "straight dude, white shirt, losin' his hair." The sweet old lady had run down a "youngish fellow, dressed nice, fancy white shirt with little lines of blue running through it." According to the physics professor, the man he'd encountered had been "my age, a business type I'd guess, except he didn't have a jacket or necktie. Combed his hair forward to hide where he was going bald..."

Next he retrieved copies of Dana's report on the teenage girls and Swarovsky's case. Neither of the teens had noticed what the man was wearing, but both described him as an older man, "not a bum", wearing respectable clothes. One of them thought he was bald. The woman who insisted to Paul Swarovsky that she had succumbed to a momentary rage and pushed a man in front of a train described him as "fortyish, not much hair, not bad looking but nothing special". He'd been wearing dark pants and a pinstriped dress shirt.

It could still be a coincidence. The descriptions did not tally exactly, although they were closer than he would have expected from the same group of people even describing a shared experience let alone several individual ones. He glanced up at the clock, noted that it was five minutes shy of the time he normally called it a day, and sighed heavily before dialing his home telephone number. Two minutes later, he started to reread each of the case files in more detail.

There were other similarities. All of the incidents took place on the East Side of Providence, the area that extended from the banks of the Providence River up through the Brown University and School of Design campuses, including the historical district, the wealthier residential areas, all the way to Swan Point Cemetery on the banks of the Seekonk River. The earliest incident was at three in the afternoon (Karen Slaughter), the latest at ten in the evening (the biker). In each case, the confessing "murderer" insisted that they had been provoked by some outrageous activity on the part of their victim, and that they had reacted with blind anger and violence totally inconsistent with their personal histories. In none of the incidents had they ever seen the man before, and there were never any witnesses.

It was dark outside by the time he finished the last folder and flipped it shut. Sparfa turned his head to look out through the room's only outside window as the lights of Providence sparkled in the ever deepening darkness. It was another half hour before he rose and went home for the night.

During the next two weeks, he conducted a low key and definitely unofficial investigation. He spoke to friends on the police force of neighboring communities, and while he learned of two bogus murder confessions (one in Cumberland, one in Managansett), neither fit the same pattern as those in which he was interested. Dana never mentioned the incidents again, and neither did Sparfa, but he noticed that she was unusually withdrawn for several days, then gradually returned to normal.

He began to worry that he was becoming obsessed over a series of coincidences, but it was like a sore tooth he could not stop probing. Any report of criminal activity from the East Side aroused his interest, and when he could find an excuse to do so, he drove slowly through the area, or parked his car and walked through the Brown campus, down the neighborhood streets near Blackstone Boulevard, or among the neatly maintained monuments of Swan Point Cemetery. He began to spend more and more of his free time there as well, so much in fact that his wife asked if he was having an affair.

Although he saw individuals who fit the general description of the murder "victims" on several occasions, they all seemed perfectly ordinary, acting in predictable, even boring ways. The only violent act he witnessed was a shoving match at a bus stop that ended almost as quickly as it began.

On Tuesday of the third week, another unsubstantiated murder confession was called in, but this time the police could not interview the self styled murderer. Miki Korashi, a Japanese exchange student majoring in landscape architecture at the Rhode Island School of Design, called 911 and calmly told the officer on duty that he'd been arguing with an older man about Japanese investment in American property, that they had both been drinking heavily, and that when he had tried to break things off and return to his apartment, the other man had followed and tried to force his way inside.

A struggle had ensued as Korashi attempted to repel the intruder, a bottle of vodka had been smashed, the man's jugular subsequently cut by the jagged edge. Korashi had thoughtfully pulled the body inside the door to avoid alarming the neighbors and promptly called the police.

When they arrived, Korashi had written down the same story almost word for word before cutting his own throat. He was found lying beside his desk in a pool of blood, his own blood. There was no evidence that anyone else had been present, and none of his neighbors had heard any disturbance.

Two weeks passed quietly, so quietly that Sparfa wondered if the phenomenon was over, or if the most recent "killers" just weren't bothering to report their crimes to the police. He spent an increasing amount of time on the East Side, both on duty and off, and although his colleagues on the force didn't appear to notice his continuing obsession, the same was not true of his wife, Colleen. They began to quarrel almost daily about the amount of time he was spending away from home, and although on several of those occasions he promised to work fewer hours, there was never any measurable change in his behavior. Sparfa could not explain, not even to himself, just why the chain of probably unrelated events was so fascinating, but he had a growing conviction not only that they were related, but that they were important to him personally.

During a particularly bitter fight, Colleen flew into a rage and told him she'd been seeing another man. Sparfa didn't know if it was true, or if she was simply lying in order to hurt him, but it didn't seem to matter. He left the house without another word, intent upon getting as drunk as possible as quickly as possible.

It was force of habit that brought him to the East Side, where he parked three blocks from Algy's Zen Pub.

Although Sparfa often drank socially, he was a fanatic about self control, always chose beer or wine, nursed each drink through several rounds. But this time he was reacting to blind anger and a sense of loss.

Through some transitional process that he never afterwards remembered, he joined three other men as they made their way systematically up and down Thayer and Hope Streets, visiting each and every bar and club along the route. A large portion of the evening was lost in some dark alley of his memory and never did emerge, although he would attempt to dredge up those recollections many times in subsequent years.

He did, however, remember the way it all ended.

The unaccustomed excess of alcohol finally wrought its revenge and he vomited painfully into the shrubbery surrounding a private school. The purging of his system left him, if not sober, at least aware of his surroundings and his situation.

"You sure screwed up good this time, Al old boy," he told himself, carefully sitting on the cement retaining wall.

"Everybody's entitled to a lapse now and then." It was a man's voice, from the darkness near at hand. Sparfa vaguely recognized it as that of one of his recent companions.

"Tell that to my wife." He pressed one hand over each ear, trying to hold his suddenly throbbing head together.

A figure emerged from the shadows, sat down on the concrete wall a meter of so away. "Woman trouble, huh?"

"She sinks...thinks...I've been having an affair. My wife does."

"They're all alike, the bitches. They get their hooks into you and once you're married, they do everything they can to humiliate you from then on."

His present domestic problems notwithstanding, Al Sparfa remained deeply in love with his wife, and the urge to defend her emerged even from within a haze of alcohol. "She's not like that. My wife's a good person. She just doesn't understand..."

But his companion ignored him, his voice gradually rising in volume and passion.

"Every time you say something to another woman, they're ready to cut off your balls, and if they don't catch you doing something wrong, they make it up. There's not a one of them worth the rope it would take to hang 'em."

Sparfa was increasingly uncomfortable with the tenor of the other man's remarks, and he felt too lousy to be patient or tolerant. "Look, that's not the way it is."

Once more he was ignored. "That holier than thou attitude of theirs is a load of crap. While we're slaving away at work, they're home getting bored, trying to figure some way to get another unsuspecting guy between their legs. And then they have the nerve to accuse us of screwing around." The man made a disgusted sound and spat on the sidewalk. "The only way to deal with them is to understand them. When my wife walked out on me coupla years back, I learned my lesson. Now I do 'em where I find 'em and move on, never let them get their hooks into me."

The voice was shrill and pedantic at the same time, an annoying sound that made Sparfa's head hurt even worse than it already did. He felt a surge of anger, no, fury, recognized it as an amalgam of frustrations, his wife's refusal to believe in his fidelity, the ineffectiveness of his investigation, the recent loss of a chance at promotion. He told himself to get up and move away, but when he attempted to rise, his legs were so unsteady that he plopped back down immediately.

His companion had not missed a beat. "I could tell you stories, my friend. There's a minister's wife in Central Falls who made it with me on a pew in her husband's church. I screwed a superior court judge's wife in her swimming pool while her husband was taking a nap in the bedroom. I've made it in the bedrooms of doctors, lawyers, politicians, businessmen, and policemen. They're the worst of all, the ones married to cops; their husbands work long hours and they get bored all the time. There's one bitch right here in the city I've been seeing just lately who screws like a mink, all the time telling me how her husband's not man enough for her."

Sparfa felt a flame ignite inside his head, was already turning toward the other man as the last, damnable words came forth.

"Yeah, that Colleen is one of the best I ever made it with. But I'll bet she keeps her husband's balls in a locket some place."

That was when Al Sparfa drew his service revolver and fired it. Twice. The first caught the man in the forehead, knocking him backwards. The second penetrated the underside of his chin, the slug emerging from the top of the skull. He was a better shot drunk than sober.

It was while he was standing over the cooling body, shocked realization of what he'd done rapidly dissipating the alcoholic haze, that Sparfa noticed that the man he had killed wore a pinstriped shirt and grey slacks, was middle-aged and slightly balding.

He had surprisingly little difficulty moving the body to his car, which was fortuitously parked only four blocks away. It was eleven o'clock, most of the streetlights in the area were out, the man's body was surprisingly light, and he only saw two other people during the next fifteen minutes, a pair of college students too intent upon each other to pay much attention to two drunken men staggering along the opposite side of the street.

Sparfa took route 195 headed east, exited once he was across the border into Massachusetts, then followed a series of almost random turns that brought him deep into farm country, along a deserted section of lightly wooded grasslands.

He doused the lights and drove off the road into a fallow field, behind a row of trees. Then he waited.

The body propped up in his front seat continued to cool until it was approximately the temperature of the night air. Sparfa sat there silently, moving once every fifteen minutes to briefly examine the corpse. At three o'clock, its temperature started to go back up and the bloodstains began receding from his clothing. The dead man's chest began to rise and fall a few minutes before five, and the heart started beating again exactly on the hour. Somewhere along the way, the horrible disfiguration of the head had slowly begun to heal, but it was too dark for Sparfa to notice any of the details, and by then he was dozing off for brief periods, so he never saw exactly how this was accomplished. The face was nondescript, but only slightly resembled the man he had shot the night before.

The sun rose at 5:32 AM, and so did the man's eyelids.

"Good morning." Sparfa felt as though he'd been drinking drain cleaner all night. "I don't suppose you'd mind telling me what exactly is going on here?"

The look of confusion in the other man's eyes was clearly genuine. "I don't understand. Where are we? Who are you?"

Sparfa withdrew his wallet and flipped it open, revealing his badge. "I'm a police officer. Now how about filling me in?"

"Fill you in? What do you want to know?"

"First of all, just who exactly are you?"

"Why I'm..." The look of confusion suddenly grew much more intense. "Why, I don't know. I can't seem to remember..."

"Let's see your wallet." Sparfa felt a flash of annoyance, but not, happily, the intense emotion of the previous evening.

As it happened, the man carried no wallet or any other means of identification. In fact, his pockets were empty, there were no tags on his clothing, not even brand labels, and his insistence that he had absolutely no memory of anything prior to his awakening seemed to be genuine.

Abruptly, Sparfa reached across, grabbed one of the man's hands, raised it to eye level. The tips of the fingers were a simple, undistinguished surface. No fingerprints.

"What are you?"

The expression remained one of complete disorientation, but this time Sparfa thought he spotted a darker intelligence moving within the eyes, rippling through the muscles of the face.

"Why, I'm a man, of course." The sun was fully revealed just above the horizon now, hot rays striking the car. With the coming of daylight, he...or perhaps it...seemed to grow more confident. "Am I under arrest, officer?"

Sparfa shook his head. "You're not a human being; I can't arrest you."

Now the man thing smiled and for the first time, a cool, cautious intelligence seemed to be revealing itself. "Well, if you can't arrest me, I think it's time for me to be going. Thanks for an entertaining evening." The passenger side door opened.

Without haste, Sparfa drew his revolver. "What happens if I shoot you now, knowing what you are?"

In the act of rising from the seat, the man thing turned to face him. "Why, I don't actually know."

Sparfa managed to put three bullets into its chest before the body tumbled out of the car.

He opened his own door and stepped out. His head still felt horrible, his stomach was filled with acid, and his legs trembled beneath the weight they were called upon to support. Unsteadily, he walked around to examine the thing he had shot.

The body was still recognizable, but only because of the clothing. His earlier shots to the head had returned, along with a host of other wounds, as though the man had been stabbed, struck by heavy stones, pierced by knives, run down by automobiles, and thrown in front of a train. Already, the shape of the corpse was growing blurry around the edges, less opaque, even the clothing fading, dissolving into the flesh it covered, and within a few short minutes, it had disappeared completely.

Al Sparfa stood motionless in the field for almost half an hour before returning to his car and driving home.

He shaved and showered, was pleasantly surprised to discover Colleen making breakfast, apparently prepared to try to work out their problems. She didn't even blink when he told her he was going into work early.

An hour after he showed up, Sparfa was called to the interview room to conduct the interrogation of a murder suspect. Captain DiFilippo met him just outside the door.

"What's up, Captain?"

DiFilippo made a rude sound. "Probably another psycho. Claims he committed a rape murder last night, buried the body, but couldn't live with it and decided to turn himself in."

Sparfa sighed. "Who's the victim?"

"Well, that remains to be seen." The Captain scratched his head. "We sent a team out to where he said he'd buried her, and someone sure had dug a deep hole and filled it in." Sparfa suddenly realized he knew what was coming next, and that he didn't want to hear it. But the Captain said it anyway.

"The thing of it is, there was no body in the hole, we have no reports of anybody missing, and there's no evidence that a crime took place at all. I think he's just another nut case, but he seems so rational, you know?"

He did know.

SCYLLA AND CHARYBDIS

Kim defied her parents for the very first time when they told her to stay away from Scylla and Charybdis. She'd noticed the two gargoyles on her way home from school one day, was convinced she'd learned rather than invented their names, and chose the two as her very best friends. Charybdis was a bat winged lion with a blocky head, muscular body, and perpetual frown; Scylla had a vaguely human torso with twisted limbs curled up within the shelter of his wings, fingers and toes unnaturally long. They would not have looked out of place in a painting by Bosch, but Kim didn't think they were scary at all.

She was nine years old, a precocious reader, invariably polite, friendly, and well behaved. Her parents sensibly allowed her as much freedom as seemed safe, and their present stance was disconcerting.

"But why can't I go see them?" She wasn't angry, even now, just puzzled. "I wasn't hurting anything."

The older Turners fumbled for an explanation. "They belong to Mrs. Trent, Kim." Her mother was always the first to answer difficult questions. "It's her house and she doesn't want kids playing there."

"But I wasn't playing. I was just sitting."

"It doesn't matter what you were doing, Kim. She has a perfect right to tell you to stay off her property."

Although she'd wanted to argue the matter further, Kim had already worked out the dynamics of her family. If she persisted, she could only make things worse.

"Okay, I won't bother her anymore."

For a second, her mother's eyes clouded, as though she sensed the duplicity, but her father was anxious for a quick, painless resolution.

"That's all we ask, Kim."

Later that same day, she confirmed her resistance to the new limit on her freedom of action.

"I'm going to Perry's." Her voice was casual but her eyes

were wary.

Audrey Turner glanced out the front window. "It's starting to get late," she said doubtfully.

"It's only a few blocks. I'll be back before it gets really dark."

"Could you pick up a bag of chips, kiddo?" Her father fumbled for his wallet, pulled out some bills. "Get yourself an ice cream or something. Audrey, you want anything?"

"No...I guess not."

Strictly speaking, Sheffield House, owned by Mrs. Trent for the past ten years, was not on the way to Perry's Convenience Store. But Kim detoured through an empty lot onto Main Street and slowed cautiously as she approached the oversized brick and stone building. The only light was in the back kitchen.

Kim stopped at the gate.

Scylla and Charybdis flanked the front steps. Although they were clearly conceived of as a set, there were subtle differences. Scylla's eyes were mere slits, intense, staring as though directly into the heart, while Charybdis surveyed broader horizons, eyes wide and all seeing. Scylla had sharper tusks and claws, but Charybdis boasted thicker muscles. Kim favored Scylla, whom she thought of as friend and protector, and for his sake she tolerated Charybdis, whose rage seemed all encompassing.

"They're monsters," Billy Gale insisted. "My dad says they killed a man once. Tore him up and ate his heart."

Not true, according to her father. "They told that same story when I was a kid. A workman did get killed while they were uncrating the statues; one of them fell over and crushed him. It was just an accident."

"You wouldn't hurt me," she whispered into the growing darkness. "I know you wouldn't."

And for the next four years, she visited the two gargoyles clandestinely, usually in the early evening, sometimes during the day when she was sure Mrs. Trent was out shopping or visiting one of the neighbors. With a quite unchildlike tenacity, Kim studied the woman's habits, learned how to predict her movements. The elderly woman never had reason to complain about her trespassing, probably never suspected it. But Kim visited her bizarre friends at least twice a week.

They were simultaneously comforting and unsettling, reassuring and frightening. Kim huddled against Scylla's side, concealed from passersby on Main Street, and felt his strength like the glow of the radiator in her bedroom. She would like to have read to him, small pay for the joy of his company, but it was usually too dark, and in any case she didn't want anyone to hear her. But she whispered softly, revealed her secrets to friends she knew would never betray her trust.

Then one summer, workmen started erecting a wrought iron fence around the property. It was as though someone had slipped a knife into her heart.

"It can't happen," she told herself, even as she watched them dig the holes for the upright posts.

That same night, Mrs. Trent was killed.

Most ten year olds don't read the newspapers, but Kim devoured them page by page, everything from editorials to letters to obituaries to wine reviews. Everything in fact except the comics page. "Too dumb even for kids."

And so she knew as much as her parents about the murder. Gladys Trent was not so much killed as smashed. "Massive trauma" was the official description. Apparently an intruder had forced open the front doors and bludgeoned her to death while she lay in bed, shattering every bone in her body.

The crime remained unsolved.

Mrs. Trent died intestate, her savings ended up in the pockets of two opposing law firms, and the house in Managansett was more a liability than an asset. None of the presumptive heirs could be sufficiently stirred to force a resolution. And so the property remained vacant for the next fifteen years.

But not unoccupied.

For her thirteenth birthday, Kim received a fifty dollar gift certificate good at the local bookstore. Her parents were immensely proud of her accomplishments. "She's a better reader than I am," her father bragged to his colleagues at work. "And the amount she retains is phenomenal." Her teachers had mixed feelings. Some worried about her social skills and Mrs. Amaral had accused her of plagiarism. "This paper could not have been written by a twelve year old, Mrs. Turner. It's far too sophisticated." Her peers were less kind. "Kim's a weirdo," Billy Gale insisted. "The only time she doesn't have her face in a book is when she's talking to the monsters at Sheffield House."

Kim left The Book Nook with a bag full of recent horror novels. A year earlier she'd discovered Stephen King and, to her parents' dismay, she'd been devouring stories about vampires, ghostly children, demonic possession, and satanic cults ever since.

"Don't you think you're overdoing the horror stuff a bit, Kim?"

"No," she'd replied after a thoughtful silence. She was always "Kiddo" to her father unless he was being serious about something, and she respected his intentions even when she disagreed.

It was a Saturday morning, late spring, the sun was bright, the sky clear, and Kim felt on top of the world. She carried her bag down Main Street to Sheffield House, pushed through the overgrown hedge that blocked the front entrance, and greeted her only two friends silently.

Scylla and Charybdis responded in kind.

Kim brushed the dirt away from a section of the front steps and sat down, trying to decide which of her books to read first. She no longer read aloud, understanding that it was not the words that were important to her visits but rather her intentions, the moments of sharing.

The intruders arrived just as the story was getting interesting.

There were six of them, Billy Gale and his friends, her primary tormentors at school. Billy's peers regarded him with either fear or loathing, but many were drawn as well by his undeniable charm. His ability to catalyze hatred toward the outsider was in its way as remarkable as Kim's reading skills. She thought he'd probably end up as a politician.

"What do YOU want?"

Kim hoped she sounded disinterested. It wouldn't do to let Billy know he was annoying her. It would only encourage him.

"Keep your shirt on, Kimmy. We're just looking around." He glanced up into Scylla's impassive face. "Ugly fucking bastard." Two of the boys tittered at the obscenity.

"Takes one to know one." The words escaped before Kim could catch them. Don't provoke him, she told herself. If he gets bored, he'll go away.

Billy just smiled, came a few steps closer, stopped just beyond her reach. His friends spread out to either side, one climbing up onto Charybdis, straddling the leonine back awkwardly because of the shrouding wings. Kim glanced that way, wanting to order him off, knowing that would only amuse them further.

"This is private property."

"Oh?" Billy glanced at his friends, reassuring himself he had an audience. "Did your parents buy it for your birthday or something?"

"No, but someday I'm going to buy it myself." Kim closed her book and shoved it back into the bag, angry with herself for having been provoked into revealing something she'd never told anyone before. She WOULD buy Sheffield House one day; she knew it with absolute certainty.

"Well, then someday you can tell us to go away and we'll have to do it. But today I think we'll just stay for a while."

It was clear to Kim that Billy's purpose was to tease, and with that realization came the solution. If she left, there would be no reason for Billy and his friends to stay either. And she could come back later, once they'd found someone new to torment.

She stood up abruptly. "Stay then, but I'm going."

Billy's face betrayed just a hint of anger as she stalked past, but before she reached the street, he'd recovered.

"I bet we could knock the heads off these things. They'd look great in my room."

Kim hesitated. Most likely it was an idle threat. But Billy had a violent reputation - the broken front window of the Managansett Inn, toppled gravestones in the cemetery, a fire started in the basement of one of the vacant low income housing units.

Ignore him, she told herself. He won't do it if you walk away. And perhaps that was true, but one of his friends had already picked up a heavy stone and was using both hands to pound it against Charybdis' comparatively slender throat.

"Stop that!" She whirled around, dropped her birthday books, and stalked back. "I'll tell your mother, Kevin. You know I will."

Kevin hesitated, the stone poised for another blow. A thin, jagged crack stretched from one of Charybdis' knobby shoulders to the other.

"No one cares, Kimmy." Billy had picked up another stone, and was poised to attack Scylla in similar fashion. "No one but you."

And as the rest of the boys searched for weapons of their own, Kim realized that Billy was right, that the two gargoyles could be smashed into dust and no one but herself would care. But she did care. She cared very much.

She managed to draw blood from Billy's cheek before two of the other boys pulled her off. He glared at her furiously, raised his hand as if to strike her with the stone he'd been using on Scylla. Kim heard cries of triumph from the rest of his gang, who were industriously pounding away at Charybdis.

"Watch this, bitch!" With exaggerated care Billy climbed to Scylla's back, rose to his feet, spread his legs to achieve a precarious balance, and raised the stone two handed above his head.

"Say goodbye, Kimmy."

She closed her eyes, refusing to accept what was about to happen, and time froze, even when she felt them release her arms, even when she heard the screaming and realized something had gone terribly wrong.

It was several seconds before she dared to look. Under other circumstances, she might have screamed along with the boys.

Billy Gale would never bother her again. Somehow he'd lost his balance and fallen forward across Scylla's head. One of the curled horns had taken him directly under the chin, striking up into the brain.

Kim wondered if she should feel pity, but in fact her only emotion was a fierce joy, a joy that passed only when she turned and saw that Charybdis had gone as well. His massive head had shattered against the stone steps when it fell to the pavement. The boys had scattered by now, headless in their own fashion.

When the police arrived, they thought she was crying about Billy.

Adolescence modifies behavior. At seventeen, Kim might have been very popular if she'd made an effort. She was smart, attractive, and accepted if not particularly liked. Most of her evenings were still spent reading, although horror fiction was now only the first among many of her interests, and she still visited Scylla at least twice a week. Although she dated occasionally, she'd never been particularly interested in boys.

Until Scott Nicholson moved to Managansett.

Scott was clearly from a different world. He was sophisticated beyond his years, good looking, athletic - although he didn't participate in school sports, intelligent - although he only read non-fiction, and self assured. Kim knew he had dated Valerie Gohannon, Tanya Gorham, and Mary Zydecki, the three most sought after girls in the school, and for the first time in her life, she envied them. So when Scott stopped by her locker to ask for a date, she was nearly incoherent.

The evening was magical. Scott's manners were impeccable and he seemed generally interested in whatever she had to say, so much so that she ended up saying a lot more than she intended.

"I'm jealous," he said at last. "I don't think I've ever played second best to a statue before."

Kim laughed, but it was slightly brittle. She worried that her confessions had been perhaps just a bit too weird, and that she might have revealed too much. "Don't worry. You're much better looking."

"Still, I'd like to meet this Scylla. Where'd you say this place was again?"

And so it was that they walked together beyond the well lighted downtown of Managansett, out toward the cemetery and the overgrown acreage that contained Sheffield House.

"It's pretty dark in there; you won't be able to see anything. Maybe we could come back during the day some time."

They were standing on the sidewalk, just outside the gates.

"Come on. We walked all the way out here, didn't we?" And Scott was tugging on her arm, pulling Kim through the unruly hedge.

"What happened to the other one?" Scott gestured toward Charybdis after examining Scylla in the moonlight.

"Kids. It happened a long time ago."

"No one lives here, huh?"

"Not for years and years. Can we go now?"

Scott ignored her. "What's it like inside, do you know? Can we get in somewhere?"

"I don't think anyone's been in the house since I was a kid."

Still holding her wrist, a bit more tightly than she would have preferred, Scott led her around the side of the building. "If I can get one of these windows open..."

Kim hovered between panic and anger. "Scott, I want to go now. I mean it."

He yanked her arm unexpectedly so that she turned to face him, caught her other wrist before she could react. "Cool it, Kim. Look, if we can get inside, there's no way anyone can see what we're doing. It's a pretty night, I like you a lot and I thought you liked me too."

"I do." But she didn't sound that way, and wasn't sure she felt that way either. There was something wrong, something had changed in just the last few minutes.

"So what's the problem? I think this could be really special if we let it."

He released her wrists then, and for a second Kim thought she'd been over reacting, panicking simply because a good looking boy enjoyed being alone with her in the dark. She had even opened her mouth to apologize when she felt his hands on her again, one catching the belt of her slacks, the other pressing insistently against her left breast.

"Cut it out!" She tried to pull away, but Scott tightened his grip at her waist and jerked her forward. His other hand tightened possessively.

"No more bullshit, Kimmy."

It was the hated diminutive of her name that spurred her to act even more than his unwelcome touch. Kim lifted her knee sharply, just as her father had taught her, and Scott fell away, gasping with pain. She whirled and rushed headlong into the darkness, scratching her cheek and snagging her clothing as she pushed through the bull briar and mock orange that had once bordered a well kept garden.

Scott made no effort to pursue, not even after he'd regained his composure. But he did call out to her.

"You blew it, Kimmy! I really kind of liked you, you know. We could have had a great time together."

She crouched in the darkness, out of breath, unwilling to answer.

"You might even have had fun. I'm pretty good at making

love. Lots of practice. Valerie and Mary and the others could tell you."

He moved away from the building, started back toward the front yard. But he paused and called out once more before leaving. "Guys talk, you know. Everyone's going to assume I had you, and I won't tell them otherwise. In fact, I think I'm remembering some details already, like how you weren't a virgin after all and insisted on giving me a blowjob first."

Kim bit her lip and lowered her head, willing him just to go away. And he did. And an hour after that, so did she.

Her parents were both sitting at the kitchen table when she came out for breakfast the following morning, and she could tell right away that something was wrong.

"How did your date go last night?"

"OK." Kim avoided her father's eyes while she poured herself come coffee.

"We didn't hear Scott drop you off."

"No, I...we walked back. It was nice out."

"Kim, we heard some bad news this morning." Her mother's voice was crisp and matter of fact, the tone she always adopted when she had something difficult to say and wanted to get it over with. "There was an accident last night. Scott is dead."

Kim's head came up sharply. "Dead? But I don't..." She looked away, not wanting any hint of her immense sense of relief to be noticed.   "How did it happen?"

"Hit and run," answered her father. "His car smashed into something up on Reservoir Road."

"Was anyone else hurt?"

"Apparently not. In fact, the other vehicle drove off and left him. But there must have been a lot of damage. They'll catch whoever's responsible."

But they never did.

Kim lost her parents during her sophomore year of college. Their airliner crashed after being struck by lightning shortly after takeoff. The estate was large enough to pay for the rest of Kim's education with a little left over. But she dropped out instead, and used the money to buy Sheffield House.

There was enough left to cover living expenses until she found a job at a local company, Eblis Manufacturing, as an inventory clerk. By the time she was twenty-six, Kim was Production Control Supervisor, with a high enough salary to allow her to restore the ground floor of the house, though the upstairs remained closed up and largely unusable.

Her next project was Charybdis.

She visited the Rhode Island School of Design and paid to have several busts modeled. Although she had described what she was looking for in great detail, even provided sketches, Kim rejected each of the completed models. Some of the likenesses were quite close and many were extraordinarily well done, none contained the specific spark of identity she was looking for.

"No, I can't explain exactly what's wrong, but when I see the right one, when I see Charbydis, I'll know it." The students shook their heads and took her money, and some even tried again, but Kim began to lose hope.

And so Scylla maintained his silent vigil alone.

Kim had just rejected another group of busts the day she was summoned to Chet Muir's office to discuss infrastructure. Muir had been hired only a month previously, replacing Alan Daniels as head of Production Planning. Although Kim tried not to make hasty judgments, she considered Muir a mental lightweight, wondered how he would ever make intelligent decisions about the complex systems used at Eblis.

"Hello, Evan." She nodded to the other man in the room, troubled by his presence. Evan Conner was an ambitious, ruthless mid-level manager. The bad feelings caused by his reorganization of the inventory control function still lingered.

"I wanted to talk to both of you together," Muir said quietly, "so that we'd all have the same understanding of what we need to do."

Kim glanced at Conner, wondering how much conversation had taken place before she'd arrived. There was a self satisfied look on the young man's face that she instinctively distrusted.

"As you may know, I've never understood why inventory control and production control were two separate functions in this company. I've decided therefore to combine them into a single department, which Evan here will head."

Kim blinked, wondering if she'd heard correctly. "I don't understand," she said finally. "I can see merging the two departments, but what qualifies Evan to run them?" She turned briefly in his direction. "Nothing personal, Evan. You do an excellent job. But you don't have any experience with the CPix scheduling system, you've only worked with one of the product lines, and there's only six people in your department. I've supervised thirty people for the last two years and I know CPix inside out."

"Naturally I expect you to continue to administer those systems until you've brought Evan up to speed, Miss Turner. And I don't want you to think of this as a demotion. In fact, I've convinced top management to simply freeze your salary for a few years rather than reduce your wages. And this way you won't have to put up with me any more." He laughed unconvincingly.

"That's not the point. I have wider experience and more seniority. If anything, Evan should be reporting to me, not the other way around."

"Well, I'm sorry you see it that way, Miss Turner, but you have to understand that as a manager I have to make these decisions based on lots of...intangibles, and I'm afraid my decision is made."

She wanted to quit, wanted to storm out of Muir's office in a rage, leave them to struggle through the intricacies of CPix on their own. But Kim knew how tight her budget was, and she had no reserves. She needed the job. So she resigned herself to being Evan Conner's assistant for as long as it took to find a new position.

Three days after the reorganization was announced, Evan Conner didn't show up at work. Calls to his house went unanswered. His ex-wife had no idea where he was but expressed the hope that it was someplace unpleasant.

The following morning Evan Conner's body washed up on the shore below the reservoir.

"The police think he fell off the dam," Muir explained to the assembled staff. "Apparently hit the rocks on the way down and broke his back. He was dead before he hit the water, mercifully."

Kim became "acting" department head with no change in pay, and while the modifier never left her job title, there was never any serious attempt to replace her.

Another set of models was rejected. Kim began to suspect that nothing would ever satisfy her, that she'd somehow conjured up some unrealizable standard that could never be met. Two or three of the models had been photographically perfect renditions of Charybdis as she remembered him, but that's all they were, images. The spirit of whatever had made Charybdis himself was missing.

When the weather permitted, she spent most evenings sitting a few feet away from Scylla, her chair angled so that she couldn't see his decapitated mate. Still a voracious reader, she'd sit until the dimming light made her squint, then set the book aside and just glory in the moonlight until finally slipping inside for the night.

Kim took a week of vacation in early spring, spent two solid days excavating what would eventually be a pair of gardens flanking the new patio she was having built. Exhausted by early evening, she settled into her usual chair beside the front steps and attempted to read, but found herself nodding off almost immediately. Kim rose, stretched, and walked over to Scylla, pressing her cheek against the cold stone.

"See you in the morning, old friend. I'm beat."

The carriage path had been cleared and paved to make a driveway, where her Toyota looked like a cub nestling at the side of its mother, a dusty cement truck waiting for morning when it would pour her new patio. Chet Muir had been replaced, and her new boss had added labor reporting to her responsibilities, along with a healthy salary increase, so she'd accelerated her restoration plans.

She locked the door behind her, doused the lights, and climbed the stairs to her recently renovated bedroom. The heat was thick and oppressive so she opened the oversized windows, letting in the cool night air. Ten minutes later she was fast asleep.

It was pitch black and considerably cooler when she awakened, disoriented, listening intently for whatever sound had disturbed her slumber. She lay propped up on her elbows for several minutes, but the house was silent. Or rather, its noises were the old, familiar ones.

She was thirsty.

Halfway down the stairs, Kim realized something was wrong. Light from the living room spilled into the hallway and one of the ground floor windows was wide open. She'd locked them all before retiring for the night. Half asleep, her mind didn't process the information quickly and she continued down the steps unthinkingly.

The intruder had pressed himself up against the staircase, and now he leaped up and caught her by the hair. Kim tried to pull away, lost her balance, and fell down the last dozen steps, landing painfully on her hip.

He moved toward her menacingly.

The intruder was the ugliest man Kim had ever seen, his face distorted by a twisted nose, a huge wen that ran across his browridge, an asymmetric mouth that didn't quite conceal the uneven teeth within. His skin was pockmarked with the aftermath of triumphant acne and his hair was long and unkempt.

She twisted away when he tried to kick her and scrambled to her feet, but not quickly enough. Powerful arms wrapped themselves around her body and she was literally thrown against the wall. The impact drove the air from her lungs and she slid slowly to the floor, struggling to draw breath.

There was a thundering sound from the front of the house, someone pounding on the door.

"In here! Help!" Kim barely managed to get the words out.

The intruder turned and started toward the open window, but Kim impulsively lashed out with her right leg, hooking his ankle. For a second he hovered on the verge of balance, then fell to the floor.

Snarling, he rose into a crouch, one hand holding a knife. Kim tried to stand up but he was too fast, his free hand catching hold of her throat and smashing her head back against the wall. When she opened her eyes, her vision grew blurry.

"I will not faint," she told herself, trying to regain control of her body. The knife flashed before her eyes and she realized the man was smiling.

There was a scream of tearing metal, then a tremendous crash as the double front doors flew open. Kim turned her head toward what she hoped was a rescue, caught just a glimpse of a charging shape before her attacker smashed her head into the wall again.

She carried a vision of her friend Scylla down into the darkness.

Kim woke up to daylight, stared at the ceiling in confusion until the discomfort of lying on the floor convinced her to get up.

The sun was well up in a cloudless sky. There was an unfamiliar rumbling from outside that she didn't recognize until she looked out the window and saw that the construction crew was pouring concrete for the patio.

She searched the house very thoroughly even before getting dressed. There was no sign of any intruder. At first she wondered if her memories of the previous night were simply a particularly vivid dream during which she'd walked in her sleep. But then she noticed that her television and VCR had been moved to an alcove near the open window, and the front door locks were broken, the metal literally torn out of the wood.

Kim showered and dressed and walked out the kitchen door into the side yard.

"Morning, Miss Turner." Dade, the crew boss, tipped a non-existent hat in her direction. "Hope we didn't wake you or anything. I rang the bell but no one answered."

"That's all right." She walked past him to get a better view of the work site. "How's it coming?"

"Right as rain. I see you changed your mind about the pathway." He sounded mildly disapproving.

Kim ignored him because she'd already noticed the same thing. To preserve her view of the handsome white birch trees in the rear of the property, she'd located the patio approximately ten feet from the rear of the building itself. There'd been two possible routes for a walkway and she'd finally chosen the one on the west side of the house.

During the night, someone had filled in the trench and dug a new one, on the east side.

"Hope you didn't do all that yourself, Miss Turner. We'd've been happy to fill it in for you with a backhoe."

She shook her head vaguely. "No, that's all right. A friend of mine helped me and I needed the exercise."

It occurred to her that the filled trench was just the right size to contain a human body.

With a cup of coffee in her hand, Kim examined the wreckage of the front doorlocks. "Have to get these fixed," she told herself, then swung open the door and stepped outside. Scylla remained as impassive as ever, but she thought there was some very subtle change in his expression. Satisfaction, she thought.

Kim usually averted her eyes from Charybdis' truncated figure, but this time it was Scylla who made her feel uncomfortable, so she turned to the side.

Her coffee cup shattered against the stone steps, spraying hot coffee over her ankles. Kim didn't even notice.

Charybdis had a new head, molded in cement that still glistened wetly in the sunlight. It wasn't much like the original, but it fit somehow, the protruding forehead, unkempt mane, snaggletoothed mouth, raspy complexion.

Kim raised her hand to the smooth stone, swept it over a muscular haunch, across the arched back and massive shoulder, let her fingers just barely brush the underside of Charybdis' new chin. She looked into the eyes and saw something there, something that she'd missed for many years.

"Welcome back, Charybdis," she said softly.

BAD FEELINGS

"Why did you nail Mrs. White's cat to the porch, Danny?"

The ten year old had been staring into his lap ever since arriving in Doctor Lane's office and he didn't look up now or give any other sign that he'd heard the question.

Ellen Lane sighed. "Do you know why you're here, Danny?"

"To get better." His voice was low, unemotional.

"Then you know what you did was wrong?"

"Of course I do." His head came up, eyes met hers firmly for a second before dropping back. "I'm not a dope."

"No, you're not. You're very smart." Smart enough to have avoided being caught. Something within the boy was crying out for help.

"Did Mrs. White do something that made you mad?"

"Nope."

"Did the cat scratch you? I know how much that hurts."

"Nope."

"Were you mad at your mother or father? Did you think this would make them sorry?"

"Nope."

"Well, why did you do it then?" A note of exasperation had crept into her voice. Ellen didn't understand this boy. She'd talked to the parents; they seemed first rate, loved each other and their son, no emotional problems she could detect. But Danny was a cipher even to them, unemotional, bland.

"Had to."

"You had to, huh? Why did you have to?"

Danny just shrugged.

Ellen repressed the urge to go over and shake the boy. "Danny, we all feel the urge to do bad things at times. You don't have to be upset about that. We're not in control of how we feel about things. But we must be responsible for what we actually do. You know what you did was wrong."

"Yes." His voice was almost inaudible.

"Well, my job is to help you to learn to handle those bad thoughts. Would you like to be able to do that?"

"Yes." Louder this time, the first actually emotional tone in his voice. And Danny had raised his head, was staring at her with naked longing.

Ellen realized she'd found the key. "Do you have bad feelings a lot?"

"All the time." Danny's eyes darted away, but he didn't drop his head. "There's something...inside of me...that wants to do terrible things to people."

"Because you're mad at them?"

"No."

"No? Then why?"

"Just because." He licked his lips and squirmed in his seat. "I told you, it's something inside of me wants to do it. I don't want to. I hate the things I do sometimes."

"Then why do you do them?"

"Because...because there's this bad thing inside of me and if I don't do things to keep it happy, I'm afraid it'll get out and then it'll do really bad things. Terrible things."

Ellen tried to keep the satisfaction from showing on her face. At last she'd gotten the boy to give shape to the inner turmoil that was tormenting him. At last she saw the way to relieving that tension and helping the boy adjust.

"Danny, have you ever played with balloons?"

"Sure." His voice was tentative, obviously puzzled by this change of direction.

"What happens if you blow a balloon up too much?"

"It pops."

"Well, people are a little like balloons sometimes. If we keep our feelings all bottled up inside, there's not room for all the other feelings we have each day and pretty soon there's so much inside that it has to get out."

"But the stuff inside me is bad. I can't let it get out because it might do something horrible like I told you."

"That's because you keep it all inside you until there's no more room. You have to let it out a little at a time, every day, so that it doesn't get all tight and crowded inside you like it is now."

"I don't know..."

"But I do know, Danny. And right now I want you to let out all the bad stuff inside you and promise me you'll never let it get stored up like that again."

Danny looked uncertain, but more hopeful than at any time since she'd started treating him.

"It's all right? You promise?"

"I promise. Just let it out and you'll be fine."

Danny nodded and sat back and his body began to quiver and shake and then something dark and scaly and slimy with lots of claws and teeth burst out of his warm flesh and did some really terrible things.

But Ellen Lane wasn't around for most of that.

TIME TRICK

Tiny terrorists issued forth from their hiding places and spread out through the neighborhood, extorting candy, trampling flower beds, filling the night with their shrill cries. Liz glanced out through the front window and saw that the street lights had already come on even though it was barely dusk. None of the marauding trick-or-treaters were in sight, but she could hear them from the next street over. It was only a matter of time.

The window was smaller than she would have liked, limiting her view, but it was HER window. For the first time in her life she was living in her own house, not one belonging to this or that set of foster parents. She was eighteen and legally entitled at last to the proceeds from her parents' estate, and while it was not enough to support her indefinitely, it had been adequate to allow for a used car and this house on the north side of Managansett. The mall job didn't pay a whole lot and she'd be living from paycheck to paycheck, but it was worth it to be on her own, to be able to make up her own rules for a change.

It had possibly been foolish to buy the house. The lawyer had suggested that she conserve her cash and rent an apartment, but she hadn't wanted to be a tenant again. If she wanted to write on the walls, she could do it. If she wanted to sleep in the dining room, that was up to her. Inside these walls, she was President and Congress and the Supreme Court combined.

She'd never felt that she had any real control of her environment before now. Some of her foster parents had flatly refused to allow her to change anything even if she wasn't sharing a room with another fosterling. "You'll only be here for a while, Elizabeth, and the next child might not like what you've done with the place." Others had not expressly forbidden it, but their displeasure had been obvious. "Oh, you moved the dresser. Was there a problem with where it was?" It hadn't taken her long to realize that she wasn't part of the households where she stayed. She was a transient, a visitor. Only once had she been subjected to any actual cruelty, and that only briefly, but the indifference had been, if anything, even worse, because sometimes she felt guilty about resenting the people who were taking care of her.

Very little about her childhood had been normal. She had never been allowed to go out on Halloween for example. She'd managed perhaps half a dozen dates during her teenage years, never the same boy twice. It wasn't that she was always forbidden to socialize – that had only happened once – but she was shunted from home to home, from school to school, with such regularity that it was hard to make friends.

That would all change now, she was sure. With her own house and a settled existence, it was only a matter of time. There was a nice boy only a little bit older than she was working at the mall and they'd talked a couple of times already. Liz knew she was no beauty, her wardrobe was pretty plain, and she had a tendency to keep to herself and not participate in conversations, but she'd made a positive effort with him and it seemed to be working.

The house was small, but it was the only acceptable place that she'd found within her budget, and she didn't own much more than a closet full of clothing. It had come furnished and it would take years to replace the aging leftovers, furniture so covered with dust that she'd discarded some of it. The house had been empty for more than ten years, according to the real estate agent, and the bank had dropped the price dramatically just to get rid of it.

"What's wrong with it then?" Liz had felt her heart sink. It had sounded too good to be true, and perhaps it was.

The realtor shuffled his papers and looked uncomfortable. "The house is structurally sound, if that's what you're worried about. The bank even replaced the roof a couple of years ago, and the boiler in the basement is brand new. The outside will need to be painted pretty soon, and you saw the water stains on the bathroom ceiling."

She nodded. "And the yard is tiny and the lot has an odd shape and it's all by itself at the end of a road. I remember all that. Is there something more?"

He sighed. "Yes, and the law says I have to inform you of this, even though it really doesn't matter. Not to most people anyway."

Liz mentally braced herself, wondering what it could be. Termites? A highway project that would claim the property in a couple of years? A basement that flooded every time it rained?

"There was a death in the house. A murder. The couple that lived there ten years ago killed one of the neighborhood children.

They were caught burying the body up near the Reservoir." He picked up a single sheet of paper and slid it across the desk to her. "That document summarizes the incident. You'll have to sign at the bottom indicating that you've been informed."

Liz felt an enormous sigh of relief. She wasn't superstitious, wasn't even religious. She'd been taken to so many different churches, even a synagogue once, that she'd decided the whole religion business was just a tent show, a ruse to separate the credulous from their pocket money. "Is that all?" She had picked up a pen and signed it without reading it.

The realtor had looked relieved and never mentioned it again, but there was a copy of the document attached to her mortgage papers.

Liz checked her preparations for at least the tenth time. A large bowl of candy sat on a small table strategically located beside the front door. Two bags held in reserve because she had no idea how many visitors she might have. One hundred fifty candy bars. That should be enough, surely? She fretted over the possibility that she'd underestimated and did a quick mental inventory of her pantry. There were some apples. And she had a jar full of quarters in her bedroom. But that would be her last resort. The quarters were her fun money – reserved for movies, dining out, and other special treats.

"Oh my God! The pumpkin!" Liz rushed out to the kitchen. On the table were two freshly carved pumpkins. She'd cut lopsided faces into both of them. She wasn't particularly happy with the first – but the second looked just fine. She picked it up, smiled at her own artistry, and carried it back to the front door. Two children in clown costumes raced down the street, not looking her way, as she stepped out onto the small porch and placed the pumpkin at the top of the steps. She took her cigarette lighter from her pocket and lit the thick candle she'd placed inside, then backed away to examine her handiwork.

The doorbell rang about ten minutes later. Three small children, a witch and two Lord of the Rings characters, held up plastic bags and slurred their demands into one word "trickertreat". Liz felt disproportionately pleased with herself as she dispensed chocolate bars under the watchful eye of a dark haired woman who stood on the sidewalk. With their prizes secure, the children raced off and Liz retreated inside. She thought about turning on the television, but she was childishly excited by the whole holiday atmosphere and left it off, hovering near the window instead to watch for her next band of costumed visitors.

They came in flurries over the next half hour, sometimes one group arriving before the previous had gone. The flow slowed after that, and a few times she'd opened the door to find visitors as tall or taller than she, sometimes not even wearing costumes. She wanted to say something to the teenagers, but she had always shied away from confrontation so she handed them a candy bar wordlessly and let her smile slip slightly. And at least one of the guys had been good looking.

By the time full darkness had fallen, traffic had slowed to a trickle, and she no longer felt any excitement. She was paging through a magazine when she heard a thump from the front porch. Liz cocked her head, waiting for the doorbell, but it didn't sound. Puzzled, she set down the paper and walked to the door, easing it open.

The porch was empty and dark beyond the pool of illumination from the small bulb over her head. No kids. She almost closed the door, but something looked wrong. It took a few seconds for her to realize that it was too dark. The candle in her pumpkin must have gone out.

Liz opened the storm door, stepped outside, and saw her pumpkin, or what was left of it, splattered across the cobblestones of the front walk.

"Damn it!" she said aloud, her eyes suddenly stinging. She descended the steps and crouched, retrieving the largest of the fragments, piling them up, then carrying them into the house. They went into the garbage can beside the sink. The short walk had seen her sorrow mutate into anger, and she snatched up the standby pumpkin and marched back to the front of the house, placing it on its predecessor's spot. It took a few seconds to find what remained of the candle where it had rolled under a bush, but she raised it triumphantly and within seconds a severely misshapen face was radiating pale light.

Still angry, she closed the door but didn't let it latch, and stood directly behind it, silently daring the culprit to return for a repeat performance. A few minutes later she heard footsteps on the porch and giggles, but then the doorbell rang and a ghost and a tramp were demanding their due. Liz smiled and complied, but the smile was slightly forced and she felt little of her earlier pleasure.

After they were gone, she resumed her post behind the half closed door, knowing that she was exaggerating this out of proportion. The interval this time was much longer, and she leaned her forehead against the cool surface of the door, almost dozing, then suddenly alert. A board on the porch had just creaked.

She waited for the next sound, and the tension built so quickly and acutely that she felt a completely irrational urge to shout or scream or do something to break the silence. Just as she was about to open the door and confront whoever her mysterious visitor might be, she heard a sudden plop and splatter and knew the second pumpkin had joined its brother in cobblestone oblivion.

Furious, she pulled the door wide and hit the storm door with the palm of her hand so hard that the grass rattled in its frame. It bounced open and she swept through.

Standing at the top of the stairs, looking woeful in her pink ballerina costume, stood a skinny young girl of perhaps ten or eleven years, with big dark eyes and dainty features, and a tiny but perceptible heart shaped birthmark on her left cheek. She looked up at Liz with an expression of terror and her voice trembled. "I'm sorry. I just wanted to look at it and it slipped. I didn't mean to."

Her anger was so strong that Liz lunged toward the girl, not knowing exactly what she meant to do, frustrated that her pleasant mood had been so completely ruined. The little girl flinched away, stepped back, and teetered precariously on the lip of the porch. Liz's fury vanished in a split second and she reached forward, trying to grab the girl's arm and pull her back to safety, but the youngster must have interpreted that as an even greater threat because she jerked backward and now her fall was inevitable. Desperately Liz tried to rush to the rescue, but tripped over her own feet. Her shoulder banged painfully against one of the porch support beams and she bounced away, saw the ground coming up and closed her eyes just before she hit.

"Are you all right?"

Liz rolled over onto her back, feeling disoriented and more than slightly sore. Her head and shoulder hurt, and she'd banged her hip somehow. It took two tries before she could sit up, and when she did, she looked down at herself in shock.

The elderly woman standing on the porch above her leaned even closer. "I asked if you were all right, dear. You took quite a fall."

Liz shook her head, ignoring the woman, and tentatively touched the torn hem of her skirt. She was dressed as a ballerina, with a pink skirt and tights, and ruby red shoes that pinched her toes.

"Let's get you up and see how bad the damage is." The woman came down the short flight of steps and took Liz's left arm, carefully but firmly lifting her to her feet. Liz made no effort to resist. She still didn't understand what had happened and was halfway convinced she'd hit her head and was dreaming.

"I don't understand," she said at last, and then closed her mouth firmly because the voice hadn't sounded like her own.

"You must have hit your head and rattled your brains a bit, young lady. Come inside and let me clean you up."

Dazed and confused, Liz let herself be led into the small house.

It looked like her home, but at the same time it didn't. The rooms were recognizable, but the furniture was different and it was arranged oddly. No, she realized, at least some of the furniture was exactly the same. She remembered that couch because it had been a real chore to move it to the opposite end of the living room, but the colors hadn't been quite so bright. And the large mirror on the wall was just the same, except that hers had a crack in the lower right corner and this one seemed to be in perfect condition.

A tall, thin man who looked every bit as old as the woman came in from the kitchen. "What's this then?" His voice was gruff and unfriendly.

"Nothing to bother about, John. This young lady had a little accident on the porch. I'll just see to her. You go back to your book."

"Finished it," he said with a snort, then walked past them both and sat down on the couch.

Liz stood in the center of the room, staring fixedly at the mirror, staring at the impossible figure within. Her reflection was that of a skinny young girl in a badly torn ballerina outfit. Her face didn't remotely resemble the one that greeted her each morning. But it was familiar, familiar because of the heart shaped birthmark on one cheek.

What was going on here? Was she in a coma? She'd seen something like that in a movie once. But this felt so real. She couldn't believe it was a dream.

The woman returned, carrying a wet washcloth. Liz didn't resist as she ran it over her face, cleaning off the smudges of dirt. "There now, you look better already. You should be more careful, dear. You could have been seriously hurt, you know."

"What was she doing on the damned porch anyway?"

"It's Halloween, John. She was out trick or treating. Or just tricking actually. She smashed my pumpkin."

"Told you not to waste your time. Kids never appreciate what you do for them."

Liz wanted to say that she hadn't broken the woman's pumpkin, hadn't even seen it, but she wasn't sure of anything just at the moment.

"Serves her right then," he added grumpily. Liz glanced briefly in his direction and noticed that he was staring at her fixedly.

The woman was fussing with her costume. "I'm afraid there's not much I can do with this, dear. I might be able to pin it up temporarily, but it looks like a total loss to me." She raised the cloth again and dabbed at the bruise on Liz's forehead. "I don't think I've seen you around here before. Are you new in the neighborhood?"

Liz didn't know what to say. If this was all an illusion, it didn't matter. If it was real, she didn't know the answer. But it couldn't be real, could it?

"And out all by yourself? Does your mother know where you are?"

Before she could think, Liz answered her honestly. "My mother's dead."

"Oh, I'm so sorry to hear that. You live with your father then?"

Liz shook her head. "He's dead too." She didn't want to talk with that odd, little girl voice she didn't recognize, but it felt worse to remain silent.

"Then you must have family here in town."

Liz shook her head. "No, I don't have anybody." She wanted to cry, missing her parents as badly now as when she'd been newly orphaned.

The woman turned to her husband. "Did you hear that, John? The child's all by herself. Doesn't have any family at all. Isn't that a shame?"

He grumbled noncommittally, but Liz found the sound oddly unsettling and moved a step away from him.

"Maybe you could come and visit us for a while. We have an extra room, you know. John and I both love children. We really do. Except when they're being bad, of course. We've had lots of children come and stay with us and we all have a wonderful time unless they're bad, and then we send them away. But we're always very sorry when we have to do that and we look forward to our next little visitor."

Liz felt the same uneasiness that she'd experienced once or twice when she'd been moved to a new home. "I think I should go now. Thank you for your help." She took a tentative step toward the door.

"Nonsense. You can't go walking out with your clothing torn like that. You're hardly decent. We have some things from one of our earlier children downstairs. John will take you down there and you can pick something out to wear."

"I really should go. I'm supposed to meet some of the other kids." It was the first thing she could think of and she knew it was inadequate. And then the man was gripping her wrist. She hadn't even noticed him when he rose from the couch and now it was too late to run.

She let him lead her to the basement door. Liz glanced back over her shoulder; the woman was beaming at her. "I'll see you shortly, young lady."

The stairs were exactly as she remembered them, but the basement was not. Someone had paneled most of it at some time in the past, but it had been in terrible shape when she'd moved in. What Liz saw now was well maintained, almost new. She brushed against a heavy wooden bench covered with a variety of shiny tools, hammers, saws, wrenches. One corner had been partitioned off into a small area like a dark room. John led her there, still holding her skinny wrist tightly as he fished in his pants pocket and brought forth a key ring. She wondered why they kept the door locked.

Inside was a generic child's room. There were bunk beds in one corner, stuffed animals scattered around on shelves and elsewhere, a heavy wooden box marked "TOYS" and a small dresser. There was a closet against the far wall, lacking a door and displaying a variety of girls' and boys' clothing. But there were other things in the room as well, things that made her mouth go dry.

"You can find something to wear in there, no doubt," John said gruffly. "I'll be back for you presently." He retreated through the door and started to close it, but Liz stepped forward and stood on the threshold.

"I'd rather have the door open, mister." She tried to sound as subservient as possible.

He gave her a searching look, shrugged his shoulders. "Suit yourself." Then he turned and started up the stairs.

Liz found a pair of jeans that fit and a shirt that was only a little bit too big for her. There were no shoes, so she had to keep the impractical red dancing slippers. There were no windows and when she walked around the rest of the basement, she found that the ones she remembered were covered over in this earlier version of the house. She went back to the tool bench, hovered for a few seconds, then retreated to the room, trying to decide what to do.

Liz knew she was in trouble. The rings set in the wall looked almost ornamental, but they were heavy and seated deeply into the concrete. There was a wicker basket full of rope sitting in one corner, and the ceilings were covered with thick, acoustic tiles. The door had been heavy, solid wood, and the walls were thick enough that there must be some kind of insulation inside. There was only one reason she could think of to insulate an interior wall, and she'd seen it only once before.

At the house where she'd been beaten as a child. The house where she might have died if her case worker hadn't actually made an effort to keep track of the children assigned to her.

She was sitting on the lower bunk when John came back, one hand resting next to the pillow. He looked her over cursorily. "You look like a boy dressed up that way," he complained. "Hilly wants you upstairs now. Come along."

He turned away, obviously expecting her to follow meekly behind. She did follow, but only for a few steps. Then she swung the hammer she'd concealed beneath the pillow with all the force she could muster. It struck him solidly on the back of the head and he pitched forward against the stairs. His face hit one of the risers and his head bounced once, slowly came to rest. There was one long exhalation of air and then he was silent, and motionless.

Still clutching the hammer, Liz carefully stepped over him and started to tiptoe up the stairs.

"What's the problem, dear? I thought I heard something fall." The woman, Hilly, was standing at the opposite end of the hall as Liz stepped through the doorway.

"I'm going home now," she said with as firm a tone as she could manage, the hammer held concealed behind her back.

"Oh, we wouldn't want you to do that. It's late and a young girl like you shouldn't be out on the streets alone. That would be very naughty."

"I don't care. Get out of my way. You can't keep me here."

"Oh but we can. We're adults, after all, and you're just a child. Children can't be allowed to make their own decisions." The woman was slowly coming closer. "Only wicked children think that they know better than their elders, and wicked children have to be punished, you know. It's for their own good, the good of their souls." And she came another step closer.

Liz couldn't wait any longer. She brought the hammer out from behind her back and raised it threateningly. "Get out of my way!"

Hilly gave her a remorseful look. "Well if you feel that strongly about it, dear, then go."

Liz edged past the woman, her back pressed against the wall, the hammer ready. But not ready enough. Just when she thought she was safe, the woman moved faster than Liz ever would have expected, grabbed the hammer with one hand and Liz's shoulder with the other. Shouting with rage and terror, Liz managed to pull free, but she lost the hammer and her footing and fell onto her sore hip. Fortunately, Hilly lost her balance as well, falling across Liz's legs.

Liz pulled free, rolled over, and scuttled toward the door on her hands and knees. She heard a cry of rage from behind her and then something heavy pressed against her back and there was a hand in her hair, tugging so hard that she cried out in pain. She squirmed and kicked and managed to slide out from under the woman's thickset body, rolling away across the hardwood floor until she reached the couch. She reached up, grabbed the arm, and pulled herself to her feet, just as Hilly did the same and rushed toward her, shouting angrily.

Without thinking, Liz crouched and threw herself at the woman's ankles. She struck solidly enough to jar herself, heard a cry of dismay, and then a solid thud and the sharp crack of broken glass.

With one hand clutching her sore shoulder, Liz stood up slowly this time, exhausted and in shock, and turned to see the old woman crumpled on the floor. Her face was turned to the side with eyes open and staring, the side of her head resting against the large mirror, whose glass now displayed a large crack in its lower right corner. Liz stared at the body for several very long seconds before turning away.

It took three tries to get the door properly unlatched, and through it all Liz imagined John crawling up from the basement, reaching for her, and when she finally got it open, she raced outside in complete panic, not watching where she was going. She leaped down the stairs and started toward the street, and something soft and slippery moved under one foot. She had a split second to remember the smashed pumpkin before her legs went out from under her and she was staring up at the stars, and then something hit the back of her head really hard and the stars went out, all at once.

She opened her eyes after some indefinable period of time and the stars were back. Her head hurt, her hip hurt, and her back hurt, and she thought she was going to faint when she sat up. But fear lent her strength and she staggered to her feet, turning to stare back in terror at the open door behind her.

But no one was chasing her. The night was quiet except for some traffic noises from over on Waverly Street. Her hands were all gritty and she reached down, brushing them clean against her corduroy slacks, and realized that she wasn't wearing jeans. "What the hell?"

Liz ran her hands over her face and then her body and realized she was a woman, not a child. She began to laugh, feeling foolish and relieved all at once. "I fell and hit my head," she told herself. "I remembered what the real estate man told me and had a dream about it. That's all."

Dream or not, she re-entered her house cautiously, walking slowly from room to room, assuring herself that she was alone and that everything was back the way she remembered it. Even then, she felt jumpy and something compelled her to open the cellar door and descend into the basement.

It was also as she remembered it, poorly maintained, the remnants of the paneling mildewed and stained. There was a stack of crumbling cardboard boxes in the corner where she'd placed the child's room in her dream and she walked over to them, curious. She'd already thrown out several cartons filled with moldy clothing and linens, crumbling paperbacks, and other detritus, but she hadn't gotten around to this particular stack.

The top box was full of magazines, stiff with age and mildew. The second held a wicker basket full of rope.

Liz pushed it away so violently that the entire stack tilted and fell with a crash onto the floor, spilling out children's toys and other, unidentifiable objects. And where they had stood against the wall, she saw something else, a metal ring. She felt suddenly sick, turned and fled upstairs, locking the door behind her.

The following morning, Liz was waiting at the door of the bank when it opened for business. She was first in line at the service desk and a brisk young woman in a green suit escorted her back to collect her safety deposit box and lead her to a cubicle. She thanked the woman absentmindedly, seated herself, and emptied the box onto the counter.

The mortgage was part of a thick sheaf of paper, but it only took her a few seconds to find the document she wanted. She held it in both hands as she read it, frowning, then read it again, more slowly. It was a standard disclosure letter, but there was no mention in it of the murder of a young girl. There had indeed been a murder in the house, however, two murders in fact. John and Hilda Hochleitner had been found dead on November 8 when concerned neighbors notified the police that no one was taking in the mail. There had been no sign of a break-in and the police believed that the killer had been known to the victims, but no one was ever arrested.

Liz felt dazed as she put the papers back. A different woman escorted her out, but Liz was so preoccupied that she never even looked in her direction until they were back in the lobby.

"Please come again, Miss Appleton."

Liz glanced up and nodded just as the woman turned away, and her reply froze in her throat as she saw the side of the woman's face.

There was a distinctive heart shaped birthmark on her cheek.

REMNANTS

I believe in ghosts, but I don't think they're the souls of the departed. I think they're something much worse.

Our early summer move to Managansett was a succession of tiny traumas that began the day I announced my reassignment. Karen did her best to conceal her unhappiness and soothe Jennifer and Danny, but I wasn't fooled.

"I could turn the transfer down. We could stay here in Michigan."

"It would mean the end of your career, Alan, and you know it." She sounded angry, as though I'd forced her to play a noble role and cheated her of the right to sulk.

"It's only temporary, a year or two. Just long enough to integrate the new company into our corporate structure." Eblis Manufacturing had narrowly avoided terminal bankruptcy for several years, a good product line but obsolete equipment, inefficient systems management, and a really appalling turnover rate. But the company fit nicely into our long term marketing plans.

Karen just nodded, not meaning it, not believing me, but resigned to the inevitable. Danny balked at first, his voice cracked by the onset of puberty and the rush of emotion. But I promised camping trips in New Hampshire and swimming on the beaches of Cape Cod. Jennifer was not so easily pacified, not even by the prospect of shopping trips in Boston or New York City or tickets to see the Celtics at Boston Garden.

"All my friends are here!" I could have written her dialogue in advance, remembered similar objections I'd voiced when my father had been rotated from Fort Devens to Fort Sill.

"You'll make new ones." Had I really said something that banal?

"I don't want new ones! Peter Cole just invited me to the junior prom and I think he's going to ask me to go steady..."

I tuned her out after that. It's not that I didn't care, didn't sympathize. But there was nothing I could do about it, not really, and frustration raked its fingernails across the blackboard of my ulcer.

A few days later Karen dropped her grandmother's chocolate set while she was packing it in excelsior and cried herself to sleep that evening. Jennifer's grades dropped so sharply we were called in twice for conferences with her teachers. Our moving van was sideswiped by a truck en route to Rhode Island, arrived a day late and with significant damage to our furniture. Danny was intermittently car sick on the trip, I earned the first speeding ticket of my life, and Jennifer refused to eat properly for two days.

But we finally made it.

The house dated from the 1890's but it had been kept in good repair. It was actually considerably larger than we needed. There were eight rooms on the second floor, and half of the full sized attic had been finished off as well. The other half was crowded with the debris of other lives.

The real estate agent offered to take care of it. "I could hire some local people to cart it all away if you'd like, Mr. Meadows."

"Don't bother." We wouldn't need the space in the short run, and I didn't plan to be around for the longer one.

We settled in, awkwardly at first, what survived of our possessions inadequate to fill the yawning depths of those oversized rooms. Karen's reservations were swamped by her anxiety to have the house looking presentable. "Just don't bring home anyone from work for a couple of weeks. Give me a head start on this."

That was an easy agreement. I was the corporate axe man, after all. If any of my new co-workers came to visit, it would probably be to throw stones through the windows. But I didn't say that to Karen.

Danny adapted quickly, but Jennifer continued to sulk, made only desultory attempts to unpack, never left the house except under duress. At least she was eating again. I relaxed a little, convinced she'd meet some of the local teens and be back to her usual obnoxious brashness before the summer ended.

On the Thursday of our third week in Managansett, I decided to take an afternoon off. There wasn't anything specific I wanted to do, but the atmosphere at Eblis had become openly rancorous. There'd been promises of job security during the acquisition process, but no one took them seriously, and I'd already tentatively decided who would have to go. But even those worth salvaging were resisting change with the tenacity of bull terriers.

Karen had announced plans to take the kids on a day long shopping trip to Providence and the malls, so I expected to have the house to myself for a therapeutic afternoon of doing absolutely nothing constructive.

As soon as I closed the front door I heard someone moving around upstairs.

The Toyota was gone, but maybe one of the kids had decided to stay home, although Karen had been determined to include them, particularly Jennifer.

"If she has to make decisions about things for her room, it'll help her to accept the move."

Possibly something had changed her mind after I'd left for work.

By the time I reached the top of the stairs, there was no question that the sounds came from Jennifer's room. Dancing, I thought, although there was no music.

Her door was half open. I brush knocked it with my knuckles. "Jennifer? Is that you?"

"Dad? C'mon in. You're home early." It was Jennifer's voice, but it wasn't. Deeper, older, and distant.

I pushed open the door, hesitated on the threshold. My daughter was standing beside her bed, wearing only the garish kimono I'd bought for her in Hawaii. It was open in front, revealing far too much.

"Christ, Jennifer, cover up!" I averted my head, angry, disturbed. I was aware of the changes transforming my daughter's body into that of a woman, but this was the first time they'd brought a responsive rush of adrenaline.

"What's the problem, Dad? I mean, it's not like you haven't seen me naked or anything."

There was no movement on the periphery of my vision; she was making no effort toward modesty.

"That's not the point and you know it!" My voice trembled, embarrassment, confusion, even shame. I was suddenly terrified that I'd have an erection, that she'd see it.

I bolted from the room, heard a faint sound from behind that might have been laughter.

During my career, I've personally fired close to a hundred people, ordered the termination of five times that number. I've had people beg me to spare their jobs, break down into tears, offer bribes, utter threats. On one occasion I was physically attacked, and on another watched a middle-aged man suffer a fatal stroke. Every instance caused me some degree of personal distress even though I only acted to keep the healthy part of our work force employed and productive.

But that brief encounter in my daughter's bedroom left me shaken and irresolute. I was sitting in the living room, drinking brandy, when Karen drove up.

As soon as she came through the front door, she could read my anxiety.

"What's wrong, Alan?"

"We need to talk."

"What happened? Something at work?"

"No." I fought to keep my voice calm. "It's Jennifer. She's..." But I never finished that sentence.

"What's Jennifer? What did I do now?" My daughter had stepped through the door after her mother, carrying bulging shopping bags in either arm and wearing the new designer jeans that had been the pivotal enticement for her participation in this jaunt.

I glanced up at the ceiling, my mouth dry. Not for one moment did I believe that I'd been fooled, that my daughter had somehow given Karen the slip, returned to the house for our little scene, then rejoined her for the trip home.

"Sorry, I must've fallen asleep on the couch and had a dream." But it hadn't been a dream. I wasn't sure what had happened earlier, but I'd been awake.

Karen glanced at the brandy bottle and her eyes narrowed just the tiniest bit. "You look like you're coming down with something, Alan," she lied. "Let's get you off to bed."

I cooperated, retreating from my own family, particularly Jennifer, who would never seem quite the same to me again. We didn't talk about it that evening, and the next morning, Karen pretended to have forgotten the entire incident.

But I knew she hadn't. Wouldn't.

The house began to look a little more like home during the next few days, and I pushed my unpleasant experience into a cloistered recess of my mind. I could even meet Jennifer's eyes again. Karen made pointed comments to the effect that I was working too hard, so I agreed not to go in at all on Saturday despite the backlog sitting on my desk.

"You could make a start on cutting down the brush in the backyard. A little exercise might clear your head."

She was right. I started hacking away at several years' worth of unbridled chaos early that morning, hardly pausing to eat, drink, and pee, and only quit when the sun dropped so low I could no longer see what I was doing. A long hot shower made me so sleepy that I was in bed by eight o'clock.

I woke at midnight.

Karen was asleep beside me, hadn't disturbed me when she came to bed. I could hear her regular breathing, familiar, comforting. The house was otherwise silent except for the usual murmurs and the brushing of tree limbs against the gutters and flashing.

My throat was dry so I carefully slipped out of bed, found my slippers in the dark, and padded over to the adjoining bath. The first glass of water when down fast; I was more deliberate with the second.

There was a small diamond shaped window in the bathroom wall that overlooked the rear of the house. The sky was clear, the moon nearly full, and I leaned forward, wondering how the day's work affected the view.

The thicket was a shadow of its former self, crowding around the edges of the land I'd made my own. I gave a little grunt of satisfaction, was about to turn away, when something moved across my field of vision.

Someone was walking down there.

I'm not a fan of horror films, films of any kind for that matter. Never had the time, nor the inclination. But I've seen enough of them to know that you never, never go outside alone at night when you see a mysterious figure walking about. Instead, you call the police, report a prowler, then lock and bolt all the doors. I'm a reasonable person, so I descended to the ground floor, confirmed that the doors and windows were secure, and made no effort to investigate personally. But I didn't call the police. Instead I made my way to the back pantry and climbed over a pile of boxes to peer out the most advantageously situated window.

No sign of the intruder, at least not until I turned my head toward the tiny patio at the periphery of my field of vision. There was a woman sitting on one of the new chairs Karen had ordered from Sears, her face averted.

Mystified, I backed away, mentally reviewing the geography of the house. The dining room window seemed the best bet, and I hastened in that direction, almost tripping over my own feet in the process.

I used two fingers to move the curtain slightly to one side, leaning close to the glass. The view was better from here, but I still couldn't see her face. I could, however, see what she was doing.

There was a large, well kept cat sitting in the woman's lap, allowing or perhaps demanding to be petted. My mysterious trespasser was obliging, her fingers stroking the fur just behind the ears. I could almost hear the purr, my imagination providing the sound that could not reach my ears through the thick glass.

The cat's shrieks a moment later penetrated with no difficulty.

The woman had suddenly tightened her grip, pressed fingers deep into throat and chest. She half turned in my direction, arms straining with effort, and the cat literally burst apart. Blood sprayed in a wide, brief arc.

My hand clenched so tightly that the curtains tore away from the window. I felt numb, unable to move, watched in complete disbelief as the woman tossed the tiny corpse to one side and turned toward me.

I saw her face.

It was Karen, my wife, Karen who captured spiders in Tupperware and escorted them out of the house and who swatted flies with open regret. But Karen was upstairs in bed. I'd just left her, hadn't I? The need to confirm that belief broke the trance and I bolted, fell and banged one knee in my haste to get upstairs, nearly wakened her by turning on the light in our bedroom.

She threw her arm over her eyes, mumbled something inarticulate, and resumed her regular breathing. Karen, inside, not standing on the patio with blood dripping from her fingers.

I spent the rest of the night sitting in the living room, with the lights on, and when the sun finally came up I ventured outside and searched fruitlessly for any trace of blood stains or a tiny mangled corpse.

Personality is not a continuous process. It seems so to us because we see patterns in the behavior of others. When someone performs an act "out of character" we view it as an anomaly, an aberration, rather than an implicit part of the mosaic of a person. But what if we're all masses of conflicting emotions and desires, held in check by some internal monitor that occasionally fails and allows one facet of the mosaic to escape? What if the most extreme, radical elements of our personalities create a sympathetic resonance in the world around us? Surviving remnants of emotional crises long past. And what happens when someone sensitive enough to feel that lingering presence wanders into range?

There was no history of ghosts in our house. I asked carefully, making a joke of it. When I called Healey, the real estate agent, he sounded defensive until I explained that I was only satisfying a promise to my son, who thought he'd seen something.

"No, Mr. Meadows, I can truthfully say that I don't know of anyone dying in that house in living memory. Before my time, maybe; the place is over a hundred years old after all. But no ghosts, no murders, no suicides. Maybe your son smoked one of those funny cigarettes."

The neighbors confirmed his assertion. An elderly widow named Kingsley seemed particularly willing to talk. "The Nicholsons weren't nice people though, I'd have to say. He hit her occasionally, you know. Right out in the yard more than once. And the kids were wild. Their daughter was on drugs during high school, never did finish. And the boy was a real hellion."

Nicholson died peacefully in a hospital, which Mrs. Kingsley thought particularly unfair. His daughter was killed in an automobile accident in Providence, and the wife and son had both moved on.

The family had owned the property for thirty years.

"Maybe we should look for another place to live." I dropped the bombshell over dinner, trying to make it sound casual.

"What in the world brought that on?" Karen was looking at me as though I were a stranger.

"I don't know. Our stuff just seems lost in this mausoleum, we're only using half the house as it is, and it'll be a real bear to heat over the winter."

"Oh, fine, I'm just getting my room looking good and you want me to move again." Jennifer shook her head and stared at her plate, adopting this new martyrdom. Danny kept glancing back and forth among us, trying to decide if he needed to pick a side.

I decided to defuse things quickly. "All right, it was just a thought. We're staying."

Apparently I was the only one disturbed by our new home.

Several days passed, and I began to wonder belatedly if I had not perhaps hallucinated both incidents. The possibility that I was suffering from the stress of my new job - which was turning out to be the greatest challenge I'd ever faced - seemed plausible, and obliquely reassuring. At least that explanation was a rational one.

"Things aren't going well, are they?"

I rarely discussed work with Karen. We had an unspoken and longstanding agreement that the things I was required to do to maintain our high standard of living were to be kept separate from our personal lives. I never brought work home, although I often stayed late, and reciprocally there was nothing of my family in my office, no pictures, no mementoes.

"I've dealt with obstinate people before," I confessed, "but never to this degree. And they're remarkably adept at undermining the changes I'm making. If they'd put half that energy into their real work, they might have been buying us out instead of the other way around."

It had rained two weekends in a row, so I'd made no further progress clearing away the jungle behind the house. In fact, I'd lost some ground. Wisteria had erupted from under the sod, and the surrounding bull briar had sprouted fresh growth challenging my enterprise.

"Time to get up, Danny."

He grumbled and rolled away from me. Danny had never been good about mornings; I couldn't begin to count the number of times he'd been late to school.

"Remember? You work in the yard with me today and we go to the beach tomorrow."

His unintelligible reply sounded enough like surrender that I left him to sort himself out while I went to survey the battlefield. The brush was remarkably thick, so many runners and vines and branches tangled together that there was no way to determine which stems led to which foliage. I used long handled clippers to cut through as many as I could comfortably reach, then grabbed a rake and struggled to pull the severed portion free. By the time I'd dragged away the first fresh fatalities, I was already soaked with sweat.

Danny was standing a few feet away, watching intently.

"They won't go away no matter how hard you stare at them," I said shortly. "Grab that other rake and help me with this."

I turned my back, assuming he'd do as he was told. Danny had a tendency to whine and complain, but he was basically a good kid, and I could count on one hand the number of times he'd defied me, even in minor ways. I was wrestling with a second snarl of briar when something subliminal alerted me, half turned and raised the rake as the blade of a shovel sheered toward my head.

Danny pulled back just before contact, shifted his stance, and swung again.

This time I was better prepared, intercepted the shovel with the tines of the rake, hoping to jerk it out of his hands. But there was no jar of contact. Impossibly I had missed, and I stiffened in anticipation of the impact against my face, eyes involuntarily closing.

Nothing.

"What the hell?" I wasn't angry; I was on the verge of tears.

Danny dropped the shovel and retreated from me, his back pressing against the wall of thorn bushes.

"What the Christ was that all about?" I dropped the rake and advanced on him, so close that the more expansive branches snagged my clothing.

His face was blandly expressionless when he opened his mouth as though to answer.

His tongue was green and there were barbed thorns protruding from it on every side. The tongue wriggled out of his mouth as I gasped and recoiled, and then more creepers appeared, from his ears and nose, emerging from beneath the folds of his clothing, then bursting out of his eyes sockets with a tiny pop of aqueous fluid. In seconds his body was a mass of writhing foliage that gradually quieted, settled back, and became indistinguishable from the bull briar and wild rose.

"Dad? Are you all right?"

I had fallen to my knees, my clothing torn in a dozen places by thorns, and I can only imagine what my face looked like. Danny was standing just beyond reach, sleep still visible in his eyes, a piece of toast forgotten in one hand.

I forced myself to find the breath to speak. "Yeah, Dan, I'm fine. Just fell and jabbed myself in about a thousand places is all. Help me get out of this."

That afternoon, I hired a local contractor to finish the job.

The ghosts...visions...hallucinations...whatever increased in frequency after that, although they were of such short duration that I remained constantly uncertain. I'd hear Nancy calling or Jennifer giggling suggestively or Danny crying out in pain, and sometimes I'd catch a glimpse of one of them, at a window, out in the garden, at the far end of a darkened hall. I could no longer tell the real from the imaginary unless I touched one of them.

They couldn't hurt me physically, it appeared, couldn't manifest themselves as solid flesh. But they caused me countless tiny torments, moments of fear, grief, disorientation, or shame.

I decided to confront them, perform my own personal exorcism.

To do so, I must first remove my family from the scene so that I could conclusively separate illusion from reality. As far as I could tell, no one else was experiencing anything out of the ordinary. Karen knew that I was under unusual stress, but I think I'd convinced her that it was the job that was responsible. She expressed sympathetic concern, but honored our agreement not to discuss these matters. Neither of the kids seemed to have noticed the way I constantly watched the shadows, remained alert to subtle sounds.

"How would you all like to spend a week on Cape Cod? I've rented a little beach front cottage."

Danny thought it was a great idea, and Jennifer showed more enthusiasm than I'd expected.

"It'll do you good to get away from your job for a few days," agreed Karen.

I'd rehearsed this in my mind dozens of times during the previous three days, but my mouth was still dry. "I won't be able to go with you, I'm afraid."

The kids just looked confused; Karen was openly angry. "What's going on, Alan? You need a vacation more than any of us. Why can't you go?"

"Things at Eblis are critical right now. I can't leave, Karen."

"Then why rent a place on the Cape?"

I sighed theatrically. "Look, the Cape has been booked solid for months. One of the managers at work has kidney stones and can't take his vacation, so I offered to buy out his reservations. I'd come if I could, and I will try to make it for the weekend at least. All right?"

Clearly it wasn't, but Jennifer and Danny took my side for selfish reasons, and Karen finally gave in, silently promising retribution.

They drove down on a Sunday afternoon. The house seemed particularly silent after they were gone, but it was a tense, irritable silence.

The night passed uneventfully.

I cut work short on Monday, announced I was taking Tuesday off, and ignored the ripples of surprise - and relief - that resulted.

The house was empty and silent. No, just silent. I knew there was someone or something waiting for me. I tried to act normally, unconcerned, vulnerable to suggestion. A change into casual clothing, a cold beer, the television mercifully silent, no CD player blaring from upstairs. I sat on the couch, pretended to read a magazine.

They didn't keep me waiting for long. Footsteps, light but deliberate, walking the corridor above my head.

"You might as well come down. I'm too pooped to climb the stairs just for a teaser."

Silence.

I flipped a page, then another. There was a familiar creak, the second stair from the top had a loose board. I resisted the temptation to crane my head around for a look.

"Don't be shy. I don't bite."

More footsteps, running this time, down the stairs, across the short hall behind me, into the kitchen. I sighed. Apparently we were going to play hard to get. Discarding the magazine, I rose and followed, making no effort to hurry.

Danny was standing in the center of the room, holding a broad bladed knife in one hand. No, not Danny. Some leftover moment of anger or hatred that manifested itself in the image of my son. That's all it was.

"Be careful. You'll hurt yourself." I concentrated on remaining calm. If these manifestations were born of strong emotion, then perhaps that was also what sustained them. Certainly every incident I'd experienced had been designed to evoke a powerful reaction.

The Danny thing advanced toward me, raising the knife to striking position. My automatic reaction was to flinch, retreat, and I did so hastily, knocking the telephone from its shelf in my haste. But then I remembered myself and stepped forward, plunged my outstretched hand into his...its chest.

I was alone in the kitchen. The image hadn't faded; it had just ceased to be.

The house was silent for the rest of the evening.

I woke to the sound of running water, Karen drawing her morning bath. On the verge of dropping back to sleep I remembered that Karen was in Hyannis. Waiting only long enough to allow my pulse to slow and my thoughts to clear, I rose, donned slippers and a bathrobe, and crossed to the bathroom door.

The tub was full, overflowing in fact, although my feet remained dry when I stepped in the puddles. There were five drowned puppies in the tub, another in the sink.

"Hurry up in there, will you? I've got a lot to do today." Karen's voice, from behind me, in the bedroom.

I retraced my steps, found her sitting on the foot of the bed, wringing the neck of a small bird.

"Karen would never do anything so cruel," I said quickly, feeling the emotion beginning to build, fearing that I would lose control. I reached out to touch her face and she was gone, like the image of Danny before her, a brief look of accusation her only parting gift.

The day passed into darkness before the next, and final manifestation.

All day I'd anticipated her appearance, and I was anxious to have it over with. The images of Karen's cruelty, Danny's violence, had never rung true; their power diminished by the inconsistency. Jennifer's sexual awakening, and to my shame my involuntary response to it, were more disquieting because they were closer to the truth. No, I never molested my daughter, not even in my thoughts, but sometimes, in unguarded moments, my body proved traitor.

It was a hot day, I hadn't bothered to run the air conditioning, and I was taking a shower before bed. When I stepped out, groping for a towel, she was leaning against the door, wearing cutoffs and a white halter top. One strap had fallen from her shoulder.

"Miss me, Dad?" She let her eyes trail down my body.

I felt myself responding, decided to end it quickly, lunged forward to touch her. With a silky sliding motion that was in itself sexual, she eluded my touch, retreating into the other room. "You'd like to touch me, wouldn't you?"

I hesitated, then threw on a bathrobe and followed.

She was lying on the bed, one bare knee crossed over the other. "Can I sleep with you tonight, Daddy? I've been having bad dreams."

"You're not my daughter." I tried to ignore the tremor in my voice. "You're not Jennifer." I advanced slowly, trying to seem casual.

"But you'd like me to be, wouldn't you?"

"I'd like you to leave me alone." I was close, only a step away from the bed, but she rolled off the other side and stood facing me. Both straps had fallen now and she stood with her hips angled provocatively.

"Why don't you come outside with me, Daddy? I don't have anyone to play with here."

She drifted out into the hall, not walking exactly, and slipped out of sight.

"Damn it!" I wanted to follow but I was afraid to. Temporizing, I shed the robe and put on slacks and a pullover, then descended to the ground floor, trying to rein in my emotions. She was standing by the front door.

Counterfeit or not, she was the image of my daughter, correct in every physical detail. How had she gotten to be such a vibrant, attractive young woman without my noticing? Or perhaps I had noticed after all, just never admitted it to myself.

"Why don't you come over here?" I wanted her close, close enough to touch, one touch and she'd be gone, and I'd be free. One touch.

"You'd like to touch me, wouldn't you?"

I blinked. It was as though she'd read my mind.

"Would you like to touch me here?" She pulled the halter up from her breasts, letting them fall free, and I caught my breath. If I'd been able to move in that moment, I might have ended it then, but I froze. "Or maybe somewhere else?"

"Why are you doing this?" I whispered hoarsely, struggling for calm.

"Because you want me to. You've wanted to for a long time, but you keep pretending not to know." The door never opened, but she was gone.

My hands were shaking with emotion, heart beating so rapidly I could feel it as a positive pressure in my chest. For the first time I began to doubt my own ability to prevail, wondered if I should leave the house, get in the car, drive away and never come back. But then anger replaced, or at least masked the complex emotions Jennifer's image had evoked.

I picked up a knife from the counter and followed the phantom of my daughter into the darkness.

She was waiting for me, standing at the edge of the woodlot that separated our property from the reservoir property. Her white halter top was a beacon in the moonlight, and I followed, walking at first, then running. I heard her laughter, familiar but alien, as she raced ahead of me, following the footpath we'd explored earlier, the narrow trail that cut across the undeveloped watershed land and down to the main road that led to our neighborhood.

The chase couldn't have lasted more than ten minutes - it wasn't that long a path - but it seemed endless. Just before we reached the main road, she stopped, only a few meters ahead of me, and turned in my direction.

"You want me, don't you? Admit it, Dad, you want to screw your own daughter."

I stumbled to a stop, physically arrested by her accusation, then started forward more deliberately, the carving knife ready. "You're twisting everything. I love my daughter."

"Yeah, but you'd like to love her even more, wouldn't you? Isn't that why you're always trying to get her to dress more ladylike, so you can sneak a look at her legs every once in a while?"

"It's not like that." I was close now, almost close enough.

"Confess, Dad. Isn't that why you used to spank me so much when I was younger. Isn't that why you always made me pull down my pants first?"

My vision blurred as I lunged, but she moved again, at the last possible moment, disappearing around a curve of the path. I had to wait until my breathing returned to normal, but then I continued, determined to end this.

We were above the main feed to the reservoir now, a narrow, fast moving current that roared as it thrashed its way over a forest of jagged rocks. The Jennifer image was just ahead, standing on the very edge, facing away from me.

I broke into a run, determined to end it now, closed the distance quickly but, at the last moment, a rock turned under my foot and I fell, arms swinging madly, hoping I was close enough to strike before I fell. I think I almost felt the impact - she was so much more real than the others - but then I hit the ground.

The breath rushed from my lungs.

When I recovered my wits and sat up, there was no sign of the counterfeit Jennifer and the night sounds seemed perfectly normal. I felt drained, emotionally and physically, sat with my legs curled under my body, head down, trying to recover my strength.

Someone touched my arm.

"Dad, are you all right?" It was Danny, his expression cautiously alarmed, and I felt the warmth of his hand. A real hand.

"Danny? What are you doing here? You're supposed to be on the Cape with your mother."

"Yeah, but we kept trying to call you and the line was always busy." I remembered the accident with the phone the previous day. "She made us come back to find out what was going on, but then the car broke down right in the middle of Prescott Street, so she sent us to get you."

Danny glanced around. "Where's Jennifer? She got ahead of me when I stopped to take a pee."

"Jennifer?" I turned away, glanced in the direction of the rushing waters fifty feet below.

She didn't answer.

THE INCORRUPTIBLE

"What do you suppose could have done this, Tom?" Matt Riley walked around the body, keeping his distance though his face was impassive. He wasn't about to let his companion know that he felt sick. "Some kind of animal?"

Tom Sharpton was squatting down beside the corpse, his nose wrinkling at the smell of death. "No animal I ever heard of could've done anything like this. Had to be a man." The two friends had been riding southwest from Cimarron City on their way to Piedmont where they'd heard there was work for the asking. They had taken a short detour because a flash flood had washed away the trail and had stumbled into a shallow valley which seemed to lead in the right direction. They hadn't expected to encounter another man, living or dead, particularly dead in such a gruesome fashion.

Sharpton glanced up at the sky. "That's funny."

Riley followed his gaze but saw nothing but a wispy cloud. "What're you talking about?"

"No buzzards. This here body was killed some time yesterday, I'd guess, and it smells nice and ripe. So where are the buzzards?"

"Maybe we scared 'em away."

Sharpton shook his head. "We would've seen them flying off. They wouldn't have gone far." He stood up and looked around. "And this body hasn't been touched."

That wasn't quite true. The body had been touched quite a lot. It was clearly a man, and a white man, but his own mother wouldn't have known him now. The body had been dismantled rather than dismembered. All of the fingers and toes were separated from the limbs, which had in turn been severed from the torso. The head had been removed as well. It stood on a flat rock with its ears, eyeballs, tongue, and teeth laid out neatly in a circle around it. The fingers and toes were arranged around the base of the stone, each one propped up against it to that they pointed to the sky. The torso was intact, sort of; the ribs had been caved in and most were broken. The internal organs had all been pulled out and were drying in the sun and the man's clothing had been shredded. Sharpton and Riley had been forced to approach on foot; their horses would not come near the body. Neither man realized that the man's heart and his sex were both missing.

But in the sense that Sharpton meant it, he was right. No scavengers had disturbed the scene, not even flies.

"Injuns?"

Sharpton stood up. "A skinwalker might do this, I guess, but I don't know why. Some kind of ritual."

Riley moved one hand to the butt of his Colt and looked around warily. "Do you suppose whoever done this is still around?"

Sharpton removed his hat and scratched his head. "Might be. I suppose we ought to bury the poor soul. I don't fancy carting him to the next town in this condition.."

Riley's eyes were darting around nervously. "I say we just leave him as is and tell someone about it when we get to Piedmont. Can't do anything more for him now and I don't feel like meeting whoever's responsible."

Sharpton sighed, but nodded. "Okay, but let's take a quick look around. Could be he wasn't alone and someone might need help."

Riley looked like he was going to balk, but he finally nodded. "All right, but Spencer is going with us." He walked to where they had tied the horses and removed a carbine from its sheath and cocked the hammer. Sharpton followed and retrieved his own rifle, a more modern Winchester.

The valley had narrowed considerably at this point and their route had become increasingly crowded with stunted trees and low brush. The two men moved together with practiced skill, close enough to cover one another, far enough apart to avoid making a single target. They had learned to watch each other's backs when they'd fought in the Confederate Army and they found peacetime no less dangerous than war.

It was Riley who spotted the tracks. He waved to Sharpton but made a sign to indicate caution. Sharpton tensed but didn't hesitate and reached the other man in less than a minute.

"Someone's been this way," Riley whispered. "At least ten mounts, two of them shod."

"Indian ponies."

"I told you it was injuns. They must have ambushed that poor soul and taken his horse."

"Two shod horses. There might have been someone with him."

Riley was sweating and it had nothing to do with the heat. "Odds are four to one or more against us. I say we fold our hand and let someone else deal with them. The other man's probably dead already anyway."

Sharpton would have liked to agree, but he'd lost his brother to Comanches when they were both in their teens. He knew he couldn't just ride off and not try to help if he could. "Let's just take a look and see what there is to see. If they've skedaddled, we won't be able to catch them anyway."

But they hadn't. There was a side canyon, more of a ravine, that twisted back and forth for a way, then straightened out. When the two men came around the last bend, they could see smoke rising from a campfire and a moment later a horse whinnied. Riley and Sharpton found a gradual rise with good cover and carefully made their way to a vantage point from which they could look down into the camp.

"Cherokee?" asked Riley in a voice so low Sharpton could barely hear it.

"Choctaw. Hunting party by the looks of it. No war paint, no squaws."

There were eight men near the fire and a ninth over beyond the horses, which had been tethered a surprisingly long way from the campsite. And they had a prisoner.

At first Sharpton thought the Cherokee had tied up one of their own. The hair was long and black and the skin had been burned dark by exposure to the sun. But the clothing was wrong and when he looked more closely he realized the prisoner was a white woman. She'd been tied between two trees with her arms outstretched.

"Can't leave her like that," he said aloud, without meaning to.

Riley grunted but nodded. "We're damn fools but I guess you're right. See any firearms down there?"

At first all Sharpton could spot were some bows and quivers, but then he saw what was probably another Spencer propped against a tree, and the ninth man came back from dealing with the horses and he was carrying another. "At least two of Spencer's brothers."

Riley massaged his bristly chin. "We can probably get at least four of 'em before they scatter."

"That leaves five and we might not get all four from this distance." Riley would have to reset the hammer after each shot with the Spencer. Sharpton doubted he'd get his second man before they reached cover.

"Then I reckon we got to get ourselves closer."

They had just started to crawl through the brush when the woman screamed. It was a cry of pain not panic and her voice was deep, almost mannish. The two men froze and Sharpton lifted his head to see what was going on. Flies buzzed around his face, some of them biting and drawing blood, but he paid them no attention.

All nine men were gathered around the woman now and one of them was standing very close to her. He held a skinning knife in one hand. The woman had stopped screaming but she was still conscious; he could see her straining against the ropes.

Riley had angled off toward the horses, hoping their restless noise would cover any sound he might make. Sharpton couldn't see him anymore but he trusted his partner's judgment. He wished that they had never left the original trail, but there was nothing to be done about it now. The man with the knife pressed it against the woman's left wrist and she screamed again, and there was anger mixed with the pain. Sharpton was close enough to see the weal where the blade had touched. They had heated it in the fire before using it.

He found a good spot, close enough that he wouldn't miss, with a low stump to provide some cover. Riley would need another minute or two to get set, so Sharpton chose his primary and secondary targets. The man with the knife would die first. Even as he made the decision, the brave turned and seemed to look directly at Sharpton, who now saw the jagged scar on the man's forehead. He hoped to place his first round right in the middle of it.

And then all hell broke loose. Either Riley had been careless or one of the braves had unusually sharp eyes. There was a shout and then confusion and then two barked reports as both Riley and Sharpton opened fire. Both shots were on target, but Sharpton's first choice had moved and he had to be satisfied with one of the others. His second shot dropped a man with a bow, but his third missed. Most of the party ran toward the horses and Riley rose up behind a tree and methodically fired his remaining six rounds, dropping one and wounding a second. Sharpton was on his feet and running and he snapped off three more rounds to cover Riley while the other man reloaded, or more likely drew his Colt.

Three of the Choctaw reached their horses and galloped off. Two more disappeared into the brush. The four who remained were all dead but the man with the scar was not among them.

Sharpton wasn't taking any unnecessary chances. He used his sheath knife to free the woman and dragged her to the ground while he reloaded. There was nothing but silence for a minute or two, then a rustling off to his right. He tensed and raised his weapon but it was Riley.

"They hightailed it, I guess. I got two for sure. How about you?"

"I did all right. We need to get out of here. There are still at least five of them and they took the rifles." He turned to the woman, who hadn't spoken a word. "Do you think you can walk, ma'am? This isn't a safe place to be."

She wasn't exactly pretty, he realized, but she'd do. Strong features, dark eyes set deep in her face, and she didn't look the least bit frightened. "Is this all of you?"

"Just the two of us. We didn't think you'd like it if we went back to town for help first."

"No, I surely wouldn't have."

Riley went to see if he could retrieve one of the extra horses, but those that hadn't borne riders had run off along with the rest once the lead was untied. The three of them retraced the route to the main canyon where Riley promptly began to curse fluently. Their own mounts were gone. "No tracks but ours. Something must have spooked them."

"Nothing to be done about it now." Sharpton looked around. The sun was dropping toward the hills in the distance. "We need to find shelter for the night, some place we can defend if we have to."

The woman hadn't spoken since they'd started walking but she cleared her voice now. "There's a cave up that ways a little." She nodded toward the opposite side of the valley.

"That'll have to do. I'm Tom Sharpton, ma'am, and this foul mouthed jackass is Matt Riley."

"Nice to meet you both." Her voice was level and emotionless.

"And you are?" he prompted.

"Oh! Sorry. My name is Cynthia, Cynthia Rose."

"I'm sorry about the fellow you were with. We found his body over there behind those trees."

"That was my husband, Frank." She didn't seem particularly broken up about her loss, but Sharpton decided she might be too shocked to react just yet.

"Did those injuns do that to him?" asked Riley. "Cut him up like that?"

"Why, I don't know. I suppose they must have."

Sharpton glanced around. "We can jaw about it later. Right now I'd feel a lot better if we were under cover."

The cave was right where she'd said they'd find it and it was large enough to accommodate them nicely. Sharpton would have liked to start a fire at the mouth, but decided there was no point advertising where they had camped. The woman seemed to have withdrawn into herself and he figured that was normal, that she'd need to adjust now that she had leisure to think about what had happened to her, might happen to her yet if they weren't careful. There was a brook nearby so they could drink but they had nothing to eat and no blankets. They also counted up their ammunition and weren't happy. Even with the handguns, they only had about thirty rounds between them.

"First watch," said Riley quietly. The woman had retreated deeper into the cave and was curled up in a small alcove.

"All right." Sharpton wanted to talk to Cynthia Rose and find out more about what had happened, but when he reached her she was sound asleep. Probably the best thing right now, he decided, and tried to find a relatively soft spot for himself.

He woke knowing that something was wrong. He had slept too long. During his adult life he had probably slept outside as many nights as within buildings and he knew the time by the sound of the insects, the feel of the air, the look of the sky. Riley should have wakened him a long time earlier. He uncoiled slowly and checked his weapons. The woman had turned onto her side but was still asleep. Very cautiously he moved to the mouth of the cave.

There was no sign of Riley, but his Spencer leaned against a rock and his Colt lay on the ground not far away. Sharpton called his name a few times, then gathered up the weapons and retreated almost to where the woman was sleeping. He stayed awake until morning.

They found Riley just after sunrise. At least Sharpton assumed it was Riley. The body was dismembered and arranged identically to that of Frank Rose. Only the clothing was different. He was about thirty feet from the cave mouth and there was no evidence of a struggle. Both weapons had been fully loaded when Sharpton found them, and a shot would have brought him running from even the deepest sleep.

The woman regarded the body impassively. She'd already seen her husband like this, Sharpton realized. A dismembered stranger couldn't be worse than that.

"We need to move. They know where we are." He scanned the opposite hillside but nothing moved that shouldn't be moving. "Can you handle this?" He offered her the Spencer. She looked at it, nodded, and casually cocked the hammer. Satisfied, Sharpton put the extra revolver in his belt. "We need to get high enough that we have a chance of seeing them coming. And they will be coming."

She nodded. "They have horses."

"I don't think a horse can climb that hill unless it's a lot easier on the other side. But even without the horses, they'll run us down if they want to. If it comes to that, don't hesitate. Shoot at the chest if you can; it's a bigger target."

"I can shoot straight," she said matter of factly. "I've killed a man before this."

His eyebrows rose but he showed no other reaction. "Then let's be on our way."

The climb was even more difficult than he'd expected, but whenever he looked back, she was right behind him. She wasn't much more than a girl, he realized, at least on the outside. On the inside, she was full grown and strong enough to be a man.

It took all morning to reach the crest, and then it was a little easier walking along the spine of the hills, although not a whole lot. There were no brooks up this high, but it had rained briefly during the night and twice he found small puddles of water where they could get down on all fours and partially quench their thirst. The woman sat down when he decided they needed a rest but she never asked for one first. He was impressed.

They walked all afternoon and Sharpton's stomach had given up rumbling by the time he decided they should start looking for a place to spend the night. "Don't suppose you know about another cave up this way?"

They hadn't exchanged more than a dozen words since setting out. Sharpton wanted to ask her about what had happened when the Choctaw jumped her and her husband, but he figured she wouldn't want to talk about it just yet and the fact was he needed all his breath for the walking and she probably felt the same. There would be time enough if they made it away safely, and it wouldn't matter if they didn't.

At the very last minute he sensed the ambush and brought up his Winchester but it was too late. Something hard struck him in the side of the head and he thought he might have heard a single gunshot before everything went away but maybe he just imagined it.

When he came to, he was sitting with his back to a tree. His wrists were tied behind his back and his ankles were similarly secured. Night had fallen but there was a fire burning not far away and he could see shadows jumping around him. He looked around cautiously, planning to feign unconsciousness if necessary. He saw the woman first. Cynthia Rose was back where she had started, tied between two trees facing him from the opposite side of the campfire. A Chocktaw was feeding wood to the flames and two others conversed in low tones not far away.

Sharpton tested the knots. He knew something that his captors didn't know. He had a trick thumb that was constantly dislocating itself. If he could manage to ease the process along, he might be able to work his hands loose. In any case, it seemed to be his only option.

The hushed conversation came to an end and the two men approached the bound woman. Each of them, Sharpton realized, carried a makeshift wooden club. He had a sudden presentiment of what they were going to do and even as they swung their arms he opened his mouth and screamed. "NO!"

There was a double crack as they broke both of Cynthia Rose's kneecaps. She screamed and once again Sharpton noticed that it seemed to carry more anger than pain. This was one stalwart woman, he decided, and he was more determined than ever to save her. Of course, that was only if he managed to save himself. That possibility seemed to recede suddenly as one of the men turned and walked around the fire and toward him. The third man stood up now, a burning faggot in each hand, and started toward the woman.

Sharpton closed his eyes when the screaming started again, but a hand caught him by the hair and jerked his head up. He opened his eyes and stared into the face of the man with the scarred forehead, who now squatted in front of him.

"You do not understand what is happening, white man. You should not feel sorrow for that one."

"Since when do Choctaw braves make war on women?"

The scarred man smiled. "That is no woman. She is Kalona Ayeliski."

"Her name is Cynthia Rose. That was her husband you killed down in the canyon. And it was my friend that you killed at the cave."

The scarred man shook his head. "Their blood is not on our hands. It is their killer which we have bound and which we will drive out of this land."

She screamed again and Sharpton could see that they had set her clothing on fire and that it was spreading to her hair. "You're killing her!"

A shake of the head. "Not so. She wears the face of one of your women but that is not who she truly is. We saw what she did to the man in the valley and knew her for what she was. I told you she is Kalona Ayeliski and she cannot be killed. Her flesh and the flesh of her victims can never return to the earth from which they came. But she can be driven away, at least for a time. We would have done so already if you and your friend had not interfered."

Sharpton thought quickly. "You sound like you're an educated man. You don't believe that nonsense, do you?"

The other man smiled. "I am called Joseph Moshulatubbee and I have been to your white man's school. I learned many things there but there is more knowledge than can be found in your books. This," he gestured back toward the bound figure, which was now wreathed in flames," is one of those things the white man has never learned."

"You ignorant savage!" One hand came free and then the other. The skinning knife was stuck through the Choctaw's belt pouch. Sharpton waited until the man's attention was diverted by another long scream from behind, then brought both arms around, a fist striking the man on the jaw while the other hand grabbed for the hilt of the knife.

The other two Choctaw were intently watching the woman burn and Moshulatubbee was too stunned to cry out. Sharpton leaned forward awkwardly and silenced him permanently by cutting his throat. It took only a few seconds to cut the ropes on his ankles and then he was on his feet and stalking the other two. At the last possible second, one of them sensed that something was wrong and started to turn. Sharpton stabbed the other in the center of the back, planning to pull the knife out and face the remaining man, but it caught in the bone and would not budge.

The other Choctaw was on him, his own knife out, and Sharpton desperately caught him by the arms. They struggled without speaking for a few seconds, then toppled to the ground where they rolled and punched and fought like two badgers. Sharpton felt an incredibly sharp pain in his left thigh but forced himself to ignore it. He was larger and perhaps more determined and definitely luckier because the Choctaw struck his head against the bole of a tree and was stunned. Sharpton staggered upright and kick the downed man repeatedly in the head, then stooped to pick up the knife.

He staggered to the woman's side but he could see that he was too late. Her hair had been burnt to the scalp, her clothing was almost completely gone, and her flesh was charred and smoldering wherever he looked. But he could not leave her that way and he cut the ropes, catching her and lowering her gently to the ground. Then he started back toward the last Choctaw with murder in his heart but he almost fell before he reached him. His leg was going numb and he realized that he was bleeding heavily. He managed to stanch the flow substantially by knotting his bandanna around the wound, but he was growing weak. Before he lost consciousness, he would have to dispose of the surviving Choctaw.

When he crouched over the unconscious man, he discovered that he could not cut the man's throat in cold blood. So instead, cursing his soft heartedness, Sharpton bound him with the same ropes from which he'd freed himself and then he sat down to catch his breath. And passed out.

When he opened his eyes again, he felt a pervasive chill and realized that he might well be dying from blood loss. There was no possible way he could walk to civilization in his present condition and he doubted the Indians had brought their horses up onto the ridge. Maybe he could get the survivor to tell him where they were tethered, trade his life for the information. It was his only chance.

The fire had burned low but it still illuminated the small clearing. Sharpton turned to where he had left the bound man and saw a figure crouching there. He blinked, unable to see it clearly until it turned and looked at him. It was Cynthia Rose, naked and covered with scabs but unmistakably alive. She had even gotten some of her hair back, though it was much shorter than before. How could that be? Sharpton tried to speak but his mouth was dry and he couldn't manage more than a croak.

And her hands weren't right. The fingers were much longer than they should be and they seemed to come to very sharp points.

Then he looked more closely and saw that he wouldn't be getting any information from his prisoner. The man's head sat on the bare ground, surrounded by his eyes and tongue and teeth. The arms had been removed from the torso, although the legs were still attached.

The woman stood up and looked at him. "You're awake! That's much better. It's always better when they can see and hear and feel." She looked back at the corpse at her feet. "He had a brave and tasty heart and he has brought back most of my strength. But it was not enough."

She started toward him and her hands reached out. "I am still hungry."

LINE EDITS

We all live in our own individual worlds, some of them more individual than others.

As lives go, mine has been a fairly pleasant one. I sold my first novel the year after leaving college, and by the time I was forty

I was confident enough of my continued income from that source to resign from retailing and write full time. Although I don't make enough to live a life of leisure, there's enough left after the bills are paid to indulge most of my whims. I married at twenty-two, bore two children who turned out quite well, and my divorce a few years ago was amicable. Frank and I are still good friends; we even date occasionally. Our lives and interests, however, have diverged too far for us to live together.

Mary Wentworth, my best friend, has not had such an easy time of it, although casual observers would certainly describe her as "successful" in life. We were one of those rare pairs of college roommates who genuinely liked each other. She introduced me to Frank and helped me get my first job as a stock clerk in the small gift shop where she ran a cash register. She was my Ellie's godmother; we'd been maids of honor at each other's weddings and had even shared an apartment for a year before Frank and I finally decided to stop dancing around the subject and get married.

Mary's life was a mirror image of my own during those years, but the reflection was distorted. She married Bob Wexler six months after my wedding. He broke her nose – for the first time – the day I gave birth to Ellie. The Wexler's had two children, Robert Jr. and Ashley. Robert was killed by an off duty police officer shortly after his sixteenth birthday when he tried to rob a convenience store. Ashley made it to seventeen, then died of an overdose of that year's drug of choice. A few months after that, Mary sued for divorce, ended up in a hospital when Bob violated a restraining order, and was only saved further problems when he lost control of his muscle car and splattered his brains on a bridge abutment.

Mary had continued to work in retailing all through her marriage – necessarily since Bob flitted from job to job with relentless regularity. The unpleasantness of her home life meant that the long hours required were not a particular burden. She had a natural talent for the job, was steadily promoted, and was managing three chain stores at the time of Bob's death. The one good turn he did Mary was to forget to remove her as chief beneficiary on his current employer's insurance plan. With that and the savings Mary had carefully hidden over the years, she was able to buy her own store – Artisan Gifts, which featured both major name merchandise and art items created by local artists. Managansett wasn't a big shopping town, but the bulk of her business was mail order and she did reasonably well. She had an elaborate web site and a strong presence on Ebay.

Not that her luck had entirely changed. She had constant problems finding good help, among other things, suffered from migraine headaches, and the building she'd purchased was constantly in need of small repairs. The two of us had lunch at least once a week – I live only six blocks from her shop – and there were times when I thought she must have been cursed by some evil spirit. The pipes burst in the store basement one winter, ruining a great deal of stock, and the insurance company delayed payment for almost a year. She caught her chief buyer taking kickbacks from suppliers and she was physically assaulted by a customer on one occasion when she caught the woman shoplifting. A drunk driver totaled her car while it was parked in front of the store and his insurance had lapsed. There was an error in her property tax assessment and it cost so much in legal fees to get it corrected that she almost would have been better off accepting the higher rate.

Then there was the stroke.

Mary and I are the same age, young enough that we shouldn't have to worry about bursting blood vessels and aneurisms. One of her employees knew me well enough to call and explain that Mary had collapsed at work and had been taken away in an ambulance. Since I was as close as Mary had to family – her parents had both died while she was in her teens – I was out the door within seconds. I might as well have taken a shower and changed clothing first because when I arrived, nobody would tell me anything.

"I'm sorry but we can't release that information to anyone except the immediate family."

"I realize that, but is she all right?"

"I'm sorry."

"Can you at least tell me if she's alive?"

"Mrs. Wentworth was admitted at 2:05 and taken immediately to intensive care. I have no other information which I can give you at this time." The nurse softened a bit. "Once a member of the patient's family arrives, we'll be able to bring them completely up to date."

"She doesn't have any family. I'm all she's got. And it's Miss Wentworth."

A professional frown. "Has Miss Wentworth completed a medical power of attorney in your name?"

"No, not that I know of."

"Then I'm sorry but we can't release any patient information."

"Can I at least see her?"

"Not at present."

You get the idea. It was seven hours before I was allowed a brief glimpse into her hospital room. She was on a respirator, surrounded by chirping machines and blinking lights and glowing readouts. I barely recognized her.

Fortunately, she made a complete recovery. Or did she?

Two months passed before Mary could return to work even on a part time basis. Her assistant manager was brand new and Mary didn't trust her, so she asked, or I volunteered, or some combination of the two occurred simultaneously. So I returned to retailing for a time, performing adequately if not brilliantly.

I noticed some slight changes when Mary came back on a limited basis near the end of her convalescence, but they were things I had expected. She tired quickly, was easily distracted, and occasionally had to search her memories for a name or other fact. On the other hand, she was more relaxed than I had seen her in years, perhaps because of the medication she was taking, perhaps because the stroke had made it clear that she needed to live life a little less intensely than she had in the past.

The first hint of trouble came two weeks after her return to work, and I took no particularly notice of it. By then Mary was working about half of her normal shift, and I was coming in for a few hours a day just so she wouldn't be tempted to overtire herself. Mostly I did paperwork because Mary had always hated that part of the job, was much more at home working the floor, greeting customers, evaluating her sales people, or planning changes to the displays. Although she sold general giftware, her specialty was figurines and sets of characters. You know, Noah's ark and various animals, licensed products from Disney or Lucasfilms, pilgrim villages, even elaborate sets of toy soldiers. Their construction was equally varied – porcelain, crushed stone, pewter, brass, crystal, even wood carvings and straw figures.

Each of her floor people was responsible for cashing out customers, answering questions, general cleanup, and so forth but each was also required to maintain a specific display area. Customers sometimes moved items to the wrong place, or knocked them over, or bought a floor sample when we couldn't find a boxed piece in stock. And they needed to be carefully dusted or even cleaned with a damp rag in some cases. Kids with greasy fingers were a constant problem.

For some time, Mary had been unhappy with Doreen Potter. Doreen wasn't a bad worker, but she wasn't particularly good either. She always did the minimum required to get by, and she didn't always pay as much attention as she should. It was a common problem because most of the young people Mary employed were only marking time, waiting for their "real" careers to get started. About half of them were fated to remain in retail despite their best efforts, but they all had much loftier ambitions.

The problem was that Doreen had an instinct for survival that kept her just shy of the point where Mary felt justified in firing her. Certainly she could have trumped up some excuse, but that wasn't her way. She had a strict, if not always predictable, sense of honor in such matters. So Doreen had lingered for almost two years and Mary had fretted and refused to act.

We were close to the point where I would feel comfortable reverting to my own life, which I desperately wanted back, on a full time basis. Mary had started doing more of the paperwork, and now when I came in, it was only to double check that everything had been done – because Mary was still occasionally forgetful – and reassure my friend that she was doing all right. I went through the printouts and summaries rather cursorily and I almost missed the odd omission. I had simply glanced through the work schedules and was getting ready to leave when the anomaly struck me and I picked them up again.

Doreen's name was missing from the list.

That wasn't necessarily reason for alarm. She might be taking her vacation early. I shrugged, put the paperwork back on the desk, and went out to find Mary and tell her I was leaving. She was tidying a row of orcs surrounding a pewter castle.

"I noticed that Doreen is out next week. Do you need me to come and help?"

Mary adjusted the last of the ugly little figures to her satisfaction. "Doreen? Doreen who?"

"Doreen Potter. You know, Daniel Boone's stockade, gargoyles and dragons."

Mary frowned. "Oh that Doreen. No, she doesn't work here anymore. She passed away."

I was stunned. Doreen couldn't have been more than twenty five years old. "What happened?

Mary shook her head. "I don't know exactly. Cancer, most likely. She was always going outside to smoke."

The second incident also seemed innocuous at the time. One Saturday night, Mary thanked me for all of my help and told me that she felt fully restored and full of energy. Although I had enjoyed managing the store for the first few days, the novelty had worn off quickly and I was greatly relieved to know I could go back to devising my own work schedule. I was still a little worried about Mary though, so I asked her to lunch on the following Wednesday.

We had arranged to meet at Cassidy's, a little coffee shop that had opened optimistically on one of the busiest corners on Main Street. Since even the busiest corner in Managansett is rarely crowded, they were struggling and it was never difficult to get a table. When Mary came in, I almost didn't recognize her. She was dressed in black from head to foot, complete with veil, although that was pulled back from her face. My first thought was that she'd just come from Doreen's funeral and I asked her about it as soon as we were seated.

"No, I'm afraid it's John's wife who has passed away this time. We're really not very close but under the circumstances I felt I had to pay my respects."

I had to think furiously for a second to realize who John might be. Mary was on speaking terms with her sister, Ruth, who lived in Providence, but she and her brother John had already been estranged when Mary and I were in college. I never heard the details because she clearly didn't want to talk about ot, but I did know that Mary loathed his wife Helen with an intensity that was almost scary. They hadn't spoken in years.

Now be honest. Would either of these events have set off any alarms if you were the one who experienced them? Of course not. And neither did the third incident, which was admittedly slightly more troubling.

I hadn't been to Artisan Gifts in almost a month but I was downtown running an errand and I'd had to cancel our lunch together earlier that week because I was running late on a project. It was almost noon so I decided to stop by to see if Mary was free. She was out on the floor and when I spoke to her she was immediately enthusiastic.

"Sounds great. Just let me get my purse."

I was walking around the shop, looking for new merchandise, when I noticed that the Metternich angels were gone. Neither Mary nor I really liked this line – the angels were constructed of ceramics and plastic and were designed to look as though they were made of cut glass, but the overall effect was crude and the colors were too bright. Angels were always big sellers, so they had been prominently displayed in the store for as long as I remembered. Now their place of honor was occupied by a quite nice set of imported porcelain figurines and potted plants whose leaves were made of jade. They were actually quite attractive and when Mary returned, I told her so.

"But what did you do with the angels?"

"Oh, they're on closeout. Metternich discontinued the line."

That surprised me. "Why in the world would they do that? They've been popular for as long as I can remember."

"I guess they finally saturated the market."

See? Nothing alarming about that encounter either. But there was a follow up that might have tipped me off that something was wrong. I was in Providence, shopping for shoes when curiosity drew me into a local gift shop. If I saw anything in giftware that looked new and interesting, I always told her about it. In this case, there was nothing to report. Everything in the store was old hat, the variety offered was far inferior to Mary's, and the displays were disorganized and needed dusting. One of the worst of these was a full table of Metternich angels.

"Beautiful, aren't they?" A saleswoman had come up from behind me in that stealthy way they're trained to adopt. "And very collectible."

"Only because they've been discontinued."

She shook her head. "Oh, you don't have to worry about that. This is one of our most popular lines. In fact, they're adding several new figures for the Christmas season."

I repeated that I'd heard Metternich was dropping the angels, forcefully enough that the woman went behind the counter and showed me the company's new winter catalog. Sure enough, eight new angels were being added to the already large array. "I guess I must have misunderstood," I said lamely.

This time I was a bit concerned. Mary had been seriously ill and it was entirely possible that her memory was playing tricks on her. Or it could have been a perfectly ordinary misunderstanding. It certainly wasn't something I was going to make into a big issue, but I told myself to be watchful for other signs of trouble.

The sign came all too soon, but it wasn't anything like what I expected.

Another few weeks had gone by and I'd pretty much forgotten the angels incident. Mary seemed perfectly all right. Her conversation was familiarly dull, her energy level had risen back to normal, and she was optimistic because the Christmas shopping season seemed to have kicked into gear a little earlier than usual.

"I'm getting so many orders over the internet that I may have to hire a part timer to help Jack with the packing and shipping. Unless you're looking for a little extra money over the holidays?." Mary had never quite understood how I was surviving as a writer. Since my books didn't make the best seller lists and weren't on display in front of all of the chain bookstores, she assumed I was a struggling artist. In fact, I was doing quite well. My latest advance had been my best yet and I was still earning royalties on more than a dozen previous books. I was probably making as much or more than she was.

We were walking along Main Street, trying to decide between the coffee shop and Nikki's Place. There were only a handful of people out walking because it had turned chilly, but I recognized the woman just ahead of us. It was Doreen Potter, very much alive. She was staring at a display of handbags in the window of Handleman's so she didn't see us. I was so startled that I shrank back, trying to digest this anomalous bit of information. I expected Mary to react similarly, but her steps never faltered. She strode full tilt into Doreen Potter. And passed through the woman as though she wasn't there.

Okay, so this was something I couldn't ignore. I stopped dead in my tracks while Mary continued on. Doreen continued to stare at fake leather handbags as though nothing in the world had happened. Neither woman appeared to be aware of the other. Was this a ghost? I'm not the superstitious type, but I felt a momentary lurch in the fabric of my personal reality. She certainly seemed solid enough.

Mary stopped abruptly and turned back to me. "Are you coming or not? I'm famished."

So I caught up to her, already beginning to doubt what I had just seen. "Did you notice that woman back there? That was Doreen Potter."

Mary made no effort to look back. "Can't say that I noticed anyone. Who's Doreen Potter anyway?"

"She used to work for you. I thought she died."

"Obviously she didn't, if you say you just saw her. So many of these young people come and go, I can't keep track of them all."

I was troubled all through lunch, but Mary didn't appear to notice. When we were done, she went back to the store and I went home to work, but didn't type a word. I didn't make the connection with the angels then, but I did start to think about Mary's sister-in-law, a nagging little thought. You see, I'm a compulsive reader. I read the newspaper from the headlines to the comics every day, including the obituaries. And I'd never seen an obituary for Doreen Potter or Helen Wentworth.

I told myself I was being silly, but I still looked up John Wentworth's telephone number. A woman answered.

"Hello, may I speak to Mrs. Wentworth."

"That's me. Who is this?"

I hung up.

I was a long time getting to sleep that night. Something was wrong with my friend's memories. Perhaps Mary had suffered some sort of unsuspected brain damage as a consequence of her stroke, something the doctors hadn't spotted, or that hadn't manifested itself until she was no longer under their eye. The encounter with Doreen Potter I dismissed as an optical illusion because it wasn't physically possible. No, it had to be that Mary was having problems with her memory, either confusing events or hallucinating. She believed that her brother's wife had died, that Metternich had discontinued its biggest money maker, and that Doreen Potter had never worked for her. It never occurred to me at the time that all three of these were annoyances whose removal from the world would have pleased her. It never occurred to me because, of course, they still were in the world. Just not in Mary's world.

A few days later Mary invited me out for dinner. This had been a tradition with us since her divorce. She took me out for a fancy meal on my birthday and I reciprocated on hers. To be completely honest, I'd forgotten that mine was rushing toward me, the big fifty. When you work for yourself, at home, with few deadlines and no meetings, the time of day and the date become less of a factor. So I was a bit surprised when she called, but pleased that she'd remembered. I felt slightly guilty because I still hadn't figured out what I should do about her memory lapses. If anything, I'd decided not to worry about them. They weren't serious after all, were they? It was the same way I'd reacted when my marriage to Frank had started to unravel. If I didn't acknowledge that there was a problem, then maybe it would go away.

We had a drink before dinner and another with it. I had shrimp scampi, an old standby with me, but Mary had gotten adventurous and ordered a casserole with a long French name. As soon as it came I knew she wasn't going to like it because it had large chunks of bright green broccoli sprinkled all through it. Mary enjoys a wider variety of food than I do, but she draws the line at broccoli. "It tastes like rubber."

She plunged in and after three of four bites announced that it was wonderful. I was surprised, obviously, but decided not to comment on her new tolerance. But as the meal progressed, I realized that I'd misjudged the situation. She wasn't eating the broccoli. In fact, when she raised a forkful of casserole, everything rose except the broccoli, which somehow remained undisturbed on the plate, as if the fork hadn't touched it at all. No, she wasn't eating around it, or somehow manipulating the fork so that the broccoli was left behind. Mary wasn't even looking at her food half the time and she ate indiscriminately. But every time she raised the fork, it was completely free of broccoli. As though the broccoli wasn't there at all, just as Doreen Potter hadn't been standing in front of Handelman's when Mary had walked past.

I lost my appetite. "Are you all right, Lucy? You look a little pale."

"It's nothing. Just a little queasy." The waiter passed by and I ordered another drink. Mary was driving.

I never finished the quite good shrimp scampi and Mary expressed concern while she was driving me home.

"I'll be all right. I just need to lie down. Thanks for dinner, Mary."

You can see my problem, right? If I went to someone, Mary's doctor for instance, and told him that things she found disagreeable were no longer real to her, literally, I'm the one they'd lock up and study, not her. And if I told Mary directly, she'd never believe me. And if I insisted and really pissed her off, then maybe I wouldn't be part of her world any more either.

So I did what anyone would do under those circumstances. I dithered.

Christmas came and went. Mary and her problems receded to the back of my consciousness in a flurry of holiday activity, visits from my kids, the approaching deadline for my latest book, and a nagging flu that wouldn't go away. Mary, of course, never even caught a cold; maybe she'd stopped believing in viruses. We saw each other less regularly, but that was normal; this was the store's busiest time of year. I invited her over for Christmas dinner and she and my kids got along famously, as always. Ellie absentmindedly asked Mary how her family was doing and I held my breath.

"My sister is fine. I visited there yesterday. My brother is still keeping to himself. His wife died recently, you know."

Ellie made sympathetic sounds and I poured myself another glass of brandy.

The situation worsened in the spring. I hadn't been inside Mary's house for several months. She had always behaved a bit oddly when she was home, probably because it was the same house where Bob Wexler had abused her so many times. The slightest sound made her jump, she talked too quickly, and she almost tiptoed from room to room. I'd suggested more than once that she find herself a new place to live, but I don't think she was consciously aware of how much she was affected by her surroundings. In any case, she rarely entertained and – since I didn't like seeing her in that state – I almost never stopped in.

Since the store was open all weekend, she closed it down on Monday after the holiday sales were over. I was running an errand a few blocks away and on impulse decided to drive by to see if she was home. Her station wagon was in the driveway, so I parked behind it and rang the doorbell.

I thought she looked a little drawn when she opened the door, but it might have been my imagination. "Lucy! What a surprise! Come on in. I was just making a pot of coffee."

Now you have to understand that Mary was always an impeccable housekeeper. Even if she hadn't been, Bob would have forced her into that mold because he was always an irritatingly prissy sort of man. I once caught him running his fingers along the top of the hutch cabinet in my dining room to see if I'd dusted. Anyway, when I stepped through the door, I thought my eyes must be playing tricks on me.

The living room and what I could see of the dining room were disaster areas. The dust was thick enough to be noticeable from a distance, there were cobwebs hanging in the corners of the ceiling, and debris of various kinds – newspapers, stray items of clothing, a few food containers – were distributed randomly about.

"Come into the kitchen. It should be just about ready."

The kitchen was worse. Far worse. The table was covered with a small mountain of dirty dishes, food wrappers, and coffee cups. The sink was piled high with more of the same and there was trash on the floor. The garbage can in the corner was so full that the cover wouldn't sit flush, and there were flies everywhere.

Mary was staring into an almost empty cupboard. "I guess I'm going to have to invest in some more coffee cups. I don't know where they all get to." She finally found two and began filling them from the percolator on the counter. I stood where I was, stunned, and fought to regain control of my face before she turned around and saw my expression. I'm not sure I succeeded, but I probably needn't have worried. If it wasn't an expression she wanted to see, I imagine Mary would simply not have seen it.

She handed me the mug of coffee, black the way I liked it. "I don't have anything to eat, I'm afraid." She pulled out one of the kitchen chairs and sat down. I picked the one opposite her, my legs so shaky that I was afraid I might fall, and raised the coffee to sip.

It was undrinkable. It was incredibly strong and incredibly bitter, as though old and fresh coffee grounds had been mixed together.

"How have you been, Mary?" My voice sounded shaky. I wanted to put down the mug, but there wasn't anywhere on the table that was level enough.

"Oh, just fine. Business is down, of course, but I did quite well during the holidays." She drank coffee with evident pleasure, then set her mug down on the table. Her mug quite literally sank through a plate of chicken bones to sit levelly on the table beneath.

That was when I started to realize what was happening. Anything that Mary preferred not to see, or taste, or touch, simply ceased to exist as far as she was concerned. If I could have looked out through her eyes, I would have seen a perfectly clear table in a well maintained, neat, clean, and orderly house.

I don't remember much else about our conversation. At the first opportunity, I fled from her presence.

The end came quite suddenly. Mary had suffered from intermittent severe headaches ever since the night her husband hit her with a sauce pan full of noodles that he insisted were overcooked. Their frequency had declined over time, but she still had occasional attacks. I was with her during one of these, a particularly intense one, and I'd insisted on taking her to be checked out at the walk-in emergency clinic.

Mary was terrified of doctors, possibly because she'd been forced to lie to them so many times about how she'd acquired one injury or another, and she insisted that I stay with her throughout the exam. Doctor Meadows was quite nice, however, and she almost succeeded in putting Mary at ease. She recommended an MRI, which Mary agreed to only if I would take her. So I did.

Dr. Winslow was less people oriented, brusque and blunt. He showed us the printout of the examination and told us that Mary had something called an Arnold-Chiari malformation. "Your condition is serious but very treatable, Miss Wentworth. Decompression surgery will relieve the pressure and the procedure has a very high success rate."

Mary was still staring at the shadowy picture of the inside of her head. "You mean this little shape here…that's what's causing all of my headaches?"

"Well, probably not all of them, but certainly those intense ones you feel at the back of your head."

"How annoying," she said softly, and collapsed so quietly that both Dr. Winslow and I were taken completely by surprise.

Mary is in a nursing home now. Her doctors insist that the malformation in her brain could not be responsible for her comatose state. "Her brain activity is very close to normal," one of them told me. "It's as though she were completely conscious and only pretending not to be."

They tell me to hope for the best, that they are sure they'll find the source of the problem and correct it eventually, but they aren't particularly convincing and from time to time even hint that they are grasping at medical straws. I could enlighten them, but I won't.

You see, I think what happened is that once Mary realized that the oddity inside her head was something she didn't want to deal with, it simply joined the many other things in her environment whose existence she no longer recognized. Except this time maybe she edited out a bit too much, and what is left isn't enough to sustain consciousness. The tissue might be fine as far as her doctors are concerned, but for Mary, it's as though that portion of her brain has been completely removed.

I think she's still conscious, in a way, trapped inside her own head. Or maybe she's not trapped. Maybe she has just retreated into her own private universe, one where nothing can hurt or trouble her. In a sense, we all live in our own little pocket reality. Mary's just a little better at it than are the rest of us.

PALE LAKE

The yellow moonlight transformed the lake into a cauldron of curdled milk, with only a few scattered patches of pondweed to break the smooth surface. Ariana walked to the end of the small pier, picking her way through a thin layer of windblown debris, and took a deep breath. The cabin behind her was a relic of the past, but it was also a link to a happier time. The impulse that had resulted in the long drive through the chilly afternoon and darkening evening had grown less compelling with each passing mile, but by the time she began to regret her decision, it was easier to go forward than back.

It had been years since she'd been here and she had long since lost her own key, but the spare was still safely tucked away inside a false rock. Her sister had used the cabin fairly regularly until recently and the exterior appeared well maintained, but the interior smelled musty and she had almost retreated to her car. There was a motel not far away and she could have stayed the night in comfort there. But it all seemed like too much trouble and she'd pushed her way inside, fumbled around in the dark until she found some candles and matches, then the lantern.

It was dusty and dank, but not as bad as it might have been. She'd opened the windows to air it out, sorted through the canned goods to find the ones that hadn't long since expired, and ended up eating beans and black olives, mixed together and heated on the propane stove. She had brought bottled water.

Clean linens were sealed in plastic bags in the closet and she made up one of the beds mechanically, her mind deliberately concentrated on the matter at hand. The simple, familiar task had a calming effect and by the time she had finished some peremptory cleaning and straightening to make the bedroom habitable, unpacked her overnight bag, and changed into fresh clothing, she felt reasonably content if not happy. Ariana and her sister had inherited joint ownership when their father had died. Ariana had suggested selling the property, had allowed Bethany to talk her out of it, and had only visited twice in six years. Now that Bethany and her family were living in Seattle, it might be time to again consider putting it on the market.

The drive had been tiring but once everything had been done and she could climb into bed and pull the covers up over her head, she had discovered that she wasn't at all sleepy. So she'd walked down along the overgrown path to the lake, enjoying the symphony of insect sounds and even the faint aroma of decay from the stagnant backwater where the short, narrow pier had been erected.

Somewhere out of her line of sight, something plopped into the water. She turned her head automatically, not really interested. A frog burning the midnight oil, a pine cone falling from a tree. She couldn't even see ripples and quickly lost interest. From time to time she and Dan had planned to spend a week here, away from the pressures of their urban life together, but when he was free, she was busy, and vice versa, and now it was too late. Dan's ashes had been interred next to those of his parents and Ariana no longer had to factor in his schedule and desires when making plans.

Another plop, louder this time, or closer. She turned and stared into the milky darkness that washed against the shore to her right. Nearby trees had extended branches far out over the darkness, and vines dripped down even further like gelatinous feelers. There was a hint of mist as well, further softening the contours and changing the shape even of sound. Ariana squatted and felt around until she found a fair sized stick, then rose and tossed it out into the shadows.

It splashed into the water, but the sound wasn't quite the same. She waited for a response but there was only silence. "Go to bed, girl," she told herself, and started back toward the cabin. After a few steps, there was another plop from behind her, but Ariana didn't look back.

It was overcast when Ariana rose the following morning. She walked down to the lake, hoping to take a quick swim to wash off the cabin's dust, but the water looked less than inviting. The surface was covered with an unhealthy looking scum, which was at considerable variance from her memories of the place. In her mind, the water had always been crystal clear and inviting. The sky was darkening rapidly and threatening rain. She confined herself to a quick wash of her face and hands, sighed regretfully, and went back to the cabin. After making a shopping list, she climbed into the Caravan and drove the fourteen miles to the nearest town, Pomfret, where she was disappointed to find that the independent grocery store she remembered from her adolescence had given way to a familiar looking chain market.

Suitably provisioned, she returned to the cabin. Now that she was here, she was determined to stay for a while. Probably not the full two months of her leave of absence, but at least a week or two. Ariana felt like a wounded animal and wanted to crawl into a corner and lick her hurts until they went away. The constant calls from friends and co-workers offering their sympathy for her loss had reopened the wounds over and over again. She had brought her cell phone, but it was in the glove compartment, battery dead, and there was no electricity at the cabin with which to recharge it.

She explored the rest of the cabin that afternoon, awakening old memories. Her father's collection of fishing rods was still in its glass case in the den and there were some books and board games in a closet that she remembered from her childhood. Other items were unfamiliar, most of them probably dating from Bethany's weekends there with Bill and the kids. There were three bedrooms, a largish living area and small den, as well as a kitchenette and bathroom that were of little use to her because without electricity the pump from the well would not work. It wouldn't be the first time she'd squatted behind a bush.

Ariana closed off the rooms she didn't plan to use and started a small fire in the fireplace, even though it wasn't cold enough to warrant it. Autumn was imminent and the air cooled down quickly at night, but she was rarely bothered by low temperatures. Belatedly she remembered that she'd planned to check the exterior of the cabin to see if any maintenance was advisable, so she pulled on a sweater and went outside to squeeze in a quick tour before it became too dark.

The roof was intact, which didn't surprise her since there was no evidence of leaks inside. There was a crack in one window that she hadn't noticed from the interior, but it looked like it had been there for a while with no adverse effects. There was still a good supply of cut wood for the fireplace sheltering under a tarp. She was reassured that a year or more of abandonment hadn't done much damage.

But she also found something rather unsettling. It was the body of either a very large deer or a small moose. The bones of one, at least. They were completely devoid of tissue which suggested it wasn't a recent kill, but the skeleton seemed almost completely undisturbed. She'd spent enough time in the woods during her youth to know that carrion eaters weren't usually this fastidious. Ariana knelt and examined the bones closely, pushing at them with a stick, but it was getting dark quickly now and the shadows under the trees were like heavy wool blankets. She stood up, brushed off her jeans, and went back inside.

Although she had no trouble getting to sleep that night, she woke just before midnight with her pulse racing. There were none of the fading images of a stressful dream. She lay in the dark, listening intently, wondering if some animal had wandered onto the property. They'd had visits from raccoons, woodchucks, and even an occasional beaver in the past, not to mention deer, moose, and even on one occasion a small bear that had overturned their garbage can.

Somewhere in the distance an owl announced its presence, and there was enough of a breeze to make an audible susurration as it passed through the pines, but nothing that didn't belong. Her eyes were beginning to close and her pulse had slowed when she heard once again the plop of something falling into the water. Impossible, she told herself. The lake was a hundred yards away.

A minute later, she heard it again.

"Damn it!" Ariana sat up, knowing herself well enough to realize that she'd be tensely waiting for the next plop until she found out what was causing it. She pulled on jeans and a sweater over her sleep gear, slipped into her sandals, and stood up. The flashlight was on the shelf beside the door and a moment later she was outside, waving it back and forth. It was colder than she'd expected, or her body's resistance had ramped down while she was sleeping, and she felt a fleeting urge to return to her bed. A recurrence of the odd sound convinced her otherwise.

It was coming from the direction of the lake.

Ariana was not a fan of horror movies but Dan had loved them and she'd seen enough to know that she wasn't supposed to investigate strange noises in the darkness unless she was quite sure she was the heroine and not just a supporting cast member. But she also prided herself on her firm grip on reality and rationality; she didn't teach principles of logic to college freshmen only to ignore them in her private life. So she told herself to be careful lest she disturb some rabid animal engaged in a little bathing, drinking, or night fishing, but she also told herself she would not sleep comfortably until she knew what was going on.

The sound did not recur as she made her way to the pier. The sky had cleared somewhat and the moon was out again. Streamers of mist were rising from the surface of the water like tenuous cobras entranced by the snake charmer's flute. A mosquito hummed in her ear and she slapped at it and tossed her head, then stepped out onto the dock and played the light along the shoreline.

Everything looked and sounded perfectly normal. The branches waved a bit when the breeze perked up, sometimes sending suggestive shadows, sometimes making her jump when an unexpected movement occurred at the periphery of her vision. She heard a bullfrog croaking somewhere to her right and the owl hooted again from her left. Everything was perfectly ordinary.

Plop! It was louder, or perhaps just more distinct than it had been before, but it was not the quality of the sound that was so unsettling. It was the direction. Whatever was responsible was now between Ariana and the cabin.

It's a frog, she told herself, with an unusually loud and distinctive call. It was a reasonable explanation, but reasonable or not, she moved cautiously to the land end of the pier and fumbled in the brush until she found a length of broken branch that made a serviceable weapon. She held it ready as she slowly made her way back up the path, playing the light methodically, pausing every few steps to listen. The sound did not repeat itself, but she still ran the last few steps to the cabin door, and she made certain that the latch was in place before telling herself she was being silly.

She went back to bed, but it was a long time before she dozed off. As expected, she kept waiting for a recurrence of the plopping sound, but if it repeated itself that night, it was after she had finally drifted off.

Ariana felt rather silly the following morning. She walked down to the lake, which shimmered under a bright sun, and bathed herself quickly. The water was chilly, but that wasn't the only reason. Over breakfast - bacon and eggs on the propane stove – she admitted to herself that she was behaving like a child and decided to go fishing. As a child, she had often done so with her father, not because she enjoyed the sport but because it gave her a chance at his undivided attention for a while.

She found the same rod he'd bought for her on her tenth birthday. He'd always preferred live bait and Ariana dug in a few spots around the cabin looking for worms, but without success and had to be content with an old lure she found in a drawer. She didn't really want to catch anything, after all, didn't even care for the taste of fish. It was the emotional feedback she wanted, the blend of nostalgia and relaxation, an escape from her grief.

There was no longer a boat tied to the pier, so Ariana decided to trek around the side of the lake to her father's favorite spot, a narrow peninsula that stuck out like a hangnail. This proved to be more difficult than she'd expected. The path along the side of the lake was completely overgrown and she was forced to make so many detours that she was afraid she had bypassed her destination. But then she saw a familiar split boulder and a minute later pushed her way through skunk cabbage and reeds and onto the base of the spit of land.

She found a smooth rock to sit on, fixed the lure to her line, and cast off, pleased at how readily her body remembered the necessary motions.

Although Ariana had not really wanted to catch anything, she was rather surprised at her lack of success. After two hours, not even a nibble. Her father had routinely taken two or three perch or johnnies an hour from this spot, and she doubted anyone had fished this side of the lake since Bethany moved west. The sun was warm and her head fell forward from time to time, jerked up once or twice as she caught herself, but eventually she fell asleep and the rod dropped from her hand.

Since she no longer wore a watch and didn't have her cell phone, Ariana had no idea what time it was when she woke up. A glance at the sky suggested that it was early afternoon. She yawned, stretched her arms, then stood and shook each leg in turn, working out the kinks. Time to pack up and go back, she told herself, but there was nothing to pack up.

Her fishing rod was nowhere to be seen.

She stood on the rock, shading her eyes, expecting but failing to see it floating in the water – it was hollow plastic. It was possible that the glittering sunlight obscured it, but more likely it had drifted out a ways before being dragged down by the weight of the reel. She felt a twinge of regret; another part of her childhood had gone forever. Then she started back to the cabin.

Now that she had oriented herself, she felt she could take a more direct route, so instead of climbing back up the low ridge where the split boulder loomed, she turned and walked parallel to it. The brush had grown so profusely that she had second thoughts after a while, particularly when a reed snapped back and slapped her painfully across one cheek, but she was determined not to be thwarted.

There was a small cove ahead, she remembered, and from there she could climb up onto the more accessible part of the ridge where the ground was firmer. The cove was much as she remembered it, bordered by a mane of pebbles. Another memory from her past returned and she bent, found a relatively flat stone, and tossed it out into the cove. "A three skipper," she said aloud as it splashed three times before disappearing.

Then she caught her breath. The cove was full of bones. They were fish bones, mostly complete skeletons as far as she could tell, but there were so many of them that it was hard to be sure. The water was perfectly clear and still and if she looked she could see that the bottom was covered for as far as she could see. There were scores of them, perhaps hundreds. She felt a little chill that had nothing to do with the weather and hurried back to the cabin.

That afternoon she visited the Pomfret police department. For one thing, she wanted them to know that she was legitimately occupying the cabin so a random patrol wouldn't roust her from bed some night demanding identification. For another, she wanted to ask about the lake.

"No ma'am, no one's reported anything unusual from Pale Lake. There aren't many folks living up that way anymore and those that do keep pretty much to themselves."

That would be the cluster of shacks on the far side of the lake. Her father had warned her to steer clear of them when she was a child. "They aren't nice people, Ari. You keep your distance." He'd been insistent enough that her aversion had stuck and even as an adult she had never ventured over to their side.

"Anything about fish kills? Could someone be dumping toxic waste there?" She told him about the fish skeletons.

The desk officer shook his head and shifted in his chair. "Sometimes you get die offs from natural causes, you know, particularly in the backwaters. The bacteria level goes way up and all the fish die."

"I suppose." She thought about the moose or deer or whatever lay behind the cabin, but she didn't mention it. Animals died all the time.

"We could send someone up to take a look if you like." He didn't sound enthusiastic.

"No, I don't suppose it's important. I just thought I'd check."

"Well, if you see anything suspicious, you just give us a call." Ariana remembered that her cell phone was still dead and decided she needed to do something about it. Unfortunately, the local hardware store did not stock adaptors that would allow her to charge it from her car battery, so she returned to the cabin as isolated as ever.

Nothing disturbed her sleep that night and the following morning she felt clear headed and more optimistic than she'd been since Dan's death. Coming to the cabin had definitely been a good idea, she told herself. She spent the morning doing a more thorough cleaning and made a mental inventory of the items she'd save if they actually did sell the cabin, although now that she was here, the urge to do so was waning. It even began to seem possible that her life might continue despite her loss.

She cooked peppers and onions and potatoes for lunch and started a new shopping list. Then she put a bottle of water and some granola bars in her backpack, spread insect repellent on her face and arms, and set out to walk up to Bullocks' Point, a truncated hill where the family had gone picnicking from time to time. It was a quarter way around the lake clockwise from the cabin and was high enough to provide an impressive if not spectacular view of the surrounding area.

It took well over an hour because she was in no hurry and because she got slightly lost at one point, but once she was beyond the tallest of the pine trees, it was hard to miss. The Bullock family had bulldozed the top way back before she was born, planning to build a very large summer retreat looking down on the lake, but their financial situation had taken a plunge and the project had been abandoned. Ariana's family hadn't been the only ones to take advantage of what soon became a raised meadow, a trend that had apparently continued judging by the number of discarded soda bottles and other trash that littered the area. But no one was there now and Ariana found a relatively unlittered spot to sit for a while and munch on granola.

From her vantage point, she could see better than half the lake. Off to her right, the pier was visible, but the cabin was lost among the trees. The peninsula where she'd lost her fishing rod was barely discernible. To her left, she could make out a cluster of small cabins half hidden among the distant trees. There was a small pier there as well, but it was canted to one side and clearly unusable. The shape of an automobile lurked beside one of the cabins, but there was no other sign of habitation.

She watched on and off for almost an hour but there was no indication that anyone was living there. No smoke rose from the chimneys. Nobody came or went. Not even a dog. Not even a bird.

Ariana felt herself nodding off again and stood up abruptly. She'd been napping a lot lately and she was self aware enough to know that it was an escape mechanism. Asleep she didn't have to think about how radically her life had changed, how shallow and unappealing the future seemed. The mild euphoria of the morning began to seep away and she decided that a brisk walk back might help.

The trip back wasn't nearly as pleasant as the walk out. It was getting towards dusk and the mosquitoes were out early, ignoring the repellent she'd applied until she stopped and added a fresh layer. There was also a fetid smell that she didn't remember encountering earlier, probably the result of a change in wind direction. From somewhere out on the lake or beyond there came the bitter odor of decay. Worst of all, she began to feel that she wasn't alone.

There was no evidence for this last. She had heard no unusual sounds and had not seen any suspicious stirring in the brush. Ariana told herself that she was imagining things, but she found herself glancing back the way she had come from time to time, just to reassure herself that no one was following her, and she made several small detours to avoid clumps of brush that might have concealed a hidden menace. When she finally came within sight of the pier again, she chastised herself for being foolish.

There was something leaning against the cabin door. From a distance, it looked like a fallen branch, but as she came closer she realized it was not a natural object. It was in fact a fishing rod, the same one that she'd lost.

Ariana's pulse began to race and she spun on one heel to survey the area and convince herself that she was alone. She felt an odd reluctance to touch the rod, but finally bent over and picked it up. The line hadn't been reeled in and was badly tangled and the lure was missing, but otherwise it appeared undamaged. Someone must have found it, she thought, and returned it. A nice, neighborly gesture. But how could they have known that she was the one who had lost it?

She unlocked the cabin door and stepped inside cautiously, not relaxing until she'd done a quick tour and ascertained that no one was hiding in a closet or behind a chair. By then the alarms were considerably less strident. Hers was the only cabin on this side of the lake, after all. It was logical to think that the missing fishing gear belonged here. It must have been some thoughtful hiker, she decided.

But she made sure that the door and windows were firmly locked before she went to bed.

Ariana spent the next day shopping, had a nice lunch at a restaurant poised above the river that ran into Pale Lake, and then found a surprisingly well stocked used book store. She spent nearly an hour picking out a half dozen murder mysteries, a history of Vermont, and a few other odds and ends, during which time she was the only customer. The elderly woman who managed the store had told her to make herself at home and call if she needed help, then returned to what appeared to be a rather elaborate knitting project.

While checking out, she mentioned that she was staying at a cabin on the lake. The woman looked up at her with an odd expression. "I didn't think anyone still lived in the shantytown." Her voice had moved from friendly to cool.

"I don't. I have the cabin on the other side."

"The Foster place? I haven't seen Bethany in a long time now. Did she finally sell out?" The warmth had returned.

Ariana shook her head. "She's my sister. We both own it but she moved out west and I haven't been here in years. I came up to stay for a few weeks."

"Well then, I'll have to tell my son." She smiled broadly. "He's the mailman up that way."

"I don't really expect to be here long enough to have to worry about mail."

"That's a shame. We need some new blood around here." She nodded at the pile of books. "Particularly if you're a heavy reader. I could use the business."

Ariana laughed politely. "Well, I'll probably be back at least once or twice before I leave. There's not much else to do out at the cabin."

"You're by yourself then?"

"Yes." She looked away, afraid her sudden melancholy would show. Another thought occurred to her. "Should I be worried? I know the people on the other side have a bad reputation, but I haven't seen anyone around."

The woman shrugged. "And you won't, most likely. Ted, that's my boy, tells me they've all cleared out. Haven't taken their mail in for a couple of months and he never sees anyone around when he drives up that way. But I'd be careful just the same. There were a couple of them that were just no damned good."

Ariana paid, gathered her books, and headed back to the cabin.

She had picked up a battery powered CD player and the addition of music and a P.D. James novel she had never read made the evening a pleasant one. She drank half a bottle of wine and toasted marshmallows in the fireplace before finally crawling into bed. But she did not sleep through the night.

Her head snapped up from the pillow and she listened tensely. It was quiet now but she was almost positive that the door had rattled in its frame. The sound didn't repeat itself as she slowly climbed out of bed and picked up one of the irons from the fireplace and the flashlight from the shelf above it.

There was, unfortunately, no window which would provide a clear view of the front door. She left the chain fastened but clicked the lock and pulled it back a couple of inches, her other hand tightening on her makeshift weapon. A wisp of cool air filtered in. Ariana moved her head to peer out through the gap, using the flashlight to search the immediate area, but there was nothing to see. The breeze picked up a bit and she shivered, told herself it had either been a gust of wind or the tail end of a dream. She relocked the door and went back to bed, but not before lighting the lantern and leaving it on the floor beside her bed.

In the morning, Ariana made a cursory search for footprints but found nothing. You found nothing, she told herself, because there was nothing. You've been living in the city too long. You're spooked by the sounds of nature and you're paranoid about criminals lurking in the shadows.

But the possibility that she hadn't imagined it wouldn't quite go away, so she decided to do a little investigating.

Without a boat, she couldn't cross the lake to the shantytown and it was a long hike around, but she did have the Caravan. It took a while, and several dead ends, to find the right road, a meandering unpaved track so narrow that branches brushed the sides of the Caravan even when it was perfectly centered. Ariana began to have second thoughts because she had seen no place where she could turn around and didn't relish backing all the way back out to the pavement, but she knew the mail truck went this way and if it could, then so could she.

For most of the next half mile, she couldn't even see the lake, although it eventually became visible between the trunks of the pine and spruce. When she finally arrived at the first building, it came as a complete surprise because it was so overgrown that it was effectively camouflaged until she was right on top of it.

There was a relatively clear space at the side of the road just beyond and she pulled over, but left the engine running. Ariana slid across the seat and looked out the window toward the structure – it could not be called a house. It looked dreadful, unpainted walls and a broken window. She waited for several minutes, but there was no sign of life. Then she slid back behind the wheel and drove on.

The remaining three shanties were huddled together and very close to the lakeshore. They were in slightly better condition than the first, but hardly inviting. There was no movement or suggestion that they were still occupied. The vehicle she'd seen from across the lake had no tires and was covered in rust. There was also a place where she could turn around and she did so, but she paused once more.

"Oh, what the hell!" She killed the engine, waited another half minute, then got out of the Caravan.

It was much quieter than she'd expected. Although she did not consciously hear the insects and birds around the cabin, the background noise was continuous there. She heard an occasional chirping, probably a cricket, but nothing else except the lapping of the water against the land.

The middle shanty was in the best state of repair, or the least state of disrepair. She walked directly to the front door and knocked. She hadn't expected an answer and didn't get one. There was one accessible window on the near side and she edged around to it, went up on her toes to peer inside. It was so dark that she could make out vague shapes, but they remained unrecognizable. She wished she had thought to bring her flashlight.

The shanty to the right was just the same, except smaller, and a shutter had been nailed over the window. No response at the third either, and the overgrowth made it impossible for her to look inside. But she did find something there. The skeleton of a fair sized animal, almost certainly a dog, lay behind the building. The bones were completely picked clean.

Ariana had crouched down to look more closely when she heard a sound from somewhere behind her. Plop! She stood and whirled around in a single movement, scanning the area intently. Nothing moved and the sound did not repeat itself. Not just then. But a few seconds later she heard it again, from the opposite direction.

She moved away from the bushes, past the shanties, out into the middle of the dirt road, one hand fumbling in the pocket of her jeans for her keys. A flash of movement caught her attention, but it was a bird flying across the lake a good distance away. "Hello? Is someone there?" Her voice shook a little and she began to back toward the Caravan.

There was no answer and the silence became more than just oppressive. It felt threatening. She fumbled for the door, found the handle, and slipped inside. Fortunately, unlike the situation in Dan's well loved horror movies, the engine started immediately and she drove away, just slightly too fast.

Once she hit the paved road, Ariana chided herself for giving in to panic. There had not, after all, been anything overt to concern her. The sounds could very well have been frogs, just as she'd theorized before. Probably she should turn around and go back, complete her investigation. But what had she expected to find? It was all just a waste of time. She kept going, convinced that she'd made the decision logically and not because she was frightened. Or at least half convinced.

That evening, Ariana considered cutting her stay short. She didn't have to go back home, of course. She could wander over into New Hampshire or even Maine, find a place she could rent for a week or more, do something touristy like hiking or take a tour boat out on Mount Desert Island. Tomorrow, she told herself, I'll decide what I really want to do and just do it.

She finished the bottle of wine and went to bed.

The thud of impact brought her awake in an instant. This time there was no question; something had struck the door with considerable force. Ariana slipped out of bed, found her slippers and robe where she'd left them, and with flashlight in hand strode out into the front room. Almost immediately there was another thud and the door shook in its frame. It most assuredly was not the wind. Something heavy and solid had slammed against it. For the first time in her life, Ariana wished that she owned a firearm.

She dropped the matches and had to fumble around for them, but eventually got the old lantern going, then the new one she'd just bought. The first remained in the center of the table where it had always sat, but she carried the second over to the door and set it on a cane backed chair. Then she went to the fireplace and armed herself with a heavy poker.

Several minutes passed before the third crash. It was the most violent yet and she cried out softly and gripped the poker more tightly. As much as she wanted to know what was out there, she was also afraid to know, afraid the chain and lock would give way and that the door would open. But it didn't, and there was no further attempt to force it.

She sat facing it for the rest of the night, and never felt the slightest temptation to sleep.

Sunrise did not entirely banish her fears this time and she was extremely cautious when she stepped outside. A quick glance at the door showed no evidence of last night's assault, and if there were signs to be read from the leaves and dirt, she was not literate in that language. Ariana explored the immediate surroundings with exaggerated caution. She found only one item out of place. The skeletal remains behind the cabin had disappeared. There was no sign that they had ever been there.

For some reason this oddity changed Ariana's mood. She became less apprehensive and more curious, with a hint of anger. Someone was playing stupid tricks on her and they had pushed her too far. Thoughts of abandoning the cabin evaporated like dew and she felt a sudden sense of purpose for the first time in a very long while. This wasn't a simple animal prowling around the cabin. She was quite sure that there was an intelligent mind at work, and she intended to find out just who it was.

Ariana found most of what she was looking for in Pomfret. She paused in front of a gun shop but there was a waiting period and she didn't normally reside in the state, so she shook her head and moved on. She did buy herself a wicked looking hunting knife and she belatedly remembered that she had pepper spray in her purse. The hardware story provided a half dozen battery powered lanterns and two portable floodlights. She called the local power company and a thin voiced man apologetically told her that it would be at least a week before they could restore electricity to the cabin. "We've had to cut back on our field crews," he admitted.

She also picked up a second, sturdier chain lock for the cabin door, a spool of fishing line, and to the astonishment of the clerk at the local pet shop, an entire box full of tiny bells meant for the collars of cats. She would have preferred something a little louder, but quantity would have to make up the difference.

The afternoon passed quickly. Ariana strung lengths of fishing line from tree to tree, after threading each through a half dozen of the bells, which she later distributed more or less evenly along their lengths. Roughly they comprised two concentric rings around the cabin, with a heavier concentration near the door. A brief, strong breeze stirred a few of them, but the lines were taut enough that she was confident it would take physical intervention to raise an alarm.

Most of the lanterns were placed in various places inside the cabin, but she hung one beside the front door and a second from a tree a few feet away. Satisfied with her work, Ariana made her supper, then took the plate and a bottle of water down to the pier. She sat at the far end, legs dangling over the water, and finished the plate of stir fry while watching the sun slowly subside behind the trees.

There was no more fear. She had looked on helplessly when Dan became sick, weakened so very quickly, and died, stealing away the future she had looked forward to. Now something seemed intent upon taking away her cherished memories of the past as well, and this time she wasn't going to lose without a fight.

Back in the cabin, she washed dishes and put them away, then took a flashlight and conducted a final inspection of her preparations outside. The air was still and the sky clear; a nearly full moon dispersed some of the darkness, but not enough to matter here under the trees. Satisfied that she'd done the best she could, Ariana returned to the cabin and turned off all but the smallest of the lanterns. Then she sat in the bentwood rocker next to the fireplace and waited.

Although she had planned to stay awake for as long as it took, she was dozing when the first tinkle of the bells tickled her awake. Her head snapped up and she felt a momentary disorientation, but then the sound was repeated and she marshaled her wits and stood up, vaguely aware that the bells had been sounding for some time now. She had considered leaving the door open to better hear them, but had deferred to caution. Now she quietly undid the chain and pulled the door open. The fire iron was in her free hand and the hunting knife was strapped to her waist. Hardly the makings of a female Rambo, she told herself, but hopefully enough to discourage a secretive prowler.

It had cooled off considerably. She stepped outside, but left the door open behind her in case a hasty retreat was required. If the usual night time breeze had arrived, it was off playing on the lake at the moment. The bells were silent and she wasn't sure from what direction the disturbance had come, so she remained motionless, waiting.

It wasn't a long wait. The bells tinkled and her head snapped around, seeking a point of origin. Somewhere directly across from the cabin door, she guessed, and waited for the sound to recur. Perhaps five minutes passed before the faint sound repeated itself. This time Ariana knelt swiftly and turned on one of the floodlights. A broad beam of pale light bathed the nearby trees and illuminated a small open space carpeted with pine needles.

There was something there. She squinted her eyes, trying to make it out in the shifting shadows. It looked like a dog. It was the right size and shape, but for some reason it seemed less distinct than the objects around it, almost ghostly. But ghosts don't trigger tripwires. Whatever it was stood motionless, then slowly turned its head toward her. She couldn't make out individual features but she could tell when its jaws opened and tensed, waiting for it to growl or bark. It did neither.

Plop! The sound startled her, even though somehow she had been half expecting it. She tightened her grip on the fire iron and took a step forward. The figure didn't flinch, and it spoke, or whatever it was doing, a second time. Plop! And then it was gone.

Ariana blinked. The animal, dog, whatever it was hadn't turned and run, hadn't dropped into a crouch. One second it had been there in all its indistinct materiality and the next it was gone as though it had been a puff of smoke dispersed by the wind.

Her composure slipped a little as uncertainty gnawed at its edges. Should she return to the cabin or go forward and investigate? She actually took a step backward before recovering herself. No, if she was ever going to find out what was going on, it would be by advancing not retreating. But she'd be careful.

The floodlight was heavy but she could manage it with her left hand, although she almost lost her balance stepping over the first tripwire. Her peculiar visitor had been standing halfway between the inner and outer rings of bells and she'd kept her eye on the exact spot. She reached it a few seconds later and stood staring down at the ground. Lying on its side, perfect in every way, was the skeleton of a small dog.

Somewhere out in the night, down near the lake shore, something went Plop!

Ariana returned to the cabin and maintained her vigil until sunrise, drifting off to sleep from time to time, but she was left undisturbed. With first light, she went out to the clearing, confirmed that she hadn't dreamed up the bones, then returned to the cabin and found an old burlap bag. She gathered the bones together in the bag and carried them back, stored them in a cabinet in the kitchen, then went to bed. She slept soundly until late morning.

The rest of that day was uneventful. She walked down to the pier several times, once heard a sudden splashing that startled her, but which turned out to be a stray mallard settling down in quest of a meal. She watched as it ducked its head under the water several times, but it appeared to have no luck and took to the air only minutes later. Ariana returned to the cabin and puttered around, checked her tripwires and other preparations, and felt impatient for night to fall. The sun seemed to take its time subsiding but eventually the shadows lengthened, pools of darkness puddled in among the trees, and a brief evening breeze came and went. This time she started one of the mystery novels while sitting in the rocker, a lantern on the mantle providing adequate if somewhat shaky light.

It wasn't a very suspenseful story and she leaned back to rest her eyes for a bit and fell soundly asleep. She barely moved for the next hour and then sat bolt upright. Something had knocked against the door.

Ariana stood up so abruptly that the chair rocked back and banged into the wall. For a few seconds, she felt disoriented, the room spinning around her, but then it settled down and so did she. There was no sound except the faint hissing of the lantern and her own accelerated heartbeat.

When nothing else happened she started to relax, only to jerk upright again when there was another thud on the door. It wasn't a knock, not exactly, more of a thump as though a branch had been blown against it by a high wind. There was no wind. "Who's there?" She didn't expect an answer so she wasn't disappointed.

It took a minute for her to gather her courage and approach the door. She called out again when she reached it, with the same lack of results. Drawing a deep breath, she raised the poker above her shoulder and slowly undid the chain, carefully standing to one side so that if someone or something tried to push its way in, she wouldn't be struck by the door. The door opened on an apparently peaceful night and there was no sign of an intruder.

It had clouded over somewhat but she'd left two lanterns lit. One was flickering, apparently with a weakened battery, but the other was as bright as ever. There was nothing to see from the doorway, and when she summoned the courage to step outside, she had no better luck. At least initially.

She turned on one of the floods and slowly moved its focus across the stand of trees that faced her. Just before she reached the extreme left, she thought she saw the faintest hint of movement, but it was half hidden by one of the larger pines. Ariana took three shuffling steps to her right to alter the perspective, and saw something hastily retreat around the bole of the tree. It was not a dog. It was much too big. A bear perhaps, or a deer.

Whatever it was appeared to be at least as frightened of her as vice versa, so she moved forward slowly. "Is anyone there?" She wasn't expecting an answer, but this time she got one.

Plop!

She shifted further to the right and her quarry countered her move, remaining out of sight. Ariana felt a surge of frustrated impatience. Damning the consequences, she started forward, determined to end the suspense one way or another.

A figure stepped out from behind the tree, directly into the beam of her light.

Ariana froze, her mind not quite processing what she was seeing. At first she thought it was a man, naked, and the possibility that she was alone in the woods with a psychopathic prankster brought her to a halt. But then she realized that he – if it was a he – was not exactly nude. And not exactly a man.

It was man shaped, and she thought of the creature now as definitely an "it" because its skin, its surface more properly speaking, writhed and squirmed as though the flesh was boiling away from the bones. She stopped six feet away, apprehensive even though it had made no move toward her. As her focus improved, she felt her stomach roll over. Its skin really was wriggling furiously and not surprisingly, since she could now see that it wasn't flesh at all, not in a conventional sense. Whatever the creature was, the entire outer surface of its body was crawling with earthworms, furiously agitated earthworms by the look of it.

Ariana fell back a step. "What are you?" Her heart was beating so rapidly that she could feel it as a distinct pressure in her chest.

This time there was a physical response. The figure took a faltering step toward her and then another. Its mouth, or the part of its head that corresponded to a human mouth, parted in a bizarre grimace. Plop!

She panicked then. But it was mixed with anger as well as fear and instead of running back toward the cabin, she advanced, raising the poker menacingly. The figure took another step forward and paused, tilting its head in an almost human attitude of inquiry. The caricature just stoked her anger and she swung the heavy poker with all her might. It slammed against the side of the misshapen head and there was a silent explosion of movement. Ariana blinked, had a momentary glimpse of a perfectly ordinary human skeleton, standing erect, and then it collapsed with a low clatter as the individual bones struck one another.

She looked around frantically, spotted small foci of furtive movement as the worms dispersed, and then she was alone in the clearing, standing above a complete, though no longer intact human skeleton, and she suddenly felt a moment of intuition in which she became quite convinced that she knew where at least one of the former inhabitants of the shantytown could now be found.

She bent over and vomited drily, then made her way back into the cabin and bolted the door.

The following morning, after discovering that the human skeleton had vanished during the night, she realized that one horror movie cliché was unfortunately entirely too plausible. There was no possible way she could go to the authorities and tell them what she'd seen, at least without some substantial physical evidence. They'd lock her up and throw away the key and she wouldn't blame them. But she also realized that she really didn't want to cry for help and let someone else solve the mystery. In some peculiar way, this had become her problem, her purpose for being here, perhaps even for having survived the loss of everything she loved.

And she had a pretty good idea where to look next.

The trip to the shantytown was much quicker this time. She parked as she had before, but this time she marched directly to the center building and tried the door. It shook in its frame without opening, but it felt jammed rather than locked. A nudge with her shoulder fixed the problem, and she staggered and almost fell into the darkened interior.

There were only two rooms – the three shacks apparently shared a single outhouse across the road. Ariana waited in the doorway while her eyes adjusted. The interior was a shambles, a rude kitchen and living room combined. There was trash on the floor, the counters, and the wooden table that dominated the room. A bead curtain masked the doorway to the second room, where two mattresses lay parallel on the floor under worn and filthy bedding. There were also two skeletons here, lying one to each mattress. Ariana decided not to enter the room.

The house to the left was easier to enter and similarly furnished, except that there were no bodies. There were two more skeletons in the third house, one on the bed, one slumped in a corner. Ariana withdrew and looked around, uncertain now what she hoped to accomplish. She could report the bodies to the police if she could think of an explanation of why she'd come looking for them. If she left one of the doors open, she could claim she had thought something might be wrong and investigated. They'd be forced to act then, but that didn't necessarily mean they'd solve her problem.

She walked around outside, even poked her head into the outhouse, but didn't find anything else until she reached the crumbling pier. There was a human skeleton lying on the shore there, as if it had crawled out of the water to die on the rocks. The side of its skull was caved in as though it had been hit by something, perhaps a fireplace poker. She was crouched there when something behind her rustled in the brush. Plop.

Her courage failed her then and she bolted for the Caravan and drove back to the cabin.

She arrived so shaken that she felt physically ill. Once inside she locked the door and lay down on her bed, slowly regaining her equilibrium. Like it or not, she was going to have to go to the police. No mention of the things she'd seen in the night, of course, but with investigators searching the woods, it was likely they'd turn up something that would trigger an alarm. And if not, she was no worse off than she was already.

She rose from the bed, washed her face and combed her hair. Under other circumstances, she'd have walked down to the lake for a quick dip, but not now. Probably never again, not at Pale Lake anyway. And tonight she'd take a room in town. She wasn't being scared away, she told herself, but she needed a shower and a dose of normality. The morning would be soon enough to make decisions.

Somewhere along the way she'd snagged her blouse so she changed that as well. It was later than she'd realized and the light wouldn't last much longer. Time to get going.

She stepped outside cautiously, where everything seemed normal. Automatically she reached behind her to close the door, then stopped. If she had to beat a hasty retreat, every second might be precious. She left it open and started toward the caravan, but never actually reached it. The passenger side tire in front was flat and she cursed under her breath, assuming that she'd hit a sharp stone on one of the unpaved roads. Then she saw that the rear tire was flat as well, and seconds later knew that all four were in the same condition. Ariana moved back toward the cabin, scanning the area warily. She could walk out to the main road, but it would take hours to reach town on foot and she wasn't going to risk it in the darkness.

She was halfway back when something stepped out of the shadows. It looked like a person, but there was no doubt in her mind that this was something, not someone. Its surface was in constant motion, a cauldron of living tissue. This was the first time she had actually seen one of them so clearly and she noticed that it staggered awkwardly, as though whatever intelligence was in control was not quite sure how a rigid structure of bones and sockets should work.

Ariana took a step back and turned halfway around. She could lock herself in the Caravan until morning if necessary. But she couldn't. Another figure, slightly smaller than the first, lurched into sight. She hesitated only a second, evaluating her options, then darted forward, determined to reach the cabin and safety. An arm began to rise but it was far too slow. She ducked away, almost lost her own footing for a second, then reached the entrance and threw herself inside, whirling to slam the door behind her. Her hands were shaking but she managed to engage the lock just as something heavy and soft thumped against the exterior.

Once she had caught her breath, Ariana felt surprisingly calm. She'd seen the worst without flinching and she was safe inside, at least for the time being. All she had to do was wait until morning, then slip out and walk to town. Maybe she'd think of something to tell the police and maybe she wouldn't. Maybe she'd just have the Caravan towed into Pomfret so the tires could be repaired and then drive off. It wasn't her problem.

Plop.

The sound no longer held the terror of the unknown, but Ariana stiffened anyway. No, the sound didn't bother her at all. But something else did. It had come from behind her.

Very slowly, Ariana turned around. It had made no effort to conceal itself; she just hadn't noticed it in her hurry to secure the door. There was nothing to distinguish this one from the others and this time she was able to examine it much more closely. They were earthworms, all right, squirming furiously in an interlaced, ever changing configuration. She saw nothing at all out of the ordinary, except of course for the fact that they were using a human skeleton as what, some kind of vehicle? Or was it simply a structure that lent organization and mobility to an otherwise disorganized, unstructured mass?

It didn't approach her and she returned the favor. Instead she inched over to the table where a gas lantern and an oil lamp were sitting side by side. She lit one and then the other, fumbling blindly because she couldn't move her eyes away from her motionless but ever moving visitor. It visibly recoiled when she lit the two lamps, but only a step or two.

There was another lantern by the fireplace and she started in that direction, then stopped when the shambling form moved suddenly forward. She felt a flash of alarm that faded as she realized it wasn't advancing in her direction, but a second later she felt a fresh flurry of fear. It was headed for the door.

Maybe it wanted to escape the light, but surely it would not be able to manage the chain lock? Ariana tried to think of a way she could manipulate it from a distance and let the creature (creatures?) escape without coming near, but that proved unnecessary. When it reached the door, both arms came up and fumbled at the chain, as though it knew its purpose and function. How could that be, she wondered, and then remembered something Dan had told her, that sometimes knowledge was passed from one lower animal to another through cannibalism. Could the worms have somehow absorbed the knowledge of how chain locks worked from the human bodies it had consumed?

It seemed so, because after it had fumbled awkwardly with the chain for several seconds, Ariana heard rather than saw it disengage. The door swung open and she took a deep breath, preparing to slam it shut the moment her guest was gone. But it didn't go. Instead, the other two immediately entered.

One she could avoid, even in the confined space of the cabin. Three of them would have little trouble trapping her in some corner and doing whatever it is that they wanted to do to her. Prepare another skeleton perhaps? Ariana had no intention of finding out. Without hesitation, she picked up the oil lamp and threw it down on the floor. The glass shattered and the oil spilled, flame rushing out in every direction. She glanced up and was gratified to see that the three interlopers had drawn back. The pool of fire spread rapidly across the wooden floor, eating into the wood and Ariana added to the fray by tossing one of the gas lanterns after it.

Her escape route was suddenly clear, although she had to dash through the fringe of the fire to reach the doorway. Then she was outside and turning, reaching in to grab the door and pull it into place behind her. It latched but she had no way to lock it. But as the seconds passed, there was no attempt to open the door from inside and within just a very few minutes most of the interior was engulfed in flames. Ariana retreated to the Caravan and watched for a while, then climbed inside. Someone would see the fire and smoke and report them and the police and others would come and they'd find three skeletons in the ashes.

She knew what she would have to tell them, that three unidentified people had broken into her cabin after disabling her vehicle, there had been a struggle and a fire and somehow she had managed to get out. They must have been drunk. She had never gotten a clear look at them. She could be dazed and uncertain about exactly what had happened. For that matter, she actually was uncertain.

And what would she do then? The cabin was gone as completely as Dan, both reduced to ash and lost forever. But she felt no real sense of loss. If nothing else she realized now that the past had never actually been the way she remembered it and it was not a refuge from the present. As for the future, it would not be what she had expected. But then again, it never would have been.

THE CHINDI

"Why would someone just go off and leave this place?" Jill gestured to include not just the abandoned hogan but its surroundings as well, a sheltered spot with a magnicent view of the landscape.

Brian shrugged. "Navajo superstition. Look, see this hole cut in the side? Someone died and that's where they took the body out."

Jill frowned critically. "You're putting me on, right? There's a perfectly good door, but someone cut a hole in the wall anyway."

"It's their custom. They always take a body out through the north side because that's where evil comes from. Then they abandon the hogan because of ghosts."

"Ghosts yet!" Jill shook her head. "And you think we can learn something from studying these people? They're living in the dark ages. They're not even smart enough to build their houses..."

"Hogans," Brian interrupted.

"Whatever. They don't even think to build them with a north entrance in the first place."

"Would you want evil to be the first thing you see every morning? Anyway, they usually take the dying out to die in sunlight, but there's not always time." He wanted to change the subject; Jill was predisposed to think ill of this entire venture, and he was just providing fuel. "So is this a good enough spot to set up camp?"

"Can we fix that hole? It'd be a lot warmer than our tent."

"Sure, I guess. But it's haunted you know. There's a Navajo chindi living there now."

Jill's expression was clearer than words. He started gathering materials to make a patch.

Jill was unusually subdued the following morning.

"Sleep all right?" They'd been living together for over a year and Brian still couldn't read her moods.

"Yeah, I guess." She didn't meet his eyes. "Who do you suppose lived here?"

"Hard to tell. A Navajo wiseman maybe. They're not hermits exactly, have a strong sense of family in fact, but they tend to go off by themselves."

Brian busied himself starting the gas stove. Coffee was the first order of business today. There was a definite chill despite the morning sun.

"I want to drive into the village today, see if I can make some contacts. Blake says they're wary of anthropologists, so officially we're just on vacation, but interested in understanding Navajo customs."

"Do you mind if I stay behind?"

Brian glanced around. "Okay, if you want, but I won't be back for hours."

"I'll be fine. I like it here."

When Brian returned late that afternoon, there was no sign of Jill. He called her name several times, and when she finally answered her voice was almost swallowed up by his echoes.

She was a considerable distance upslope, sitting in a cleft of tumbled rock. It took almost half an hour for Brian to climb to the spot.

"I found something." She pointed with her chin.

It was a body, partially mummified, tucked into a narrow crevice.

"Damn!" Brian felt attracted and repelled simultaneously. "I bet that's our missing wiseman."

"He was a witch, actually. Everyone around here was afraid of him."

"Yeah, right. What'd you do? Find his diary or something?"

"Something." She stood up abruptly, started upslope. "C'mon, that's not all I found."

The climb only took about ten minutes, but the shadows were already lengthening when they reached a narrow gap between two rocks.

"There's not much room. You go first. I've already seen it."

Brian was puzzled, but did as she asked, turning sideways to slide between two planes of stone. He emerged onto a ledge overlooking a deep, rocky pit. The pit was full of bones. Human bones.

"What the hell?"

Jill touched his shoulder. "He killed them all, brought them up here and pushed them in. Most died right away but sometimes it took longer. He got more strength from them when that happened. Took their lives to extend his own. But eventually even the magic couldn't keep his body going."

"This is incredible. How'd you find this, Jill?"

"You might say I had a native guide." And something much older than Jill suddenly looked out through her eyes and Brian tried to find something to hold onto when she suddenly pushed forward, toppling him from the narrow ledge.

Brian was young and strong and it took him a long time to die.

CLEANSING AGENT

Even thought it was impossible, a toilet flushed in one of the empty stalls.

Danny jumped at the sound, whispered "What the fuck?" under his breath, wishing he had a weapon, the Magnum he'd lost in a poker game, a knife, even a wrench. He'd just finished checking out the entire men's room and knew there was no chance that he might have overlooked anyone, and the fixtures were so primitive, there couldn't have been an automatic timer.

He moved to the far wall, where a row of filthy sinks underlined a murky mirror. There were six stalls; he counted them again just as he had the first time, when he'd swung each door open in turn, revealing nothing more alarming than wads of damp toilet paper lying on the floor, dangling from the fixtures, or draped over the cracked porcelain seats. Each remained open as he'd left them, the sound of rushing water coming from somewhere near the far end, one of the last two.

"Anybody in there?" His voice sounded unnaturally hoarse, an old man's querulous inquiry, totally inappropriate for someone who had celebrated, after a fashion, his twenty-first birthday only a few months earlier. And a lifetime ago.

Another step and fresh pain blossomed just above his groin. Danny ignored it as best he could, trying not to remember the mass of bruised flesh that girdled his body, already turning grey and purple and yellow. He had no watch, and when he'd regained consciousness, there was only the vaguest sense of the passage of time. Minutes, or hours? He'd been too busy to worry about it, too busy taking inventory of his battered body and shattered self confidence.

They were supposed to be his friends, the foursome who'd turned on him treacherously just as he was about to divide up the spoils of their cooperative effort. Only Tanya had made him uneasy at times; she always looked at him as though he smelled bad. But Buzz and Dylan insisted it was all an act with her, that everything was cool, and Lizzie, well, she'd been giving him the eye a little when the others weren't looking, as though she were interested in something more than business but not sure enough to act right out in the open. He'd respected that and waited for his chance, thinking he was about to score big with one of the best looking chicks he'd ever been close enough to touch.

Well, they'd touched all right. He particularly remembered the expression on her face when she stood over him, kicking his ribs so hard it must have hurt her as well, but with a face so full of the pure joy of inflicting pain that he wasn't surprised when she kept right on with it, probably even after he'd passed out. Afterwards, they'd bundled him into a narrow closet and left him to recover or die on his own. There'd been an ominous amount of blood in his urine when he'd pissed a few minutes ago, sitting in one of the stalls, trying to pull himself back together.

The final gurgles subsided and silence returned. Danny walked to the far end of the room, supporting himself with one hand brushing across the rims of the sinks. There was no one there; he was alone in the bowels of the airport.

Danny was good at his chosen profession, a natural talent he'd nursed from a smoldering ember to a raging fire. While his newfound business partners were distracting people with their outrageous appearance and language, he moved among the crowd, collecting wallets almost at will, so many that he'd worried a security guard would notice the bulges in his intentionally voluminous clothing. But everyone was preoccupied, still wondering what had caused a passenger flight to crash on the main runway earlier in the day, and he'd been amazed at how easily things had gone.

He had removed all the cash and had been about to count the not inconsiderable evening's take when Buzz hit him from behind, and the money was falling from his numb fingers as Tanya pivoted on her heel and kicked him in the balls. It still hurt to think about it, not just the terrifying, utterly devastating pain, but the expression on her face as she did it -- not cruelty, not anger, not anything he could live with. Tanya looked as though she'd turned over a rock and found something too loathsome to tolerate, something that needed to be squashed, destroyed, utterly expunged from the world.

The stalls were still empty, all of them. There was no place to hide, no utility closet, ventilation duct, or any other feature that might conceal an unseen lurker. He was alone in the restroom just as he had been ever since he'd regained consciousness in the maintenance closet and staggered here.

There was a sudden twist in his gut and Danny turned, leaning over the sink, waiting for his gorge to rise. But although he tasted the bitterness of bile at the back of his throat, his stomach lacked the contents, or the strength, to follow through. When he was sure the spasm was over, he splashed lukewarm water onto his face, blinked rapidly, trying to evaluate his appearance in the steamy mirror.

He couldn't believe how humid it was down here; the walls were dripping with condensation, as though he'd stumbled into the stomach of some plastic and concrete behemoth. He used his sleeve to clear a roughly circular spot in the mirror, brushed at his clothing. There was blood, but not a great deal of it, and the stains were already dried. His vest was reversible and he shrugged it off, moaning briefly as bruised ribs protested this exertion. Bruised or broken? He didn't want to deal with the second possibility.

With the lighter side of his vest showing, he was satisfied that he looked sufficiently acceptable that children would not run screaming from his presence. Danny turned away from the mirror, had actually started toward the exit when the toilet flushed again. But this time the sound was altered, not a flush exactly, more like a prolonged swallow. There was something about it that suggested a living creature, something that Danny was not sure he was willing to face. Without glancing toward the row of stalls, he took a deep breath and crossed to the door, swung it open, stepped out into the corridor.

There was a painting on the facing wall, one of a number of poorly rendered murals that were sprinkled throughout Dry Plains Airport. Danny was aware of their presence without having taken conscious note of their subject matter, but this particular one was so grotesque, so out of place, that he stood transfixed for long seconds.

His eyes were drawn initially to the small pile of bones in the exact center of the scene, a horned head vaguely reminiscent of a steer, although there were subtle differences which might have been attributable to careless artistry, or which might have been designed to imply something else entirely, a species driven to extinction, or perhaps one that existed only in legends.

The bones were flanked by scattered cacti and dead trees, and in the branches of those trees sat four starkly rendered, ominous creatures, vultures, wings held close against attenuated bodies, long beaks, scaly talons clutched tightly around their perches. There was something vaguely familiar about them, so tantalizing that Danny stood transfixed, staring, until he decided he was interpreting the painting through a filter of his own preoccupation. Certainly one vulture was holding its head at the same odd angle that Dylan used when he was contemplating mischief, and another stared with the same intolerant expression he'd seen in Tanya's eyes, but that couldn't be anything other than simple coincidence.

Danny forced himself to turn away, headed toward the staircase that led up to the main concourse. He could hear the sounds of human activity, muffled, like distant thunder. Earlier, the five of them had slipped past the ropes and signs indicating that this section of the airport was "Closed for Renovation", secure in their belief that no one would be working in the small hours of a Sunday morning, that they'd be uninterrupted.

There were featureless doors on either side of the corridor, differentiated only by small, signs with block lettering. ELECTRIC, he read, PERSONNEL, MAINTENANCE, LOST AND FOUND, SATISFACTION, and SUPPLIES. Danny was several meters beyond before the oddity registered. Satisfaction? He stopped, half turned, squinting to re-read the sign in question. It still bore the same letters, clear and enigmatic at the same time.

Danny backed up and knocked hesitantly, then said "Fuck it!" softly and tried the knob. It turned easily. The room beyond was dimly lit and unfurnished. The walls were plain and unadorned, no windows, not even a calendar to break up the smooth plains of off-white, softened even further by the inadequate illumination provided by a single fluorescent light. A table stood in the center, covered with dust so thick that Danny almost failed to notice the faint outline of two objects, a torn scrap of paper and a small, metal key.

He leaned forward and blew the worst of the dust away, then picked up the paper using just the tips of his fingers, shaking it until it was relatively clean. It was a detailed black and white map of the airport with a single black "X" marked near the upper right hand corner. Danny folded it carefully and slipped it into his hip pocket, then picked up the key, still bright and shiny despite the layer of dirt, decorated with the number 216 along its stem.

There were several rows of short term rental lockers near the gift shop upstairs. Apparently one of the keys had been misplaced a long time ago. With any luck, the locker was back in service and might well contain something Danny could use, preferably cash or something he could pawn, although he wouldn't have minded even a fresh set of clothing.

He closed the door behind him when he left.

There seemed to be far more steps leading up than there had been coming down, one short flight after another, interspersed with gently inclined ramps. Danny felt as if he were plodding an endless treadmill, wondered if his strength would hold out long enough for him to reach the upper levels. And just as he was considering stopping for a while, to catch his breath and will away the throbbing pain in his ribs and thighs and the center of his forehead, he found his way barred by an imitation velvet rope, pale yellow, draped from stanchion to stanchion like stringy intestines.

There were people beyond, but fewer than he expected, most sitting or standing in small, isolated clusters throughout the concourse. The concessions were all closed except for a small coffee shop at the far end, whose lights blinked irregularly. No one sat at the counter, although a hunched form was visible in a corner booth, motionless, perhaps asleep. A uniformed man with a fixed expression of disinterest was pushing a wide headed broom across the floor, leaving small piles of debris at odd locations, following no pattern, never clearing any of the accumulation away.

Danny stepped over the cordon and pushed forward.

The locker was on the rear side of one row, facing the wall, sheltered from observation. Danny inserted the key and twisted, half expecting the lock to have been changed, but there was a slight, distinct click and when he pulled on the handle the door slid smoothly open. There was a small paper bag inside, the open end folded over and stapled shut.

Disappointed already, Danny ripped the paper angrily, expecting to find a couple of magazines or an embossed sweatshirt or something equally useless. What he did find was a snub nosed pistol, clean and well oiled, and loaded with six cartridges. He glanced around nervously, made certain that no one was watching, then slipped the weapon into the inside pocket of his padded vest, adjusted the way it fell until he was confident no one would be able to see it.

The presence of the pistol was like a powerful analgesic and much of the pain receded, his back straightened and he raised his chin, drawing from this newfound source of strength. Satisfaction, the sign had read, which right now meant revenge, and he had the instrument of that imperative at hand. Buzz and Dylan, Tanya and Lizzie, yes, most of all Lizzie, with her treacherous unspoken promises, they were all fair game now. All he had to do was find them. It never occurred to Danny that they might have left the airport, dispersed to the crumbling tenement they called home. He knew with absolute certainty that they were still around, still within reach, believing him unconscious or even dead back where they had dumped him. He even fancied he could detect a faint trace of Lizzie's perfume in the air.

But how was he going to find them?

Danny returned to the concourse, strolling with deliberate casualness in a great circle. Most of the handful of people he passed turned away rather than meet his eyes, a few stared back defiantly. The man with the broom was making a fresh circuit, rearranging the small piles of candy wrappers, cigarette butts, claims stubs, and other debris into fresh patterns no less confused and useless than before. If Danny had been in a more settled frame of mind, he might have wondered at the air of lethargic chaos that reigned tonight, might have noticed that all flights, both incoming and outgoing, were labeled on the overhead monitors as "Canceled" or "Delayed". But his own preoccupations were paramount.

He climbed an open railed staircase to the observation deck, found it abandoned, crossed to the wall of reinforced windows and stared down onto the airfield proper. Two planes were snug up against one wing of the airport off to his left, but their lights were all off and there was no flurry of baggage handlers and mechanics, no indication that passengers were boarding or disembarking. In both directions, the umbilicals designed to offload passengers were partially extended, making gentle curves like the talons of a vulture.

No, he told himself, almost speaking aloud. More like the fingers of a sleeping child. The airport is a body, he realized, and he'd crawled out of its very bowels, no, its heart, an antibody of some kind, a white blood cell on a mission to seek out and destroy invading parasites. That's what they were, all right, Dylan and Tanya and the others. Parasites. Danny had always thought of his own thievery as a game, sleight of hand, his wits and skill and agility pitted against those of his victims. No one was every hurt, not really, just inconvenienced. And he passed over those who looked as though they couldn't afford the loss of a few dollars, telling himself he acted out of compassion, never admitting that the truth was that the small potential gain was not worth the risk.

Danny had teamed up with others in the past; it always helped to have a distraction, a loud and carefully staged argument, hot coffee spilled over someone's tailor made suit, even once an impromptu folk singing duet whose talents might well have been more profitable had they been directed toward a more constructive goal. He'd always worked out the split in advance and never cheated, even on those occasions when he could have run off with the entire take. Danny had standards, what he thought of as his personal code of honor.

He'd made a mistake in allowing himself to become involved with the foursome, but they'd made a bigger one letting him survive the encounter.

The airport complex seemed even larger from up here, sprawling in several directions, the original building lost in a complicated series of additions, modifications, and then abbreviations as certain underutilized areas were closed off, their functions consolidated elsewhere. It was a bewildering maze taken as a whole, and Danny felt a brief moment of despair when he realized how easy it would be for the others to conceal themselves. There were multiple walkways between the main structures, a system of veins and arteries that rivaled the human body in scale.

Then he remembered the map.

It was still in his pocket and when he unfolded the creased paper, the semblance of a living creature was even more obvious. The two parking ramps at the south end could be legs, although certainly not those of a human, more insectlike, sharp angles at the joints and a length disproportionate to their width. The passenger terminal made up a stubby torso, no real arms although it was possible to imagine them tucked close to the chest, with only the hands and fingers extended. The cluster of restaurants, gift shops, and other concessions formed a misshapen head.

The "X" he'd seen earlier was drawn precisely over an unlabelled square next to the shallow garage where the baggage trucks were parked. Even from the observation deck, and despite the floodlights spaced evenly outside the building, Danny could barely separate its roof from the surrounding shadows. But it felt right.

It took several minutes to discover the small accessway, an unmarked door whose lock succumbed to one of Danny's other acquired skills. He descended a short ramp covered by a flapping tent, realized the wind had picked up outside, the hot, dry air filled with particles of dust that stung when they struck unprotected flesh. Hunching his shoulders, he stepped beyond the fabric, blinking as he reoriented himself.

There! The building was surrounded by a hurricane fence, but the gate was unlocked. He removed the pistol from his vest and held it against his hip as he moved quickly to the side of the windowless building. It was loud out here, he realized, not just the wind but a rhythmic thrumming that came from the external blowers of the airport's ventilation system. Canvas had been stretched between two posts to break the force of the exhaust, and the fabric billowed out, then fell back, then out again in a regular pattern that reminded him of a breathing creature.

Someone laughed inside the building. He barely heard it above the din, but never doubted the evidence of his senses. It was the familiar, unpleasantly nasal sound Tanya made when she was amused. The strangest things amused her, he'd learned, usually things that he found sad or repulsive. His fingers tightened around the reassuring solidity of the pistol and he edged around the far corner, saw the door just a meter or so ahead.

As far as he knew, none of the others carried anything more dangerous than a pocket knife, but they'd deceived him on so much else, he wasn't prepared to take any chances. When he reached the door, he hesitated, assaulted by doubts. Did they know he was there? Were they waiting for him to come inside so they could finish what they'd begun earlier? Even if he surprised them, could he subdue all four before they could react and take the weapon away?

For a few seconds, his resolution faltered. He took one step back and relaxed his grip on the pistol, but as he did so the pain returned to his body with such immediate, overwhelming force that he doubled over, barely managing to retain his hold on the weapon. It was a clear message, but from whom?

"Okay," he whispered. "I won't chicken out." And as quickly as the pain had returned, it was gone.

They were sitting playing cards when he came through the door. Dylan looked startled, his face twisting into a defensive smile as he recognized Danny. The first bullet shattered the smile forever and the second quite unnecessarily struck him in the chest. Buzz and Lizzie were already diving for cover, but Tanya jumped to her feet and lunged forward, her eyes still filled with a raging contempt that only disappeared when she fell to her knees, staring disbelievingly at the small entry wound in her chest.

"You shithead!" It was the last insult she'd ever deliver.

Buzz and Lizzie had disappeared, concealed behind a pile of wooden crates and several pieces of machinery covered with tarps. This was a storage shed of some sort, Danny noted disinterestedly, moving slowly to one side in an effort to spot his prey.

A dark shape leaped out of the darkness, swinging something wildly as it came. Danny fired without conscious thought, then a second time when the shape continued to advance. Buzz slammed into him, still moving, but fell away before Danny had time to react further, dead before he hit the floor, a length of chain still clutched in one hand.

He found Lizzie crouched in a ball behind the last row of crates.

"Don't you come near me, you goddamned asshole!"

Danny stood just out of reach, the pistol angled toward the floor but ready to rise. He wondered now what he'd ever seen in her. There was a certain wild attractiveness, but the long black hair was unkempt and unclean. Lizzie deliberately wore excessive makeup and it was badly smeared, her cheeks wet with tears, forehead glistening with sweat.

"Come out of there." He said the words softly and she ignored him, so he raised the pistol and repeated the order, this time with clear menace. "Come out of there now."

She hesitated for only a second, then stood up, her arms pressed tight against her breasts, shivering slightly despite the heat. Danny gestured toward the door and followed her out, noticing that she carefully avoided looking at the bodies of her late friends. No, not friends, companions. People like Lizzie didn't have friends, as he'd so recently realized.

"What are you going to do?" She was making some effort to regain her self control now that she realized he was not going to kill her out of hand. But what was he going to do? Danny suddenly realized that he'd spared her, up to this point, without a conscious plan. Did he intend rape? He considered it briefly, but the idea was unappealing. Lizzie revolted him now, her breasts and thighs were alien shapes, concealing alien pleasures.

"This way." He gestured toward their right, where a walkway ran parallel to the main building, then angled in under an overhanging roof.

"Where are you taking me?" Strength was flowing back into her voice with every passing second. Enraged, Danny lunged forward, swung the butt of his pistol in a short, vicious arc that intersected with Lizzie's shoulderblade. She stumbled forward with a sharp cry, nearly fell.

"Just do what I tell you," he warned when she turned to face him, torn between fear and anger.

He used the last bullet to shatter the safety glass in a unmarked door, but Lizzie didn't seem to have been counting his shots and made no effort to escape. "Unlock it," he ordered and she reached carefully through the broken glass and did as she was told.

There was another door beyond, and this one opened into a corridor he recognized. Lizzie reluctantly led the way past a double row of doors, then around a corner into a dimly lit dead end.

"Look familiar?"

Lizzie turned to face him, anger gone. "Listen, I didn't want to stiff you like that, Danny, but the others made me do it. I always kind of liked you, and I thought, you know, maybe we could've been better friends if Buzz and the others hadn't've been around." She tugged at her blouse, trying to look casual as she pulled the material taut to emphasize her breasts. "Won't'cha give me a chance to prove it?"

Danny felt a momentary weakness, something inside that wanted to believe her, but he remembered the expression on her face as she had kicked him again and again and knew it was false, another lie, and rage was a bright flame that drove away his uncertainties just as it had dulled his pain.

"Come here," he said quietly, lowering the empty pistol to his side, trying to reshape his mouth into a smile.

Lizzie nodded, still hesitant, faltered after a single step. "You wouldn't hurt me, would ya, Danny? I mean, we're gonna be, like, friends and all. Partners maybe. Without the others, there'd be less to split."

"Sounds good to me," but as she advanced to within reach, he swept his arm up and smashed the cold metal into her left cheek. Lizzie twisted as she fell away, landing on her stomach, moaning, trying to get back to her feet. Danny let the pistol fall to the floor and moved to her side.

When his right foot began to hurt, he used his left, continuing long after he had broken all of her ribs, even after she had finally slumped to the floor for the last time, motionless, no longer breathing. There was surprisingly little blood, but then most of her injuries, like his, were on the inside, where they didn't show.

Once his breathing returned to normal, Danny suddenly became acutely aware that he was standing next to the evidence that could send him to jail for the rest of his life. Or was there a death penalty here in Texas? He couldn't remember. This part of the airport seemed deserted, but he couldn't count on that indefinitely. Besides, he'd already decided on a fitting resting place.

He dragged her by the heels to the maintenance closet door behind which he'd regained consciousness some indeterminate time earlier that evening. Had it been only minutes, or hours? Danny had no watch, nothing with which to measure the passage of time. The door was latched but not locked, and he pulled it open, prepared to bundle her into the tiny space within, among the mops and brushes and cleaning supplies.

But he couldn't carry through with his plan because there was already a body inside. It seemed to be a young man, about his own age, slumped forward with head on knees, wearing baggy clothing and a vest with very large pockets. The vest was virtually a copy of his own; in fact, so were the shirt and pants.

Danny staggered away, Lizzie's body forgotten, and raised the back of his hand to his mouth, stifling what threatened to be a cry of outrage and shock. "What the fuck's going on here?" he managed at last, but neither of the two dead people answered.

He was tempted to reach forward, lift the man's head, examine the face. But every time he started to do so, his muscles cramped and his stomach threatened to rebel, and he realized he really didn't want to know. With a small, inarticulate cry, he turned away and ran back down the corridor, running so fast that he caromed off one wall, stumbled over his own feet, continued forward off balance for several steps, then crashed full length to the floor, knocking the wind from his lungs.

When Danny had the strength to rise, he felt emotionally parched, and his legs were so unsteady that he pressed both palms against the wall while his self control slowly returned. He raised his head, found himself staring into the same mural he'd examined earlier, four vultures holding watch over the remains of a past meal. No, it couldn't be the same, because there were no bones visible in this one, just a bare patch of sand. And the carrion eaters were drawn differently as well, alert, attentive, as though a fresh meal awaited them.

Danny tried to straighten up, but discovered that he couldn't lift his hands away from the wall. Mystified, he lowered his eyes, then gasped when he realized his forearms disappeared where they touched the plaster, as though his body was being absorbed into the wall. That's when he remembered his high school biology class and what happened to white cells once they were no longer needed, but his subsequent frantic attempts to pull free only caused him to fall further forward into the wall.

He tasted hot sand in his mouth in the instant before sharp beaks and talons touched his flesh.

SNEAK THIEF

Although I consider myself a competent observer, I was totally unprepared for the unique threat posed by Heather Angeli.

I remember the day she moved in. It was a humid Saturday morning in August of 1990. Jennifer, Esther, and I were sitting on the front steps, drinking lemonade and hoping for an ice cream truck. Westwood, the only rooming house in Managansett, managed to trap heat with remarkable efficiency. Only air conditioning would have made it bearable inside, and if any of us had been able to afford such a luxury, we would have been living elsewhere in the first place.

Esther was alternately enticing me toward yet another suicidal chess game and enlightening us with a no doubt accurate analysis of the demographic reasons why the Masai culture in Kenya could not survive absorption by the Kikuyu. I listened closely enough to nod at appropriate places without actually following the argument. Although I admired Esther's sophistication and insight, she was at in her late fifties while Jennifer, on the other hand, was twenty-five, attractive, and available.

Our landlady's battered Volkswagen pulled up to the curb, followed closely by a taxi, distracting me from a surreptitious examination of Jennifer's tanned knees. A young woman emerged from the cab, painfully slender, skin unusually pale for this late in the summer. Her eyes were dark with long black lashes and she walked tentatively, as though unsure of her footing. I suspected immediately that she was recovering from a long illness; she had the look of someone who hadn't been out in the sun for weeks, perhaps months.

Jeri Kaplan, who managed Westwood, introduced us.

"Heather, this is Esther Henneberg, our most senior tenant, and Jennifer Lee, our newest. Until today anyway." Esther smiled and nodded while Jennifer stood and offered her hand, which Heather accepted after a momentary hesitation. It wasn't rudeness, exactly. She seemed to be confused by social cues, uncertain of the proper response. When her head turned in my direction, I realized that behind that pallor, framed by the fine, shoulder length black hair, lurked a face of truly appalling plainness.

"And this is Alex Clausen, our writer in residence." Since

Heather's arm had dropped back to her side, I simply nodded and smiled noncommittally. To be truthful, I felt a mild revulsion toward the young woman, and while vaguely ashamed of my reaction, I was reluctant to actually touch her.

"Heather is taking the empty apartment on the second floor," Jeri explained. "I hope you'll all make her feel welcome."

Room 202 had been vacant since Paul Caldarone picked up stakes and moved on. We made polite noises of welcome while the taxi driver grumbled impatiently in the background. I offered to carry her bags upstairs and she nodded so casually, as if expecting no less, that I was mildly offended.

Upstairs, I made a hasty excuse and left while Jeri was apologizing for the poor ventilation, hurrying back outside into the comparatively cool air.

"Another inmate in the asylum." Jennifer sound less than enthusiastic as she leaned back against the railing to let me pass. Her shorts rode high on her thighs, but I still couldn't spot the tan line. She had extraordinarily good legs, perhaps her best feature, slender but well muscled, probably because she spent so much time playing racquetball.

"Poor girl looks like she's been sick," Esther suggested. In my absence, she'd started another game of chess, this time playing both sides.

I was about to organize a walk down to the corner for ice cream when I was forestalled by the arrival of another Westwood tenant, Henry Davidson. I always felt overwhelmed in Henry's presence, physically at least. His hobby was bodybuilding, and he worked out religiously both at home and at the gymnasium and racquetball club down near the Scituate border. I'm an active if not an athletic person, but I must confess to an irrational feeling of inferiority in Henry's company. The man positively radiated physical fitness. In his presence, colors seemed brighter, sounds crisper, life rich and full of potential.

"Hello, people. What's new?"

Esther gave him a brief account of our new neighbor.

"Sounds good, having a young girl around." Henry quickly realized his mistake. "Another one, I mean." He nodded to Jennifer, who smiled politely. There was some unresolved conflict between the two of them, and although neither spoke of it, the coolness was hard to miss. Which left the field open for me.

But there was a new player in the game.

I'd expected Heather to have a minimal impact on our lives, but she made her presence felt very quickly. The following morning, she told Esther about her recent recovery from a grave but unspecified illness. "I just need some peace and quiet, till I get back on my feet."

Henry was more enthusiastic, accompanied her on increasingly lengthy walks around town "to help get her strength back." Sometimes he ran errands on her behalf when she wasn't feeling up to the challenge. I never quite understood the nature of their friendship, which was not overtly sexual in any discernible fashion. On the other hand, I once caught them sunbathing in the small yard behind Westwood. Henry appeared to have dozed off but Heather was sitting upright, slowly running her fingers along his arms and legs, tracing the curves of the muscles, then echoing the motion on her own body. The systematic, almost clinical way she did it made me very uncomfortable and I slipped away before she saw me.

Heather's health and appearance continued to improve, her frame gradually filling out. While Henry remained her most frequent companion, she gained enough self confidence to take tentative steps toward the rest of us. The only lingering evidence of her physical problem was an awkward lack of coordination that betrayed itself in occasional small accidents, stumbles, a bottle of soda dropped down the stairwell, other minor incidents.

I didn't dislike Heather, but despite the healthy glow in her cheeks and some additional meat on her bones, she remained an unusually unattractive young woman. And a dull one as well. Our conversations, always brief, dealt with such compelling topics as the weather, how helpful Henry had been, what she had eaten recently, and so on. She was invariably superficial and colorless and I was puzzled by Henry's obvious infatuation. Esther abandoned an early attempt to teach her chess, Jennifer was unable to interest her in a shopping trip to Providence, and my occasional attempts at conversation had generated responses that were less than scintillating.

Temperatures continued higher than normal, but heat or no

heat, I had to get some writing done. It was cooler after the sun fell, so I spent a late August night typing until almost dawn. The following afternoon, I carried the manuscript down to the front steps to work it over with a red pencil.

"Whatcha doing?"

The unexpected words spoken inches from my ear were so startling that I dropped part of the manuscript. When I bent to retrieve the loose pages, Heather squatted beside me and offered awkward assistance.

"Sorry. Didn't mean to scare you."

"That's all right. Here, let me take those."

She was holding two pages, and I saw her eyes move from left to right, obviously reading but with a puzzled expression as though the words held no meaning for her. "What is this?"

"It's a story I'm working on. Just a draft."

"Why?"

"Why? Because this damn heat makes it hard to work." I felt oddly disconcerted in her presence, and was already rehearsing excuses to go back inside.

"No, I mean why do you write stories?"

There were many answers to that question. I selected the one I thought she'd find most convincing. "Because I get paid to do it." Pause. "Sometimes," I added in a moment of honesty.

"Can't be much if you're living here." Her eyes strayed eloquently back to the front door of Westwood as she handed me the pages.

"There are other rewards. I enjoy the act of creation. I take my experiences and shape them into a new form that other people find entertaining."

"You give away a part of yourself? Why would you do such a thing?"

"It's not a gift; it's a kind of sharing. I don't lose anything in the process."

"Are you sure?" It was an odd question, spoken with great intensity, and I was still trying to think of an answer when she stood up and left without another word.

The first tragedy came almost one month following Heather's arrival. I hadn't seen Henry for several days, but we'd never interacted regularly and I assumed Heather was still his major preoccupation. I was dividing my own time between bouts of writing and an admittedly fitful pursuit of Jennifer. Although I would not have characterized her as beautiful, Jennifer was attractive and pleasant company and responded encouragingly to my cautious advances.

My most recent novel came back with an apologetic rejection, but I had two major short story sales in the same week and all in all, I felt pretty good about life. Until Esther broke the news about Henry's leukemia.

There had been no indication anything was wrong until Henry collapsed, apparently in a faint, during a strenuous workout at the gym. He recovered consciousness quickly enough but remained obviously shaken, and two of his friends overrode his objections and bundled him over to the emergency room in Providence for a quick checkup. They admitted him two hours later.

The next few weeks were a burden for all of us. Henry's few relatives had either died or fallen out of touch, and his acquaintances from the gym seemed to evaporate as quickly as his own formerly robust health. Those of us at Westwood who considered Henry our friend informally scheduled ourselves so that someone would be with him every day, but I have to admit that the speed of his decline was so depressing, I dreaded my turns at his bedside. To her credit, Heather spent more time with him than the rest of us, sometimes riding the bus with Esther, or driving in with either Jennifer or myself. She was still unattractive and uninteresting as far as I was concerned, but with color in her cheeks and a bit more flesh on her frame, I no longer felt actively repelled by her.

But she was definitely the most boring and ignorant person I'd ever known.

"You're not being fair," Jennifer reproached me. "She's not as dumb as you make her out to be."

"Come off it, Jenny. I don't mean to pick on the woman, but sometimes I think she might even be a little bit retarded. She thought Philadelphia was a state, remember? You're more intelligent asleep than she is awake." I realized I was over reacting and took a deep breath. "All right, I'm sorry. She might not be particularly bright, but she's been a better friend to Henry than I have, so I've got no business criticizing her."

Jennifer held her glare a few seconds longer, then allowed it to soften, reached over and patted my knee. We hadn't slept together yet, but we were moving in that direction.

"Okay, so maybe there's some things she's not too bright about, but that doesn't make her stupid, does it? Esther taught her to play chess while they were keeping Henry company, and she's doing pretty well for a beginner. Maybe she just never had a chance to learn things until now."

Shortly before Henry's hospitalization, Heather had started keeping company with a young man her own age, Nick something or other; I never did learn his last name although I met him a few times. Nick struggled to survive on the meager income he earned working as a ballet dancer for the Rhode Island Performing Acts Company and several semi-professional troupes. Once it became obvious that Henry was never going to leave the hospital, Heather began to see Nick more frequently, although she never missed her turn at Henry's beside. Tactfully, she never brought her new boyfriend along.

Henry died two evenings before Christmas.

I remember it well because it was the same night that Jennifer and I first made love. Neither of us ever spoke about the unpleasant coincidence of the timing, but it remained an unspoken barrier complicating our relationship, the first indication that we had peaked as a couple, were already sliding toward the downside.

We all attended the funeral, even Nick, although I doubt he'd ever met Henry. Clearly he felt like an interloper, and I found myself sympathizing with his discomfort, attempted to involve him in a casual conversation to break the tension. Jennifer and I followed the two of them through the cemetery; Esther had gone ahead with Jeri Kaplan.

The Managansett cemetery might have been pretty if it had been better maintained; there were none of those cheerless flat expanses so common elsewhere, but rather a series of rolling slopes dotted with gravestones placed randomly in the grass. I remember at one point Nick stumbled over a half concealed marker. Heather turned and caught his arm, steadying him effortlessly, displaying an agility I would never have expected from her.

At the time, I saw it as just one more bit of evidence that she was recovering her health. Later, the incident took on much greater significance.

The new year was less than joyous. Esther collapsed in upon herself and didn't visit with us as much as she had previously, although she still showed up in the first floor lounge from time to time for a game of chess. Heather acquired an insatiable taste for the game, and invariably won on those occasions when she browbeat me into playing against her. She even defeated Esther a few times, and her willingness to listen attentively while Esther lectured her on the economic interpretation of the American Revolution or the evolution of the social contract seemed infinite.

One afternoon she asked me how Esther ever came to know so much.

"I guess she just absorbs knowledge like a sponge. She's always reading or watching PBS."

"She really amazes me. I wish I could be like that."

It seemed a perfectly innocuous conversation.

"Heather really seems to be blossoming lately," I ventured one evening in March while Jennifer and I were watching a rented movie in her room.

"So you said yesterday, and the day before. Can't you talk about something else for a change?" Jennifer sounded annoyed and I realized my comment had been less than tactful. Our affair had not become stormy, but the clouds were beginning to gather. We'd been intimate enough to discover each other's rough edges, and while I felt that our relationship grew stronger with each hurdle passed, we did occasionally quarrel.

"I'm sorry," I replied. "She's a friend of yours too, isn't she? I notice the two of you spend a lot of time at the racquetball club together."

"What's that supposed to mean?" Definitely angry now.

"It's not supposed to mean anything." I straightened up on the couch, surprised at her tone. She'd been irritable all day and I was starting to feel a little annoyed myself.

It might have turned into a serious argument, but just as we were rattling our sabers, there came a tentative knock on the door. Jennifer glared a clear warning that the subject was not closed as she uncrossed her legs and stood up to answer it.

Esther Henneberg stood just outside, her eyes glittering with unshed tears, hands clasped in front of her chest, the fingers of one hand squeezing those of the other.

"Please, Jennifer, I'm dreadfully sorry to bother you." Her voice was thin, brittle with near hysteria.

"That's perfectly all right, Esther. Why don't you come in? What's wrong?"

Esther shook her head and remained outside. "No, I don't want to impose. I just wondered if you might give me some directions." Her calm evaporated at that point and the tears flowed freely. "I don't seem to be able to find my room, you see." And then Jennifer's arms were around her and Esther was sobbing heavily, despairingly.

It was diagnosed as Alzheimer's Disease, and Esther was moved to a nursing home three days later.

Spring came and our moods lightened. Esther's absence was like a missing tooth; we kept worrying at the empty space with our mental tongues. Jennifer and I were back on good terms; the first flush of romance had faded, replaced by an easy intimacy that I found reassuring.

Heather and Nick had parted ways during the waning months of winter. He slipped on an icy staircase somewhere and broke his leg. Whatever had existed between them must have been even more fragile, because it failed to survive their separation.

Jennifer's brief animosity toward Heather vanished as well, and she finally engineered a shopping trip.

"It was like a kid in a toyshop, Alex. You should have seen her. Do you know that she's never worn makeup in her life?" Jennifer made it sound like a form of child abuse. "I'm going to have to teach her everything."

I continued to earn a living with my typewriter, turning out a steady stream of sometimes saleable stories, making just enough to pay the rent and keep food on the table. Jennifer worked three nights a week at Foodworld running a cash register, so I set aside those evenings as dedicated creative time. I've never been troubled by writer's block, so adapting my work schedule was a simple task.

And then one evening, there was an unexpected knock on my

door.

"Hi! Got a minute?" It was Heather, eyes downcast, wearing a patterned blouse with the two top buttons undone. She had filled out considerably during the past several months, and Jennifer's crash course in cosmetics had clearly been a success.

"Sure," I answered uneasily, swinging the door wide. "Want to come in? The place is a mess but I think we can find a couple of chairs that aren't completely buried in the clutter."

"I don't want to interrupt if you're busy. I know you've been writing; I could hear the typewriter from down the hall."

Heather took the seat I indicated and crossed her legs demurely. She had changed hairstyles recently, and health and physical well being had remolded her features. While I still would not have called her beautiful, there was no doubt that she had shed the pale ugliness that put me off when she first arrived. In the dim light, from the right angle, she actually looked rather pretty.

"No problem. I've reached a snag anyway. I usually take a break when that happens and let my unconscious sort things out."

"What's the problem? Maybe I can help."

I laughed, but her expression remained serious, and I was suddenly conscious of the fact that I might hurt her feelings. "All right, but you'll have to understand the background first."

My latest project continued the adventures of my recurring detective, Victoria Sanders, and the critical scene depended upon one character's ability to copy a data file from the murderer's computer. Every time I wrote the scene, the murderer came across as hopelessly inept or careless, and that conflicted with the way I'd drawn the character earlier.

"Couldn't the hero rig the computer so it made a copy of anything entered?"

I shrugged. "Not plausibly. Remember, he only has a few minutes of access before the critical scene, and the data hasn't been inputted yet, so he can't steal it until later."

"Could there be a modem? Nick had one on his PC." I was surprised she knew so much about computers; maybe she wasn't quite as dumb as I had always believed.

"Maybe, but there'd still be some kind of security system."

We talked about it for a few more minutes without finding a satisfactory solution, and I was genuinely surprised by Heather's mental quickness.

"Nick was always talking about computer stuff," she explained, "and I guess I picked up more than I realized."

I completely forgot to ask the purpose of her unexpected visit, a puzzle which didn't occur to me again until long after she was gone.

It was a few more weeks before I began to suspect that Heather was making a play for me. I suppose I should have noticed sooner, but my experience in such cases is pretty limited. Although I'm not exactly unattractive, I was rather self absorbed throughout high school and college, and dated infrequently. When I did finally notice the change in her attitude, I have to admit I was flattered.

But I remained faithful in deed if not in thought.

When Heather stopped by my room that last Friday evening in June, she told me her toilet was backed up and asked to use mine. Considering my own recurring problems with Westwood's plumbing, I saw no reason to doubt her story. I never expected her to emerge naked from my bathroom, intent upon seducing me. Jennifer was home that evening, so even if I had felt inclined to cheat on her, I would at least have locked the door first.

"Heather! What in the world..."

"I want to be with you, Alex," she answered breathlessly. "I want to share with you."

I raised my arms to ward her off as she approached, which was precisely the moment when Jennifer walked in. I can imagine how it must have looked, and I was caught so totally off guard that I couldn't even speak. Jennifer didn't say anything either, just looked back and forth between the two of us and walked away.

I did make an effort to straighten things out. While I can't pretend that I was in love with Jennifer, I valued our relationship and wanted it to continue. But I never had a chance to explain. The situation changed too quickly.

Jennifer had been bothered by the sudden appearance of a rash earlier that month, and had finally gone to see an allergist. Less than a week after the night she stormed out of my apartment, her doctor administered a fresh battery of tests and sent her to a specialist. Fortunately, the rare degenerative skin disease was diagnosed early enough that they felt confident she would recover completely, in time, and they hoped to minimize the scarring.

Jennifer moved back to her parents' home in Vermont. She promised to stay in touch, but never answered any of my letters.

I began to see Heather more frequently, but neither of us ever referred to the attempt at seduction and our relationship was strictly casual thereafter. Heather did most of the talking when we were together; although I never saw her with a book, she seemed to have absorbed volumes of new knowledge and often reminded me of Esther. Now that she was fully recovered from her illness, she acquired an undeniable sexiness, and properly made up she was pretty enough to attract the attention of passing strangers.

Heather found herself a job working with a semi-professional ballet company in Providence, apparently having demonstrated significant natural talent. If she'd been a character in one of my stories, it would have been a triumphant plot, the return from adversity and the transformation into a talented, competent adult.

But something about the story rang false, although I never suspected the truth until today.

Earlier this evening, I was working in the small sitting room which I laughingly refer to as my office. The chapter I've labored over for the past several weeks has been an endless struggle, each word resisting my efforts. I've thrown out paragraphs, even pages, without being able to force the words to flow. I haven't finished a short story in well over a month, and find it difficult to concentrate on what I'm doing. After two hours of frustration, I threw the latest version of chapter five into my wastebasket and decided to take a break and see if Heather was home.

She greeted me with her usual cheerfulness and invited me in.

"I thought we might open this?" I held up the wine bottle I'd snagged from under my sink.

"What's the occasion?"

I shrugged. "I don't know. If we have enough to drink, I might be able to think one up."

"Sounds good to me. Wait, I'll get us a couple of glasses."

When she disappeared into the kitchen, I wandered into her

equivalent of my office, the small windowless room where she kept her television. Since the last time I'd visited, she'd made an addition.

A shiny new portable typewriter sat in the middle of the coffee table.

"What's this?" I pointed with one hand while accepting a glass with the other.

"It's called a typewriter. I thought you author types were familiar with them."

"I know it's a typewriter." My enthusiasm for this meeting wilted; silent alarms were beginning to clamor for attention. "What's it for?"

"Open the wine, will you?" She ignored my question while I poured us each a drink, perhaps to consider possible answers. "Mmmm, good." She sat down and placed her glass beside the typewriter.

"It's not really a secret, Alex, but I'm a little embarrassed about it. You see, it was so interesting listening to you talk about your writing, you know, how you create people and places and control events and everything. Well, I thought that was something I'd like to try too. I know I'll never amount to anything as a writer; I don't have that kind of talent, but I thought it would be fun."

I remembered Heather's illness before Henry nursed her back to health, how superficial her knowledge of the world had been until she'd subsequently revealed a sophistication that rivaled Esther's. Nick would never dance in the ballet again, but he might someday see his ex-girlfriend appear on a stage professionally, a girl whose physical appearance had improved as dramatically as Jennifer's had declined.

And then I looked at the sparkling new typewriter and the open box of paper set neatly to one side, remembering the thirty pages of typescript I had thrown into the wastebasket just before coming downstairs.

I am very frightened.

RAGGEDY

"It was probably a bunch of kids." Detective Myers glanced down at the open grave and shook his head. "They don't respect anything anymore. And those damn horror movies give them sick ideas like this." Myers, who was unmarried and had not so much as spoken to a child in years, nevertheless felt qualified to pontificate on the subject.

Higham, the night watchman, spread his arms in a gesture that could have meant anything. "We've never had trouble like this before. This is a respectable neighborhood and I keep the gate locked after dark. Once in a while a couple sneak in to fool around with each other, but that's the only problem we've ever had. Now I've got two missing bodies."

Myers shook his head unsympathetically. "My grandmother could climb over your fence, and she's confined to a wheelchair. Have you searched the grounds?"

Higham nodded. "As best I could, but there are lots of places they could have hidden them, if they didn't take the bodies away. There's no one hanging around anyway."

Myers raised his flashlight and peered down into the open grave. The coffin was still there, the velvet lining speckled with clumps of earth. "What are we talking about? Bodies or just piles of bones?" He stepped back and moved the focus of his flashlight along the ground, picked out the marks where a shovel or shovels had been driven into the ground.

Higham shook his head. "The lady has only been here a few days, and the Armenian guy got planted this morning. That's probably why they chose these two in particular. Nice and fresh."

Myers rubbed his jaw. "Now how would they have known that, do you think?"

The other man nodded at the headstone. "Says it right there. Or they could have read the obituaries."

The detective, flustered, put his notebook away. "Have you notified the next of kin?"

"Not me. The head groundskeeper will take care of it in the morning. I called him, right after I called you."

Myers suspected it was the other way around, but said nothing. "Do you have a name and address for the family?"

Higham looked surprised, but nodded. "In the office. There's a card file. This place is too cheap to computerize."

Myers acquired the name of the widower, Andy Little, and an address close by in Managansett. This was probably a simple case of vandalism, but it was possible that someone with a grudge had targeted these two in particular. If there was a link between the two, he might be able to track it down and get some brownie points. He was tired of getting all the crappy assignments just because he'd had a little too much to drink at the cop bar and shot his mouth off about Chief Dowdell while the wrong people were listening.

He told Higham not to touch anything at the grave site, then drove through the dark streets of the mostly sleeping town to Maplehurst Drive where he was gratified to see that the lights were still on at the Little house. It was in an established neighborhood, well kept, with gingerbread trim around the windows and eaves. There was a For Sale sign on the front lawn.

Andy Little answered the door promptly. He was tall and slender with dirty blonde hair that complemented the paleness of his complexion. Myers guessed him to be well short of thirty, which made sense since his dead wife had only been twenty-six. He identified himself as a police officer and Little invited him in, his expression guarded. There was a hint of something else a well and Myers struggled to find the right adjective. Supercilious. Resentful. I don't like this man, he thought to himself. There is something inherently wrong about him.

"What can I do for you, Detective?"

"I'm investigating a case of vandalism, Mr. Little." His host's face remained neutral. "Out at the cemetery. I'm afraid your wife's grave has been tampered with, possibly by some of the local teenagers."

Little's lips thinned. "They can't leave her alone, can they?" His voice hardened when he spoke.

There was a photograph on the mantle, Little standing next to a tiny, quite pretty young woman. Neither of them were smiling. Myers blinked. "I'm not following you, sir. Who are they?" Myers mimicked the other man's emphasis.

"They are the same people who hounded her to death. I thought that would satisfy them, but apparently I was mistaken."

"What people would that be, sir?"

"The neighbors, for a start. They never liked Jennifer, probably because she was too young and pretty. Worried that their husbands might have wandering eyes, I suppose, not that any of the men were particularly civil. And the people where she worked. They were always giving her a hard time. Jennifer was a kind and gentle person, Detective Myers, and she was deeply hurt by their animosity."

"How did your wife die, sir, if I may ask?"

"Typical. Run down by a delivery truck while she was crossing a street in Providence. In the crosswalk."

"I see. I'm sorry for your loss," he added automatically. "Is there anyone specific whom you have reason to believe might be responsible?"

"No, not really." Little seemed suddenly deflated. "I don't suppose it really matters that they've taken her body. She's beyond their reach now."

Myers noted the sudden change of mood. Little's outrage had seemed masked, or perhaps the man really was exhausted and despondent. The detective was introspective enough to realize that his instinctive dislike of the man might have colored his judgment. He asked a few more questions, expressed his sympathy once more, and took his leave. But he was only three blocks from the house when he pulled over to the curb and leaned back with his eyes closed, profoundly dissatisfied. One of his talents was the ability to recall entire interviews in great detail and something about his conversation with Little bothered him. He replayed it twice before he spotted the anomaly.

How had Little known that his wife's body was missing? Myers had mentioned vandalism, but usually that just meant a broken headstone or some juvenile defilement like leaving turds on the gravesite. He sat for a while longer, then retrieved his flashlight from the glove compartment and opened the door. It only took a few minutes to walk back to the Little house, staying in the shadows as much as possible.

The lights in the front room were off now, but Myers ducked hastily behind a hedge as the garage door suddenly opened and a

Camry backed out into the street, then moved off toward the downtown. The garage door was already closing when Myers impulsively ran the few steps across the grass and pulled a garbage can forward so that the door struck it and stopped, the motor whining briefly in protest before disengaging.

I won't go inside, he told himself. That would be an improper search. I'll just take a look.

Just inside the door stood a long handled shovel. The blade was dark with clots of fresh dirt. There were other garden tools as well, but Little hadn't struck him as the domestic type. They probably hadn't been used since his wife died. Except the shovel. That had been in use quite recently indeed.

So what now, Myers, he asked himself. If Little was in fact the sicko he believed the man to be, then his dead wife's body was in all likelihood somewhere inside the house. Could he get a search warrant based on a dirty shovel? Probably not, and certainly not at this time of night. He might convince the captain to ask for one in the morning, but by then the case might have been reassigned to one of Dowdell's toadies. And if Myers was wrong and Little was innocent, it could be very embarrassing. What the hell, he thought. If I take a little unofficial look around and find nothing, it'll spare the man some additional grief. And if I do find something, I can claim that Little was nervous and evasive and that he knew the body was missing before I told him. That's enough for probable cause.

Myers crossed the empty garage and used his handkerchief to try the door to the house. It wasn't locked. With a last glance toward the street, he turned the knob and stepped inside.

He hadn't seen the kitchen before. It was fully equipped and spotlessly clean, so clean in fact that it looked like a photograph from a magazine. There were no dings, stains, or other marks on any of the plates, pans, or glasses, which were neatly stored, stacked, and sorted. Curiously he opened one of the cabinets, then another, then each in turn. There was a variety of glassware and kitchen tools, but no boxes of cereal or crackers, no canned goods, no condiments or spices. A quick glance confirmed that there was no separate pantry. Myers opened the refrigerator and then the freezer, both of which let out a cool blast even though they were completely empty. He had half expected to find the late Mrs. Little in one or the other.

Okay, so Little ate out all the time now that his wife was dead. Strange, but not beyond the realm of possibility. Myers left the kitchen.

He'd already seen the front room, the dining room was small and orderly, and the downstairs bathroom was antiseptic and the medicine cabinet was empty. Myers climbed the stairs quickly, knowing he needed to be out of the house before Little returned, and there he glanced into a second bath, two bedrooms, and a sewing room. One of the bedrooms showed signs of use, though minimal. The other did not. It was the last of these rooms that answered one of his questions, but posed several new ones.

Jennifer Little was sitting in a chair at the far end of the room, facing a state of the art sewing machine. And she was sewing. She turned to look at him when he stepped through the door, and he had not the slightest doubt that this was the solemn faced young woman he'd seen in the photograph downstairs. "Oh dear. You shouldn't be here. Andy is going to be furious."

For several long seconds, Myers could not get his brain to work. Thoughts came as disconnected flashes. This was a hoax. She wasn't really dead. This wasn't actually Jennifer Little but just someone who looked like her. He was dreaming. It was all a practical joke. He'd been drugged. All of the reality seemed to have been drained out of the world and he felt a tinge of nausea.

When she reached toward the sewing machine, he took a hasty step backward and his hand moved instinctively to his holstered weapon. "I'm a police officer. Please identify yourself."

"Yes, I know who you are. I heard you and Andy talking. And you know exactly who I am, Detective Myers." She sighed. "You have no idea how much trouble this is going to make."

Myers flinched at the word "trouble" and tried to justify himself. "I had probable cause to believe that a crime was...is...being committed on the premises so this is a legal search." It was a bluff and not a good one. He struggled to regain his composure. He might have done so if he hadn't glanced down to see what it was that Jennifer Little had been working on.

It was a very lifelike infant, or at least most of one. The head and torso were complete and the limbs were attached, but there was a long seam running from breastbone to groin that lay open revealing a hollow interior. Against the far wall, on a low table, lay the body of an older man with drawn features and a thick moustache. Unlike Jennifer Little, he looked very much like a freshly excavated cadaver. He was completely naked and there were pieces of skin missing from his body, pieces that looked suspiciously like they'd been cut out to conform to the outlines of sewing patterns.

"What the hell is going on here?" His voice was hoarse and his hand unsteady as he tried to point at the dead man.

Jennifer misinterpreted his question. "Oh, the baby. You know, we never did fit in here, just like Andy told you, but I think it's because this is mostly a family neighborhood and we didn't have any children. Andy thinks I'm wasting my time, but I believe that if we have a baby with us when we start our new lives, we'll be more likely to make friends and fit in. Don't you agree?"

Myers moistened his lips, but couldn't think of anything to say. They were both crazy obviously, husband and wife, but who had been buried in this woman's grave and where was that body? Had they faked her death to collect on an insurance policy to finance their move to somewhere else? That seemed the most logical explanation. He felt slightly better. Insurance fraud was a much sexier case than vandalism and grave robbing.

Jennifer went on brightly, unaware of or ignoring his confusion. She picked up a handful of cotton padding and began stuffing it into the tiny torso, pushing it deep into the leg cavities. "This is from Andy. He complained of course, but he really is a kind man, you know." Her hands moved quickly and the rag doll began to look increasingly realistic.

I need to call this in, Myers thought. But what the hell do I say? He had left his radio in the car, hadn't expected to do anything except look over the property from the outside.

"Now I have to do my part." She reached over and picked up a pair of shears and this time Myers drew his weapon.

"Please put down the shears, Mrs. Little."

She ignored him but made no move in his direction, threatening or otherwise. Instead she raised her other arm and with one quick slash, cut herself open from wrist to elbow. Myers shouted an expletive, expecting to see a gush of blood, but the flap of skin fell open to reveal a line of thick cotton padding.

It's a prosthetic arm, he told himself. But the shock was still so great that he stood there as though paralyzed, unable to act, speak, or even think clearly.

Jennifer pulled out a handful of the padding and began stuffing it into the doll, filling it out. It only took a few seconds, and then she was folding the two flaps together and holding them. Her foot depressed the pedal and there was a hum as the sewing machine neatly stitched a line down the seam.

Myers was beginning to think clearly again, and might have salvaged the situation even then, except for one thing.

The baby began to cry.

SALT OF THE EARTH

His horse shied away when they reached the ravine, but with half a dozen or more Navajo warriors close behind, Jake wasn't about to let her have her head. He used the spurs to emphasize his opinion and got an angry whinny in reply.

"Sorry, girl, but this is no time to get temperamental on me." The possibility occurred to him that a mountain cat might be upwind but that was a chance he was willing to take.

He noticed the quiet almost right away.

Even the sound of the wind was muffled by the steep, rocky walls on either side. The hoof beats slowed to a trot and lost their sharp percussion. He was heading due north, right into the face of evil if the Navajo were right, but he had no inclination to turn back. They'd kill him for certain, whether or not they believed Sakaja had joined him willingly. Even now, fleeing for his life, he remembered the way she had moved against his body under the blankets, and twisted in the saddle uncomfortably. Sure, he'd known she was the chief's favorite daughter, but she'd come to him voluntarily and he'd treated her gently until she'd balked after she'd already gotten him thoroughly aroused. And then she'd tried to raise an alarm and he'd only meant to quiet her for long enough to get away, but he'd underestimated his own strength and her neck was broken and here he was.

The ground rose steadily and his progress slowed even further. Jake glanced back over his shoulder. The foot of the ravine was still in sight and his pursuers couldn't be far behind. He knew their kind; they could track him for days over bare rock. He couldn't outrun them and he couldn't outlast them but maybe something would work to his advantage.

The grade began to level off as the walls closed in more tightly, forcing him toward a narrow notch. The footing grew even more treacherous and Jake crouched low over his mount's neck, willing her to place each foot with care. He was sweating with more than the day's heat when they finally reached a level spot. He turned for a final look back.

The Navajo were at the foot of the ravine.

There were eight of them, each carrying a bow and full quiver. Hunting arrows, not war arrows. Jake was a despoiler of women, an animal to be chased and killed, not an honorable enemy. Their mounts milled about nervously as if they too sensed something threatening ahead.

Oddly enough, Jake felt no imminent danger. He pulled back on the reins and his mount obediently halted, while he twisted in the saddle and stared at the men sworn to kill him. The tableau held for an uneasy minute, then another. He was within bowshot, but none of the warriors reached for a weapon. They just stared at him, silently, as if waiting for something to happen.

They seemed disinclined to enter the ravine.

Jake knew the Navajo well enough to guess what had happened. He'd wandered into one of their taboo places. Maybe some wise man had died up here and his chindi was still around, looking for a new body to inhabit. Although he wasn't a religious man himself, Jake knew the kind of grip that fear held for the Navajo. He met a preacher once who'd "converted" a band of Navajo, but even though they showed up regular at his church, they still built their hogans facing away from the north and carried their sick outside to die in the sunlight.

Thanking the god he didn't believe in, Jake turned away and urged his horse into the notch.

The ground was level for the next half mile or so, winding through a series of wind scored mounds. He found a thin, fast moving trickle of water after a bit. The water tasted of alum and made his mouth feel funny, but it was cold. He drank some, then filled his canteen. The horse lapped up a bit, stopping every few seconds to snort and shake her head.

There was no sound of pursuit. No sound at all for the most part. Jake picked up a piece of loose shale and bounced it off a nearby boulder just to break the silence. Even then the crack was muted.

He was about to remount when he noticed the stains on his chaps. "What the hell?" It was a greenish brown residue, almost like mold. When he brushed it off, streaks of color remained behind.

Ten minutes later he lost the horse.

The trail had widened and smoothed out enough that he'd picked up the pace a bit. The mare fought him at first, still balking at something she sensed ahead. Jake was ready to use his rifle if a big cat or other predator attacked, but it was a much more prosaic fate that claimed its victim.

A patch of ground collapsed under a pounding hoof. Jake alertly jumped clear as the horse rolled, avoided being crushed in the fall although he bruised one shoulder badly when he landed. The mare's right foreleg had snapped just above the hoof.

"Sorry, old girl." Jake expended one of his bullets without hesitation, then uncinched the saddle and dragged his gear into the shade of a rocky outcrop.

He had a number of options, none of them good. Reversing course was certain death. Spooked or not, the Navajo would camp where he last saw them for at least several days, long enough to be sure he wasn't coming back that way. He might be able to scale the cliffs to east or west, but there were wide bands of desert in both directions, too wide to cross on foot. North was unknown territory but he suspected these twisted ravines and canyons went on for quite a way. There were mountains beyond, but he estimated they were at least a week's hard riding, and distances out here were difficult enough to judge that it might be twice that. Even if he had a horse, which he didn't.

Jake took the line of least resistance. With his saddlebags over his unbruised shoulder, he started walking north.

The sun was starting to drop below the line of rock to the west when Jake began thinking about camping for the night. He still had almost a full canteen of water; it tasted stale and unpleasant but he'd had worse. There was enough jerky in his bags to last for a day or two if he stopped eating when the pain went away instead of when he was satisfied. He'd been keeping an eye out for game, but hadn't seen a single animal since entering the ravine. No vultures circling hopefully overhead, no snakes sunning themselves on the exposed rock, no vermin scattering at his approach. Not even a tarantula or a scorpion.

Then he saw the coyote.

It had been dead for a long time. The bones were sun bleached to pure white. Jake wasn't a particularly imaginative man, but he was not unintelligent. He saw right away that there was something wrong. The skeleton was too perfect. Every bone was exactly where it should be. No scavengers had worked at the carcass, searching for the best parts. The animal had died peacefully and laid undisturbed ever since, losing its flesh to the elements.

"Hey feller, I don't suppose you could tell me where to find some fresh water?"

Jake spoke to break the relentless silence, but his voice was hoarse and uncertain. He considered that fact, then tried again, first clearing his throat and spitting.

"The Navajo, they say you talk to them. Call you their brother. You got any brothers might come talk to a desperate man?"

The coyote didn't answer.

There was enough light that Jake could have kept on for another hour or so, but his legs were shaking and the sun had given him a spectacular headache so he decided he could resume rushing toward his death in the morning.

"You ain't the best company a man could have of an evening, but then I ain't in the mood for much conversation anyways."

Just upslope from the coyote, a shallow declivity in the rock face offered a natural shelter. Jake tossed his saddlebags into a corner and began scouring the area for firewood. There were plenty of dead trees around, all stunted and gnarly, but the wood was so rotten that a lot of it crumbled to powder in his hands. By dusk he'd accumulated what he hoped would be enough to last if he didn't light a fire until it was full dark.

The bizarre silence seemed to intensify with the coming of darkness. Jake deliberately stopped thinking about it consciously, but the eerie atmosphere of this place continued to nibble at the corners of his self possession. He finally started his fire not for the heat or light but simply to listen to the crackling of the flames. They at least seemed perfectly normal.

The rotted wood flared up with unusual brilliance, providing an almost cheerful pool of light that swept down from Jake's bedroll to where the dead coyote lay facing him. Jake's brow furrowed briefly. He'd come up from below when he'd first seen the coyote, and he could have sworn it had been facing back the way he'd come. Might there be two of them?

He uncurled his stiff legs, picked out a relatively solid brand from the fire, and made his way down the slope, past the skeletal remains. There was no sign of another; he must have been mistaken.

But that didn't seem right. Jake had lived most of his life in the wilderness; he had a good eye for detail and the wisdom to realize that small mistakes could have fatal consequences. He returned to the coyote, crouched to examine it more closely.

Something moved.

Jake hastily retreated a step, holding the flame defensively in front of him. "What the hell?" When nothing further happened, he advanced again. The skeleton seemed undisturbed but changed somehow. He squinted and lowered his head, trying to figure out just what he was seeing.

The edges of the bones had lost their sharp edges, grown fuzzy. At first Jake thought it was his eyes failing to adjust to the flickering light, but then he saw more clearly that the bones were thickening with unnatural life.

The body cavities were beginning to fill in, but the coyote was still just a sketch of a creature when it stirred and raised its head.

Jake had fought Indians and outlaws, lawmen and angry women, rattlesnakes and wolves and angry steers and wild horses. He wasn't the kind of man who panicked easily. But the sight of that unholy thing suddenly reanimated struck right past his defenses into the primitive fears we all hide within our souls. He broke and ran through the darkness, away from the coyote, away from his fire, off into the night.

For several minutes, the only thought in his mind was to get as far away as possible. Heedless of bruised shins and scraped hands, he scrambled over the rocks, sometimes climbing, sometimes sliding down a crumbling rock face, sometimes running foolishly even when he couldn't see where he was going. This headlong rush ended only when he lost his footing completely and slid down a gravelly slope, finally coming to rest with his breath gone and his panic partially abated.

The night was silent again.

Jake picked himself up and waited for his breathing to return to normal. Now that he was once more a rational creature, he realized that he'd abandoned what remained of his food and water, along with his blanket and rifle, even his gun belt. He climbed carefully to the top of the nearest slope, then scanned the horizon, hoping to spot the reflected glow of his campfire. But either the faint light of the flames had been swallowed up by the bright moonlight or, more likely, the fire had expired during his panicky flight, because Jake couldn't see anything that might guide him back.

"Just as well," he whispered softly. In the daylight, he'd stand a better chance of retracing his path, and with the darkness banished, he'd be more willing to face whatever needed to be faced.

He was crouched in a hollow, trying to doze off, when he heard the horse.

There was no question about the sound, the steady clip-clopping of iron shod hooves on hardened soil and rock. Not a Navajo mount; there was a distinct metallic sound. And the pattern of the feet was wrong, every fourth impact slightly mistimed. Jake felt ambivalent, but was too desperate to let the chance go by.

He pressed hard against a swell of rock, concealing himself in the shadows, waiting as the sound grew rapidly louder. And there, in the distance, a shadow moved, a large one, and a horse emerged from a twist in the rock and began trotting in his direction. The horse had neither saddle nor rider.

Jake was astounded at his luck. Some stray or runaway had shown up at just the right moment. He pushed away from the cold stone, started forward to intercept the horse.

And froze in astonishment.

The arrhythmic pattern was more apparent now, along with its cause. One of the forelegs hung at an odd ankle, although the animal seemed to feel no pain when its weight came to bear. This was the same mount that had reluctantly carried Jake into this place of damnation, trotting smartly through the darkness even though he'd put a bullet through its brain not twelve hours earlier.

This time Jake's panic didn't abate until he'd run square into a protruding finger of rock and knocked himself unconscious.

It was daylight when Jake opened his eyes this time. His mouth tasted sour, his lips and eyes were crusted with salt distilled from his sweat, and his muscles protested when he rolled over and rose to his knees. Blood had dried in a broad band from his forehead to his cheek, and his head throbbed with a pain so intense it made him dizzy.

Moving very carefully, Jake stood up and slowly surveyed his surroundings.

The rock in most directions was unscalable, but there was a clear path leading upslope. Jake's major concern at the moment was water; his throat felt as though he'd been eating sagebrush. High ground would provide a vantage point from which he might be able to spot either running water, or at a minimum vegetation.

Some of the cramps in his muscles faded but many remained unabated as he climbed up into the sunlight. But all pain, even the thirst, was forgotten when Jake reached the lip of a hollow and saw what lay before him.

Jake had seen the craters left by cannon fire and this reminded him a little of that, although the scale was all wrong. The depression below was at least a hundred yards across and much deeper in the center, and the edges had started to crumble with the passage of time. But it was almost perfectly circular and the slope was uniform around the entire perimeter, too regular to be entirely natural. Dead center was a man-sized lump of black stone, the blackest thing he'd ever seen. It almost seemed to suck in the light from all around it.

On the far side, just above the crater rim, a Navajo hogan had been erected under an overhanging rock.

Jake hesitated, but only for a moment. If the hogan was occupied, he might be marching to his death, but if he didn't find water soon, his extinction was even more certain. The shortest route was directly across the crater, but something warned him to go around, a silent voice too solemn to ignore.

He gathered his strength and set out.

Although there was no one in sight, the hogan appeared to be in good repair. Jake approached cautiously at the last, but he'd been exposed to casual view for the entire trip around the circumference of the crater and wariness now served little purpose. He bent low at the entrance, drew a deep breath, and slipped inside.

The first thing he noticed was the skin of water hanging from a peg, and he didn't pay much attention to the rest of the interior until he'd slaked at least the worst part of his thirst. Perhaps because he'd been so long without, the water seemed particularly sweet and fresh, with no trace of the alum taste he'd noticed previously.

A neat pile of blankets had been placed at the opposite end of the hogan, along with some beaded pipes and mats that he recognized as Navajo work. He walked slowly to the opposite end and stared down at them for several minutes, his thought processes still fogged with fatigue.

"Welcome to my home."

Jake spun on his heel and staggered, not having realized how weak he was. Although he was a Navajo, the old man who had just entered the hogan seemed too frail to pose a significant threat. His skin was dry and unhealthy looking and his hands were trembling. But Jake remained cautious nevertheless.

"Please, make yourself at ease. You have been expected, although I had thought it would be one of the People." The old man spoke good English, with just a trace of Navajo inflection.

"Who are you?"

"I am...He Who Watches, though my eyes have grown weak and I fear I will watch for little longer. You are injured, I see."

Jake raised a hand to his bloody forehead, dropped it quickly. "It's nothing. What is this place?" He gestured with his hands to indicate he meant more than just the hogan.

"This is where the gods of the sky touched the Earth, the birthplace of the skinwalkers, the playground of the Laughing God."

Jake shrugged impatiently, allowing himself to relax. "I don't suppose you have anything to eat?"

In reply, the Navajo withdrew from the hogan. Jake followed and saw that a freshly killed rabbit had been spitted and was roasting over a small fire. The smell made his stomach rumble.

"Are you alone here?" Jake crouched by the fire, watching driblets of fat drop sizzling into the flames.

"I watch over this land, as did the watcher before me, and the one before him. As will the one who comes after."

That didn't really answer his question, but Jake let it pass. His mind always worked better when his belly was full, and he'd lived among the Navajo long enough to have picked up some of their talent for patience.

They ate the rabbit in companionable silence.

When they were done, the old man impaled the carcass on a stick and carried it to the edge of the crater. Jake followed a few steps behind, watched as the remains of their dinner was thrown down into the declivity. A step or two closer and he saw that it had landed on a bare spot surrounded by dozens of other clusters of bones. All of the skeletons had been picked clean, but he was able to identify rabbits, coyotes, plains deer, even what appeared to be a wolf. He wondered idly if the old man had eaten them all.

He allowed the Navajo to clean the wound on his forehead, wincing slightly as his long hair was extricated from the bloody gash.

"You must rest a while."

Although he felt uneasy about letting his guard down, Jake recognized that his body had been pushed to its limit. After only a very brief protest, he retreated into the hogan to escape the hot sun, and fell asleep almost as soon as he lay down.

It was dusk when he next opened his eyes.

Jake emerged from the hut, half expecting to find his pursuers waiting for him, but the only person in sight was the old man, who stood at the crater rim, spreading white powder in a thin line from left to right.

"What are you doing?"

"Marking the border between the land and the sky. When the darkness comes, the spirits of the sky gods can no longer tell one from the other. But they will not cross the salt."

So saying, he scooped another handful from the pouch hanging at his waist and extended the existing line. Jake watched in puzzled silence as the Navajo completed a circle around the hogan before relenting.

"We will be undisturbed now."

Whatever Jake might have said next was precluded by a rustling from within the crater. His hand instinctively went to his side, but his Colt was somewhere back in the ravine. The sounds grew louder, more insistent, more numerous, and despite a growing conviction that he really didn't want to know the source, he moved cautiously to peer down toward its origin.

The dead creatures, re-fleshed, were stirring, moving with initial uncertainty, then with more assurance as the new forms grew solid and coherent. Jake stepped back, his heart racing, but the old man was at his side.

"They cannot cross the salt. It is of the earth and they are of the sky."

Unconcerned, the Navajo returned to the hogan and, after a while, Jake joined him, though his thoughts strayed to the perimeter constantly and he slept uneasily all that night.

The days that followed sank into a comforting routine. Each morning the two men would leave their haven to hunt for food. There was little to be found nearby, but to the north lay land untouched by the blight. There was game here though not plentiful, and the old man proved to be a fine shot with the bow, although they did better after the ninth day, when Jake found his rifle and his Colt. There were roots and berries in considerable quantity, and wild grain that they ground into paste. But each day, without fail, they travelled to the salt flat near the hogan and brought back enough to redraw the line of demarcation around the hogan.

And each night the dead things in the crater crowded around the edges and looked in.

One afternoon Jake suggested gathering up all the bones and burying them inside the perimeter, but the old man just shook his head.

"It is better to know where the sky things are than where they are not."

The old man's health continued to deteriorate and he began setting aside pieces of firewood they gathered each day for another purpose.

"When I die, you must burn my body and return my ashes to the earth."

This puzzled Jake greatly because he knew that the Navajo were deeply superstitious about death. Unlike the plains Indians, they invariably disposed of their dead by entombing the bodies in rocky cairns where they were protected from scavengers. He thought to ask, but remembering the animated corpses that spied upon them nightly, he answered his own question.

Even though he'd been expecting it, Jake was devastated by the old man's death. It came quietly, while he was spreading the salt barrier. Jake saw him fall and ran to his side, but the last breath had already passed his lips by then. There was enough wood for the cairn, and Jake was preparing the pyre when an idea occurred to him.

He thought about it some, and then he thought about it some more. When he was done thinking, he wrapped the old man in a blanket and buried him in a shallow grave near the hogan. And that night he was very careful about leaving no gaps in the line of salt.

Jake spent the following morning making several trips back and forth to the salt flat. By the time the sun was directly overhead, he had filled one corner of the hogan with salt. During the afternoon, he collected all of the skeletons from the crater and buried them inside the salt line. He spent an uneasy night despite the double line of salt he'd spread about. There seemed to be something whispering within the crater, although when he concentrated he could hear no sound at all.

Just before dawn he rose and lit the fire. A half dozen creatures stood just outside the salt line, staring at him. As the sun came up, they sank back to the ground and the stuff of their bodies receded. He collected these bones as well and added them to the mass grave.

He spent that day building a travois, using his Bowie knife to cut down two stout young trees, then cannibalized two of his remaining three blankets, sewing them with a thorn bush needle to secure them to the frame. Only three new skeletons greeted him in the morning, and he buried these as well, then returned to the ravine where he found the bones of his mare. It took two trips to carry them back to the hogan, and even then he was forced to leave many of the smaller bones behind. Then he rested until dusk, eating what remained of his food.

The sky turned pink as the sun retreated for the evening. Jake began spreading salt, but this time he consciously left a single gap in the line. Satisfied, he wrapped a bandanna around his face and began the unpleasant task of unearthing the old man's body. Even protected by the earth in which it had been interred, his flesh had begun to spoil, an acrid odor which penetrated the bandanna easily. Jake persevered, dragging the body to a point near the gap in the salt line.

"Sorry, old man, but it's needful."

Full darkness fell and the night was as silent as ever. Jake sat by the fire, keeping vigil over the body, waiting for what he knew had to come. Even so, even expecting it, he was almost taken by surprise.

The smell subsided, but Jake thought that might just be that he was getting accustomed to it. There was no sign of movement, not from a distance, though had he been closer he might have seen the falling in of the flesh as parts of it were taken away and replaced by something else, something that masqueraded as earthly life even though its origins were elsewhere. The furious activity of replacement was largely internal, and Jake wouldn't have wanted to see it even if that had been possible.

There was a sigh, like escaping gas, and Jake's head turned suddenly. Sure enough, the fingers of one outstretched hand were beginning to twitch, and there was movement in the torso, although it was nothing like breathing.

Then the old man sat up.

Jake stumbled backward as he rose to his feet, and the Colt was in his hand even though he hadn't given it a thought. The face was still recognizable from time to time, although there was a constant churning movement beneath the surface that altered the contours in an unnervingly fluid fashion. The eyes were open but sightless, the soft parts gone and replaced with something blacker than the night. And when the old man's mouth opened and something vaguely like a tongue writhed and twisted, Jake forgot his plan for the moment and fired six rounds without thinking about it.

Jake was a good shot, and all six shells hit their target, three in the chest, three in the forehead, but for all that, the old man's body didn't even shudder. It was like the bullets passed through or around the counterfeit flesh, punched holes in bone and passed on.

The old man started to get to his feet. There was a sound now, a gurgling as though something was trying to master the mechanism of speech. Jake dropped his Colt and stepped back to the hogan, reached inside for a handful of salt.

The old man was lurching toward him, one arm reaching out, and from his throat came a hideous moaning that seemed to originate in the depths of space. Jake threw a handful of salt directly into its face.

The flesh began to boil and bubble like a fresh egg dropped into hot fat. The top layer peeled back and sloughed off, exposing the next within. But still the body was moving forward, each step a bit more self confident than the last.

Jake threw double handfuls of salt at the thing, aiming for the exposed arms and legs. Oddly enough, there was no smell, neither the honest putrefaction of earthly flesh, nor any unworldly odor from the invader. Two more handfuls and one leg collapsed. The torso hit the ground heavily but the arms were lifting forward, clawing at the soil, still trying to move toward Jake. He threw more salt, furiously now, and the fearsome advance stopped only inches from the hogan entrance.

Jake wasn't satisfied until he'd completely buried the old man's remains with the last of the salt, and then he built the pyre and set it alight and with the last of the salt he inscribed a tight circle directly around the hogan, in which he slept until well after the sun rose.

The black stone at the center of the crater seemed nothing more than that, although it was honeycombed with pits and holes and tiny tunnels. Parts of it were clearly hollow because it weighed much less than he'd expected, but still enough that it took most of the day and all of his strength to drag it to the rim of the crater.

It was easier from there. Jake's travois held together almost all the way to the cliff above the salt flat, and when it failed, he rolled the black stone the rest of the way, then pushed it over the edge. Night fell while he was burying it there in the middle of the salt flat, but nothing came to watch him with eyes that weren't eyes.

But when he had finished, he still gathered enough salt to draw a circle around the hogan for the night, even though he felt that it was all over, that the unearthly life would never walk in earthly bodies again.

Or would it. An insect landed on the back of his hand and he crushed it, then peered closely. Was it really an insect, or had something else taken its form? Jake rubbed the back of his hand in the remaining salt and lay down, seeking unconsciousness.

The hum of diminutive wings filled the night. Earthly life returning to reclaim the ravine, or something else? Jake couldn't muster the courage to find out.

Sakaja's oldest brother, Wokani, spotted the white man trekking out of the forbidden place. The rest of the hunting party had given up long before, but he'd stubbornly insisted on remaining behind to avenge his sister's - and thence his own - honor. But even he had begun to believe that either the white man had escaped, or more likely that he'd succumbed to whatever curse hung over the forbidden place.

Wokani urged his pony forward to meet the man.

His heart cried out for this man's blood. He had dreamed of his vengeance nightly at first, burning off the white man's testicles, pushing slivers up under the nails of fingers and toes, pressing thorns through the tongue and eyelids. But the anger had simmered and cooled until now he felt only a sense of duty, of balance.

The white man had offended and now he must die. That was the right of it, and there was nothing else to say, no reason for anger or regret.

Jake made no effort to avoid the mounted warrior, stood silently in the open while Wokani circled him once, then dismounted, knife in hand. The warrior peered into Jake's face, saw the white residue of the salt the man had smeared all over his body, saw the tears leaking from irritated eyes, sensed the pain emanating from the numerous cuts and scratches that crisscrossed the white man's body, all liberally caked with salt.

Then he looked into Jake's eyes and saw a pain greater than any he could inflict. Wokani sheathed his knife and left him there, content that justice had been done.

A NOTEWORTHY AFFAIR

It all started when Jeff Gorham had a sudden, irresistible desire for a chili dog and the only way he could get one without going miles out of his way was to stop at the mall.

That was almost enough to kill the urge. Jeff detested the new shopping center, partly because it obscured what had once been an attractive view of Prendergast Hill, partly because the traffic congestion made his drive home from work even more difficult than it already was. He'd vowed never to spend a penny there and his resolution had lasted for two years.

But the imagined taste of a chili dog was too strong that Friday evening, and with Karen spending the summer in Europe researching her new book, his choices at home were limited to those few things he was able and willing to prepare.

He consulted the directory, made his way to Chili Wili's without so much as glancing at any of the storefronts he passed. This is a one- time deal, Jeff promised himself. Nothing's going to tempt me ever to come back.

He was wrong.

Up two flights of stairs, he spotted the food court, made his way through an already dense crowd, predominantly teenagers, eyes fixed on the blinking menu board.

"Two chili dogs with the works."

"Anything to drink?" He took one look at her and was lost.

"Sir? Would you like anything to drink?"

"What? Yeah, I'll have a ginger ale. Large."

She rang up the order and handed him some change after accepting a crisp ten dollar bill.

Jeff tried to keep his eyes averted but they kept drifting back. She looked to be in her late teens, creamy complexion, jet black hair tied in a pony tail. Shiny white blouse, red skirt, short enough that when she rose onto her toes to grab an empty paper cup, his breath caught in his throat. Her figure was a good compromise between sexy and boyish, and her face was finely sculpted and innocently open.

Jeff swung his eyes sharply to the left as she turned, holding the completed order, and thanked her with a voice that shook slightly. His legs were unsteady and the craving that had brought him here was forgotten. When he stumbled over to one of the small tables in the dining area, it was a minute or two before he remembered what he was holding, forced himself to start eating.

He finished the dogs as slowly as possible, with his head turned so that he could watch the girl without appearing to be doing so. When the food was gone, he lingered over the ginger ale, ignoring the handful of people standing around with trays or bags in their hands, searching for an empty place. But the crowd quickly grew thick enough to obscure his view of Chili Wili's, and as the connection was broken, he realized he was being foolish, stood up abruptly and went home.

Saturday Jeff was restless, decided to go for a drive. It was a genuine surprise when he found himself in the mall parking lot, but then he was walking inside and he knew exactly where he was going.

She wasn't there.

Evening shift, he realized. She works later in the day. He thought about leaving, returning later, but eventually swallowed his pride and decided to check out the mall. He found the new novel by Paul Di Filippo in paperback and bought it, then sat on one of the plaster benches to read the first chapter before heading home.

Halfway through the book, he wondered when the shifts changed. The mall was open ten to ten. Was that two five hour shifts, six days a week? If so, she'd be coming on duty within the next half hour. Jeff bought a deli sandwich, carried it halfway across the court, ignoring several empty tables, took one with a good vantage point, sat down to eat as slowly as possible, pretending to read. But she never showed up.

That night he dreamed she was in bed with him, crouched down between his thighs. In his sleep, he rose up onto his elbows as she cupped her fingers around his erection.

"What do you want?" His dream voice was raspy with emotion.

"The works," she whispered.

On Monday he checked his watch so often during the course of the day that his boss noticed.

"Are we keeping you from something important, Mr. Gorham?"

"Sorry, Mrs. Crandall. I'm not feeling well, couldn't sleep last night."

So he got to leave an hour early.

His mood brightened quickly when he reached the food court. Her back was toward him but the pony tail was unmistakable. Jeff decided he was in love.

If Jeff had paid attention to what he was eating, he might have learned to hate chili dogs over the course of the next two weeks, because he had them for supper every evening, Monday through Friday. After a while, she began to recognize him. "Two dogs with the works and a large ginger, right?"

And she'd smile and he'd nod and then he'd spend half an hour eating them at a nearby table, the longest he could manage to stall without worrying she'd suspect something.

That second Thursday he found out her first name, because the manager called her to pick up a special order. He tried it out in the car on the way home that night, speaking aloud. "Julie. Mrs. Julie Gorham."

Jeff told himself it was all just a harmless fantasy. He and Karen had been married for eight years, and they were still reasonably excited by each other. Once or twice he'd had the opportunity for brief flings, but had never been tempted. Life was complicated enough already. "I'm just looking," he told himself. "I'd never actually do anything about it."

Three days later, he wasn't so sure.

He was halfway through the first of his two dogs when she came out from behind the counter and started walking briskly in his direction. Jeff felt a bolt of panic, convinced that she had caught him staring. But she went right by, didn't even glance in his direction, headed toward the mall services sign.

The ladies room.

When she came back, he was calmer and better prepared. Her legs were longer than he'd thought; he'd never seen them from the right perspective before. Well shaped, deeply tanned. He imagined touching them, running his hand over the kneecap, up the thigh. And that's when he realized that just looking wasn't going to be enough.

Jeff had always been a good problem solver, organized, intuitive, focused. He'd survived three layoffs at work because of his tenacity and reputation for succeeding where others abandoned hope. So he decided to approach this new challenge in the same fashion.

His goal was to spend more time in Julie's company. He considered applying for an evening job in the mall, then realized this would be counterproductive. All that would accomplish would be a curtailment of his one sided assignations.

Unless. He flipped through the phone book, found a number, dialed, asked a question.

"Hiring? You gotta be kidding. Look, you want to come in and fill an application, be my guest. But we've got twenty, thirty names on the waiting list already."

No job openings at Chili Wili's then.

But she didn't spend all her time at work...

He timed Friday night's visit carefully, arriving just before nine thirty.

"The usual?" Her hair was still drawn back, but in a broad fan rather than a pony tail.

He nodded, meeting her eyes for just a second.

"Kind of late tonight, aren't you?"

"Big project." Perfect, the opening he needed to establish a legitimate excuse for breaking his original pattern. "I'll be working late two or three nights a week for a while."

When she handed him his order, she leaned over the counter, her voice low. "Don't you ever get tired of these things?"

Jeff was terrified that his voice would falter. He'd just had the briefest of glimpses inside her blouse. "Well, yeah, sometimes. They're okay."

When the PA system announced the mall would be closing in ten minutes, Jeff still had a couple of bites left. He glanced toward Chili Wili's, but Julie had disappeared into the rear.
Was there an employee's exit in back? That would ruin everything. But no, she came out just as the five minute warning sounded.

Jeff bundled his trash into a receptacle and walked out of the food court. Near the stairs he paused until he was sure she was headed his way. One flight down, he stopped to deal with an "untied" shoelace, saw her bare legs out of the corner of his eye as she passed and started down to the first level.

When she pushed through the outside door, he was ten paces behind.

The parking lot on this side was almost empty, maybe thirty cars, a few already with their engines running and headlights on. That helped because he could drop back a bit and still see where she was going.

When her Honda pulled onto the access road, he was standing behind a stanchion, perfectly positioned to read the license plate. He stood there until she turned west on Route 13, headed toward Managansett, the same way he'd be going.

Two nights later, he was able to follow her home. It was a two family house just off Main Street, directly across from the town library, only a mile from Jeff's apartment. He pulled over to the curb and watched as she parked under a tree, then climbed a wooden staircase to the second floor and disappeared inside. The interior lights went on a second later.

Jeff killed the engine and sat for a while, then decided to check out the neighborhood. It was late and he'd be expected to catch up on his work in the morning, but he doubted he could sleep right now. This was where Julie lived, the streets she walked, and sharing the same space even removed in time was exciting.

At least for half an hour or so. By then he realized the area was neither special nor particularly well lit, and when a dog growled at him from the shadows, he beat a hasty retreat to his car.

Just as he turned the key, her door opened and someone came out. Not Julie, but another young woman, tall and with lighter hair. He saw her face clearly for a second as she stood under the outside light. A minute later, she drove off in the Honda.

Jeff went home.

He spent Saturday in the library, a selection of reference books piled up on a table under the window facing Julie's apartment. The driveway was empty when he arrived, but at 10:30 the Honda drove up and an attractive Oriental woman in her early twenties got out and climbed to the second floor. Half an hour later, a fair skinned redhead came down and drove off. No sign of Julie.

Jeff gobbled down a quick lunch at a diner a few blocks away, arrived back at the library to find nothing changed. Just before five, a clearly mystified librarian told him the library was closing and he reluctantly accepted the inevitable and gathered up the pages of meaningless notes he'd taken to cover his real purpose.

On his way down the front steps, the Honda reappeared. The redhead jumped out, not even closing the car door and raced up the wooden stairs. Jeff unlocked his own car, was just climbing inside when a tall black woman stepped out onto the landing.

Apparently Julie had three roommates. At least, he thought wryly, none of them are men.

He showed up late twice during the following week, just often enough that she wouldn't find it unusual. On all five evenings, he found the Honda easily, parked in the same corner.

Although he had planned his move for the following Friday night, conditions Wednesday were too good to pass up. The sky had been overcast all afternoon, and early in the evening it started to rain. The full brunt of the storm struck as darkness fell.

Jeff arrived at nine and waited until he could park a few spaces past Julie's Honda. The ramp protected him from the rain as he got out, walked slowly down the line of cars, watching to make sure no one was around. Satisfied he crouched, drove the point of his screwdriver deep into the sidewall of one of the Honda's tires, then moved quickly to do a second. The sound of the air hissing out seemed incredibly loud to him, but with the rain thundering above, no one could have heard it unless they were within a few feet.

He tossed the screwdriver into a trash receptacle and went inside.

"Not much of a crowd tonight."

Julie blinked, glanced around the food court as though it hadn't occurred to her before. "Yeah. Must be the rain keeping them away. You want the usual?"

"Yeah. No, wait, throw in an order of fries this time. I'm starving."

When she started to cash out the register, he stood up, waited until she glanced in his direction and waved. She nodded but didn't wave back, but all he had hoped to accomplish was to convince her he'd left before she did. But he wasn't leaving, not quite yet.

Sitting in his car, he watched as she came out, ran across the narrow exposed place to the shelter of the ramp. The rain was heavier than ever and it had begun to thunder again. When he lost sight of her, he started his engine, trying to decide how long to wait. What would she do when she discovered the flat tires? Obviously she didn't carry two spares, so she'd have to go back inside the mall, try to call someone to come out and help her, a garage or maybe a friend.

He couldn't let that happen.

Jeff let his car roll forward, headlights on, turned slowly to his right and rolled rather than drove down the slight decline toward the access road. There she was, standing indecisively beside the car. In the gloom, he couldn't really see the flats, but she wouldn't know that.

The car stopped and he leaned across the front seat, rolled down the window. "Looks like you've got a flat tire there, miss."

She twisted nervously in his direction, alarm written clearly on her face, softening only slightly when she recognized him.

"Oh, hi. Yeah, two of them. And I have to get home." The last few words weren't really addressed to him.

"I could drop you off at the garage down near the interstate if you want. They're open all night." But he doubted they'd be able to get to her for a while, and there was a coffee shop where he'd just naturally offer to buy her a cup.

"No, that won't help. I mean, thanks, but I have to get home." To his surprise, she was literally wringing her hands; he'd never seen anyone actually do that before. "Maybe I could call a taxi."

Jeff was ready for that. "I don't think any of them come this far out after the mall closes. The garage is really your best bet."

"But you don't understand!" Her voice vibrated now with real panic. "I have to get home by eleven. My roommate is expecting me and if I'm not on time, she's going to be furious."

Quickly shuffling scenarios, Jeff decided he'd been presented with a golden opportunity. Fortunately, he caught himself just before offering to take her home since "you're right along the way". He wasn't supposed to know that, not yet.

"Well, I'm heading out Route 13 to Managansett if that helps. Or I can take you to the garage like I said."

"Managansett?" The sudden hopefulness in her voice was so vivid that Jeff knew she'd taken the bait. "That's where I live. Do you know where Lancaster Street is?"

He knew exactly where it was. "I'm not sure. Isn't that over near the library?"

And less than a minute later, she was sitting beside him.

"I really appreciate this. Heather can be a real bitch sometimes."

"What are you going to do about your car?"

"Oh, Heather'll take care of it. She's much better than I am in emergencies."

"Lucky I had to work late tonight. I'm Jeff by the way."

"Nice to meet you, Jeff. I'm Julie, Julie Sepharen."

Jeff had rehearsed a number of conversational ploys, not really caring about her responses, but using conversation as an excuse to keep turning in her direction. He'd left the dome light on and it gave him a great view of her legs, one knee crossed over the other. The temptation to reach over and slip his hands between them was strong enough to be painful.

He was about to ask an oblique question about boyfriends when they caught sight of the flashing lights. A minute later they were stopped.

An unhappy police officer in a totally inadequate raincoat banged on his window. Jeff rolled it down, shrinking back as rain sprayed in.

"You'll have to turn around and go back, sir. The rain's undercut the bridge up ahead and it won't be passable until sometime tomorrow." He sounded tired, as though he'd said the same words a hundred times already, as he probably had.

"But I need to get to Managansett, officer."

"I can't help that." Irritation animated his voice slightly. "You can go up to Foster and come back down Route 13 from there, or south to Scituate and back by way of Reservoir Road."

Jeff closed his mouth. "All right, officer. Thank you." He rolled up the window, secretly pleased because now they'd be together even longer. Considerably longer.

"What'll we do now?" Her voice was small, like a little girl's.

"North, I guess. It'll take a while though."

She turned in the seat, facing him squarely. "You don't understand! I can't be late!"

Jeff shrugged. "Look, I'm doing the best I can. Do you want to stop some place and call your roommate?"

"That wouldn't help!" Her eyes glittered and Jeff realized that she was close to tears. What was the problem, he wondered. What kind of tyrant was this roommate? Then Julie leaned toward him, put one hand on his thigh, innocently it appeared, although he doubted anyone could really be that naive. "Isn't there something you can do?"

Manipulation it might be, but Jeff felt a sudden rush of masculine protectiveness. "Well, there's an old farm road that cuts through above the dam. It's not paved, but they keep it clear. It'll save maybe half an hour."

"Does that mean we'll make it by eleven?"

"We should, yes."

And they would have too, except that the heavy rain had turned the road into a treacherous morass. Three times Jeff got stuck, but luckily he rocked himself free on each occasion and finally made it back to Route 13.

Unfortunately, they had at least fifteen minutes to go, and it was five minutes of eleven.

"We're going to be close, but we're not going to make it."

He glanced to his side, the first chance he'd had to concentrate on anything other than his driving in half an hour. Julie was pressed against the car door, her arms wrapped around her body, shivering even though it was still quite warm and very humid.

"Are you okay?" The light wasn't good, but she seemed very pale. "Are you going to be sick or something?"

"Just...just get me home. Please!"

He tried, risking a speeding ticket though he doubted any of Managansett's small and underpaid police force would be doing much in this weather. An accident was more likely; the road surface was covered with a film of water and he fought with the wheel on every curve.

Despite every effort, the dashboard clock read 11:08 when he pulled into the driveway, realizing too late that he wasn't supposed to know which house was hers. But Julie was in no condition to notice.

"Are you all right? You look like you're going to faint." As indeed she did. Her clothing clung to her body, soaked withsweat, and her eyes were unnaturally bright. She was trembling uncontrollably and even in the poor light, Jeff could tell that she'd lost much of her color.

"I'll be all right." She opened the car door, shifted her weight, and fell to the ground.

Jeff almost lost his footing and was thoroughly soaked by the time he reached her. Julie had risen onto her elbows and knees but seemed to lack the strength to stand.

"I'd better take you to the hospital." He crouched, put his arm around her shoulders.

"No. Just...just help me up to my room. I'll be all right once I'm inside."

He had to carry her up the stairs, her arms wrapped around his neck. She was heavier than he expected.

The door wasn't locked and there were no lights on.

"The bedroom's over there." She waved vaguely, apparently exhausted.

Jeff spotted a light switch, flicked it on with his elbow. They were in a kitchen, equipped with a small table, an old fashioned refrigerator, and a gas stove. There were shopping bags and corrugated boxes everywhere, each filled with small colored squares of notepaper.

"Where's your roommate?"

"She'll be here. Please, I need to lie down."

He set her on the bed, mattress and spring actually. There was no frame. This room was as bare as the kitchen, a bureau, the bed, a closet. A small night table held a lamp, half a dozen felt tip pens, and a transparent plastic cylinder filled with more paper squares, these as yet unused. A tall wastebasket was nearly filled with discarded sheets, each covered with hand written notes.

"Why don't you get out of those wet clothes before you make yourself sick." He hesitated. "I'll make us some coffee or something, warm you up inside."

He found the matches on a shelf over the sink, turned up one of the burners and filled a teakettle. There wasn't any coffee, but he found two cups, some teabags, and a bowl of sugar. The apartment was smaller than he had expected. There was a sitting room with a couch and chair, no television, a bathroom, and a second bedroom, completely empty of furniture.

Where did Julie's roommate, or roommates sleep? All in the same bed?

"Can I come in?" He hesitated at the door.

The answer was indistinct, so he interpreted it affirmatively.

Julie was lying down, completely naked, one arm across her face. She was still quite pale, even her hair seemed to have lightened. Jeff knew intellectually that he should be wildly ecstatic to see her like this, but instead he was distinctly troubled. There was something not quite right here. He entered the room cautiously, and as he approached the bed, saw something that puzzled him. The lines of her body weren't exactly right; she seemed almost to be...taller somehow, and surely her hips hadn't been that broad.

Abruptly, Julie moved her arm and sat up, and a complete stranger glared at him.

"Who the fuck are you?"

It was the same woman he'd seen leave Julie's apartment the night he'd followed her home.

Jeff staggered back into the kitchen as though he'd been physically attacked, shook his head groggily and lurched toward the outside door, kicking bags of tiny note paper out of his path. And then he was attacked, by a naked woman six inches taller and twenty pounds heavier than the one he'd carried up the stairs ten minutes earlier.

They staggered around the kitchen locked together in an embrace that bore no resemblance to the ones featured in Jeff's fantasies. She had an arm around his throat, cutting off his breath, and wrapped surprisingly strong legs around his thighs. Incongruously, the tea kettle began to whistle.

"Little Julie screwed up bad this time," hissed the woman. "She's always leaving messes around for me to clean up." She tightened her grip and he staggered back toward the stove, struggling to breathe. "A whole fucking year she's been with us, and not once has she even said 'thank you, Heather'."

The teakettle was loud, close, and Jeff suddenly realized what he had to do. He bent his legs at the knees as though collapsing, then threw himself backward. She screamed, either scalded by the steam or burned by the kettle itself, and her arms and legs loosened their grip. Jeff tore himself free and turned, as the woman pushed herself away from the stove.

Her eyes went to the knife rack mounted on the wall, and Jeff knew what she intended even before her arm started up, reacted without thinking. He picked the kettle off the stove and swung it desperately, spraying hot water in a broad arc before striking the back of her head.

Heather dropped to the floor, conscious but stunned.

He was halfway out the door when she called out, her voice weak but still angry. "We'll come after you, you know. Not Julie maybe, but Vanessa and Angel and Jennifer and I. You won't know we're there until it's too late."

He fled the place without answering.

Jeff was at home drinking brandy almost as quickly as he could pour it when he heard the sirens, but it wasn't until the next day that he found out Julie's apartment...their apartment...had been completely destroyed by fire.

He listened to the news all that day, but there were no reports of any bodies found in the ruins.

Mrs. Crandall wasn't pleased when Jeff called and told her he needed to take two weeks of vacation to deal with a personal emergency. Truthfully, he wouldn't have been of much use at work, and he spent most of the next week sitting in the front room of his apartment, staring down into the street.

It was still difficult for him to think about what he'd been through. The woman who'd attacked him...Heather?...seemed to have no recollection of her existence as Julie. And the others she had mentioned, were they the redhead and the dark skinned woman he'd seen from the library? Were they all the same person somehow? The notes, were they messages from one personality to another, a way of maintaining some kind of continuity? What kind of creature was she...or were they?

He tried to put the entire series of events out of his mind, but never quite managed.

Wednesday morning he had a bad few minutes when he spotted a white Honda cruising the neighborhood, but even though it passed his building twice, he wasn't able to see the license plate or the driver. Would he have recognized her even if he had?

When he woke up Thursday and glanced outside, an identical car was parked directly behind his own. Three times he started to go outside, determined to cross and check the license plate, but three times he lost his nerve.

The day passed, and so did Friday, and then the weekend. Monday morning he called the police, gave a false name, and reported an abandoned car. "It's been in the same spot for a week now," he lied, "ever since some teenagers left it there." Then he hung up the phone.

That afternoon, a tow truck took it away.

He returned to work the following week, and the week after that Karen flew back from Europe, announcing herself well pleased with the trip and ready to start the final manuscript. They ate at a fancy restaurant across from the air terminal, then went home for a lengthy and enthusiastic reunion in their bedroom.

She was up before him the following morning, rearranging the small den to serve as an office for the next few months. "I want to make a start on this while I'm still enthusiastic. See you tonight."

But when he got home, she was watching television.

"What? Already lost interest in your book?"

She glanced up from the screen. "It'll keep. How was your day?"

It was still light out when Jeff suggested that it might be cooler in their air conditioned bedroom and Karen agreed after only a momentary hesitation. Their lovemaking was less frantic that evening; Karen seemed more willing to experiment than usual, and when Jeff finally fell into an exhausted sleep, he'd managed to put thoughts of Julie and Heather and all the rest firmly out of his mind.

He'd always been a light sleeper though, and when Karen turned on her nightlight, his eyes opened almost immediately. The alarm clock beside the bed read just a few minutes before eleven.

"What's up?" He half rolled in her direction.

"Nothing, go back to sleep." Her voice was light, casual, but then changed, became harder, chilling.

"I just have to write myself a note."

TAINTED LIVES

Bram Stoker stepped off the Cadogan Steam Ferry and began walking briskly toward home, his thoughts alternating between concern for his wife Florence, who was having a difficult pregnancy, and the usual proliferation of problems that preceded each new production, in this case *The Merchant of Venice*. Henry Irving was a genius when he stepped out onto the stage, but a constant source of irritation and frustration to his co-workers on virtually every other occasion.

He threaded his way through an unusually heavy crowd, detouring around a pair of stilt dancers, stopping for a moment to admire the capering of an organ grinder's monkey, and carefully avoided a handful of street urchins who would either beg a penny or pick his pocket. A drunken mendicant was urinating into the gutter while a pair of shop girls watched surreptitiously and giggled. Stoker resolved once again to find quarters outside Covent Garden at the earliest opportunity and was so immersed in his own thoughts that he nearly ran into the elderly man standing at the corner.

"I beg your pardon," he said automatically, but when he started to move onward a wrinkled hand caught hold of his arm, the fingers surprisingly strong.

"You are Bram Stoker, are you not?" The voice was thin and raspy and very slightly accented.

"Yes, that's my name." He turned and searched the stranger's features, saw nothing familiar. A man of advanced years, certainly, tall and slight of build but with no visible evidence of infirmity. The eyes were alert, the clothing unstylish but well maintained. He carried a leather satchel in one hand and an umbrella in the other. Not a gentleman, but perhaps a professional of some sort. "You have me at a disadvantage, sir."

"My name is Van Helsing. I have been waiting for you. I wonder if I might possibly purchase for you a pint of ale." The accent was more noticeable now, and the phrasing just the slightest bit odd.

Stoker glanced toward home. "I'm afraid this is rather an awkward time, sir. My wife hasn't been feeling well of late."

"I understand, and I shall not delay you any longer than is necessary. You were recommended to me by Sheridan Le Fanu while I was in Dublin. He said that I should mention his name."

Sighing, Stoker nodded. "All right. I owe Sheridan more than one favor. There's a tavern just around the corner."

It was early but the Prancing Foal was already half filled. They ordered bitters from a table in a relatively quiet corner, and neither man spoke until they had taken their first sip. "Now what can I do for you, Mr. Van Helsing?"

"It's Doctor Van Helsing, actually. I wish you to share a burden with me, Mr. Stoker. I am not a young man, as you can see, and it is prudent that I take steps to ensure the survival of certain information in my possession. For several years, I have served as the reluctant custodian of the written record of events which recently took place here in London and elsewhere, terrible events which have never been made public. I wish to entrust these documents to your care."

Stoker became instantly wary; this would not be the first time he'd encountered a madman. "Surely you could find someone more appropriate for such an honor, sir. The government perhaps. I'm only a theater manager, new to London, and with no high connections, not a man of action."

Van Helsing shook his head. "You misapprehend my motives; I do not intend that you take up my cause to that extent. But you are a writer with a talent for organization and you could perhaps turn these fragments into a coherent narrative. I will not ask that of you now, but I beg you for a fair hearing. Take these documents home, read them at your leisure. I will revisit this establishment at the same hour five days hence. If you wish to return them to me at that time, I will bother you no further. If you have questions, I shall endeavor to answer them."

Stoker drank what remained of his pint without tasting it. "All right, I'll do as you request. But I must go now. I am needed at home."

"I will delay you no longer then." He remained seated as Stoker rose and picked up the satchel, which was heavier than he'd expected. Van Helsing fumbled inside his vest and abruptly held out his hand. Lying in his palm was a small, glass vial containing some viscous red fluid. "Take this as well. I will explain it when we meet again."

Stoker reluctantly accepted the gift. It felt surprisingly warm. "What is it?"

Van Helsing's expression was unreadable. "A sample of my blood."

By the fifth day following their meeting, Stoker was convinced that Van Helsing was demented. He had read the various diaries, journals, letters, and other documents contained in the satchel at least twice, and had even organized the fragments into an approximate chronology. Together they presented a compelling story and hinted at much more, but the central premise was clearly absurd. He remembered Le Fanu's fictional *Carmilla* and wondered if this was an elaborate joke perpetrated by that old rogue. Van Helsing had seemed in earnest, but this tale of unclean creatures and perilous pursuits was a bit too melodramatic to be credible.

Curiosity rather than conviction drew him to the appointed meeting. Van Helsing was there before him, at the very same table in fact and wearing what appeared to be the very same suit. He greeted Stoker with a slight nod and the hint of a smile.

"You have decided in my favor, I hope."

Stoker shifted uncomfortably. "I have the documents in my rooms, yes. They are intriguing, Dr. Van Helsing, but not entirely convincing. I don't suppose you have any evidence to support them?"

"No, as a matter of fact I do not. But you do."

Stoker raised his eyebrows.

"The vial, Mr. Stoker. You still have it, I trust?"

"Oh, yes." He fumbled in his pocket and held it out. The contents flowed sluggishly from one end to the other. "What is it?"

"I told you. That's a sample of my blood, drawn on September 1, 1877."

Stoker shook his head. "I'm not a medical man, Van Helsing, but I know that's impossible. Blood would long since have dried into a powdery residue."

"Normal blood, yes. But what flows in my veins has been altered, contaminated by evil. It has other unusual properties as well. Would you care to hazard a guess at my age?" After a brief hesitation, Stoker suggested a number. Van Helsing laughed. "Add more than two decades, my friend."

Stoker refused to believe that but decided not to argue the point. "And how did this wondrous transformation take place?"

"You will recall the efforts we undertook to save Lucy Westenra and later Miss Mina?"

"Of course."

"Four of us gave of our own blood to prolong Miss Westenra's life. Quincy Morris died, but John Seward, Arthur Holmwood, and myself survived. Our efforts were in vain, of course, and Jonathan added himself to our number when Mina was stricken. After the events in the Volga Pass, we thought the episode closed, but within months it became obvious to me that while our blood was flowing into the bodies of Dracula's victims, something was struggling against that tide, some sinister infection had passed in very diminished form into our bodies."

Van Helsing seemed to be growing agitated and his mug was empty so Stoker waved for a fresh round. His companion remained silent until the drinks arrived, then took a long draft from his before continuing. "It took us in different ways. Jonathan and Mina became troubled by dark dreams, dreams which they somehow share between them, full of horrible events and darkness. They disappeared the very day I drew that sample of my blood, and I have not heard from either of them since. Seward no longer sleeps, by night or day, and exhausts himself with his work in a vain effort to find ease. Holmwood began to drift into the vilest forms of debauchery, until his family responded by purchasing a captaincy, hoping the discipline would cure his spiritual ailment. He fell at Isandhlwana and has, I hope, found peace."

"And you?"

Van Helsing sighed. "I have made the best of the devil's bargain. The sun burns my skin at times and I find that I crave meat that has been warmed rather than cooked, but the discolorations have disappeared from the backs of my hands, my spine is straighter, I have suffered no illness since that day, and I enjoy unusual strength of body and freshness of mind."

Stoker was unwilling either to accept or reject Van Helsing's story out of hand. "So what is it that you require of me?"

"Only that you hold what I have given you in safekeeping. I trust your judgment as to its disposition. I am leaving England; the knowledge which I seek cannot be found here."

"Will I see you again?"

"That is only one of the many questions to which I have no answer."

One year followed another. The Lyceum and Henry Irving both prospered, and to a lesser extent so did the Stokers. With Florence and young Noel, Bram moved to larger, better quarters on Cheyne Street, overlooking the Albert Bridge. The theater was renovated and enlarged. William Gladstone became a close friend and occasional dinner companion. Stoker visited the United States and then moved his family once again. His career was set at the Lyceum, despite some changes which had circumscribed his authority, and he was supplementing his income by writing. At times he forgot about the satchel and its contents, now hidden in the Lyceum's prop room, but a taste for the bizarre was obvious in his writing and he had joined the Golden Dawn and lectured at the Society for Psychical Research.

Van Helsing re-entered his life on September 27, 1888. Stoker had no trouble recognizing him, for he appeared in no way changed from his last appearance. He was even garbed identically.

A prodigious walker, Stoker was strolling along the embankment when he saw a motionless figure ahead. His regular stride faltered when he recognized Van Helsing, but he altered course slightly to greet the other man.

"I had feared I would never see you again," said Stoker as they moved on together at a much slower pace. "You are looking well, Van Helsing."

"I am sound, Stoker, though hardly well. Oh, don't be alarmed. It's not a sickness of the body but of the soul. You remember our last conversation."

"Every word of it."

"Allow me to bring you abreast of current events. My efforts to find Jonathan and Mina have been completely unsuccessful. I have been to Capetown and have reassured myself that poor Arthur is truly at rest, but I fear for those two young souls."

Stoker hesitated before speaking, and his voice shook slightly "You appear unaltered since our last meeting."

"The evil works slowly within my aging body. The sunlight is crueler with each year that passes but I have thus far been spared the harsher ravages that have afflicted my friends. Or at least so I believe. It may be that my spirit has coarsened without my realizing it."

"What about Dr. Seward? How has he fared?"

Van Helsing turned his head away and it was several seconds before he answered. "It is because of Jack Steward that I have come to you, Stoker. He has disappeared under extraordinary circumstances. Two months ago, a patient died at his sanitarium. The body was mutilated most horribly. A Mrs. Welter, Agnes Welter, who had been in his care for several years."

Stoker digested this slowly. "Do you think Seward was responsible for her death?"

"No one has said so, but he hasn't been seen since that night and he was one of the few with a key to her cell. The last letter I had from him was strange, barely coherent. It was sufficiently alarming that I abandoned my plans and returned to London at the earliest opportunity, but by then the worst had happened. I must find him, and quickly."

"That's no easy task, even if he is still in London."

"He's here, Stoker. There's no question about that. And he's somewhere near Whitechapel."

Stoker stumbled, then stopped in his tracks, his face pale. "You're not suggesting that Seward is the Ripper?"

"I think it is almost a certainty. The surgical cuts, the timing, the exaggerated mutilations to conceal the fact that he is drinking their blood, even the name 'Jack' on the letter to the police, all point to the man."

"The letter was a hoax perpetrated by Tom Bulling, a reporter. There has been no communication from the Ripper except possibly some nonsense scrawled on a wall."

Van Helsing dismissed Stoker's objection. "If so then this reporter has made a lucky guess. I tell you I have little doubt that Seward is responsible for these killings, and I am determined to stop him. But I need your help, Stoker. I cannot do it alone."

The silence stretched before the taller man finally let his head fall forward, acknowledging his surrender. "How can we possibly find him?"

"The blood calls to the blood, my friend. We shall rent a hansom and visit Whitechapel and its surroundings. If we come close to him, I shall know it, never fear. We need only wait until he reveals himself."

"And then?"

Van Helsing sighed. "And then we destroy my old friend, or what my old friend has become."

Despite Van Helsing's confidence, they spent the better part of the next two days and nights fruitlessly walking the streets of Whitechapel, attracting suspicious gazes, lewd offers, and occasional insults. Van Helsing carried a pistol, which he kept concealed in one of the interior pockets of his cloak, and he insisted that Stoker carry a vial of holy water and a crucifix. The Dutchman was visibly disturbed by their lack of success, and Stoker's doubts about the sanity of his companion were further compounded.

They were making their way down Berner Street just before midnight when they heard a loud commotion from the International Workingmen's Club. Thinking that perhaps another body had been discovered, they cautiously approached, and discovered only that a large meeting had just ended. Several score men were dispersing, many talking loudly amongst themselves. Stoker was about to turn away when Van Helsing caught his arm.

"He's somewhere about! I'm sure of it."

"Where?" Despite his skepticism, Stoker felt a brief rush of pure terror.

"I cannot be certain. He would seek a dark, hidden place during the daylight hours. A basement, perhaps."

There were still as many as a dozen people within the building and the lights remained lit, but it was not difficult for the two men to slip past them and find the staircase to the lower level. Stoker felt conflicting emotions. It would be horribly embarrassing to be caught in such trespass, but it also thrilled him to dare such things as he had previously described in stories. The stairs were encumbered with so much debris that passage was difficult, but once their eyes adjusted to the gloom, they had little difficulty in descending. The basement was a veritable warren of small rooms, the floors were earthen, and there were no exterior windows. Van Helsing insisted that he could feel the pull of Seward's tainted blood, but their search was unsuccessful and Stoker's earlier doubts were redoubled.

The activity upstairs had almost entirely ceased when they exited into the unlighted yard behind the building. Stoker had resolved to divorce himself from further fruitless endeavors, and was therefore taken aback when Van Helsing gave a hoarse cry of horror.

Only a short distance away, a dark figure crouched over the supine body of a woman.

Even in the dim light, the man's appearance was striking. His clothes and hair were matted with mud and dried blood, and some not so dry. He wore an apron tied around his waist, as though a small part of his mind retained a hint of the fastidiousness Dr. Seward, if this was indeed the man, had shown in his previous life. His latest victim lay with her throat cut from ear to ear, although her clothing was as yet undisturbed.

"Hello, John." Van Helsing spoke calmly. Seward remained motionless and did not answer; indeed, Stoker was not sure the man was any longer capable of speech. His expression was that of a wild animal, an animal currently held at bay.

He raised his arm and Stoker saw that he held a large blade in one hand. Van Helsing slowly began to reach inside his cloak, presumably to retrieve the pistol. If so, their brief standoff was interrupted before he could act. There was a commotion at the far end of the yard and Stoker turned to see a pony cart halted at the entrance. The smell of freshly spilled blood must have alarmed the animal, which refused to enter, and the increasingly loud exhortations of the driver would likely draw unwanted attention to the area.

Van Helsing must also have been distracted, because he cried out in frustration. Stoker tensed in expectation of an attack by Seward, but the man had disappeared as though he was able to blend with the shadows themselves.

"We must not be found here!" Van Helsing whispered, already moving away with a speed startling in a man of his age. Panic lent strength to Stoker's limbs as well, and the two men were out of the yard and beyond risk of discovery within seconds.

"All is not lost, but we must hurry. I can taste his blood in the air."

They followed Seward westward, more than half a mile, concealing themselves in dark corners several times along the way. The Mile End Vigilance Committee was out in force, and it seemed that every constable in London was arrayed along their path. Stoker became disoriented until he finally recognized Church Passage. They were approaching Mitre Square.

They evaded one last constable before they caught up to Seward. He was crouched over the inert form of yet another young woman. Her throat was cut, and he had probably drunk from that gaping wound as he had the others. Seward had also cut her from breastbone to thigh, removing her internal organs and arranging them on the ground and across her body. The nose was completely severed.

He saw them from a distance and ran off, his body bent forward in an awkward, almost apelike posture. Stoker's eyes were drawn briefly to Seward's latest victim, then shifted away.

"Come quickly!" urged Van Helsing. "He must not escape us now."

The streets were wider here and better lighted. Within seconds, they heard a constable's whistle from behind as the newest outrage was discovered. Seward led them to Whitehall, where they momentarily lost his trail. Van Helsing seethed with frustration until he picked up the scent again, at the entrance to a construction site. Seward had descended into the bowels of the new and as yet unoccupied Metropolitan Police Headquarters, almost as if daring the authorities to capture him.

Forever afterward, Bram would think of what followed as an almost literal descent into hell itself. The moment they entered the building he was aware of a faint smell of decay, which grew stronger with each successive step. The light failed after the first turn and the two men halted, but even after allowing their eyes to adjust, Bram could see little and said so, his voice a strained whisper.

"My eyes are better suited for the darkness." Van Helsing pitched his voice low but it was much steadier than his companion's. "There is light up ahead. Hold onto my cloak until we reach it."

Bram followed as a blind man might have done, one hand tightly clutching a fold of Van Helsing's woolen cloak, the other in front of his face to ward off any obstruction that might otherwise cause him an injury. They moved very slowly, but once they had turned the next corner, a faint glow in the distance restored some of his confidence, and soon after that he was able to proceed unassisted.

The light emanated from a lower level, and they descended a narrow staircase with great caution, Van Helsing still leading the way. At first Bram thought it was completely silent inside the building, the sounds from without muffled by the enfolding walls, but then his hearing adjusted. Some liquid was dripping slowly but steadily in the distance, and on two occasions he detected a furtive scuffling that was almost certainly a rat. If he had been alone, there is little doubt that he would have turned about and removed himself as hastily as possible, perhaps even with some loss of dignity, but he was loathe to shame himself in front of, or in this case, slightly behind Van Helsing.

They found the lair a moment later. It was a small room, probably meant for storage but currently empty except for a straw pallet lying in one corner just past a pile of rags that might have been clothing. There were perhaps a score of candles strewn haphazardly across the floor, all lighted and flickering very faintly. Bram recoiled from the smell, which reminded him of a butcher's shop, the acrid tang of blood, both fresh and dry. Van Helsing entered but stopped almost immediately, and after a momentary hesitation, Bram joined him, moving to one side.

At first it appeared that they were alone, but then the shadows in the far corner stirred slightly and Bram realized that someone stood there, a smallish man of middle years with a thick, uneven moustache and a paunch that testified of a sedentary life style. Although Bram stiffened when he realized they were not alone, Van Helsing seemed almost to relax.

"Hello, John. It's been a long time."

There was a long pause before the answer came, and Bram was shocked to hear a reasonable, educated voice instead of the bestial growl he'd anticipated. "Abraham? Is that you? I had not thought to ever see you again, old friend."

"I would rather that it had been under other circumstances than these, in the light rather than the darkness."

Seward stepped forward so that his features were better illuminated and Bram saw that the wretch looked more puzzled than dismayed. His hair was matted and his face unshaven. Seward's head slowly turned back and forth, as though he was examining his environment for the very first time. "This? All of this is superficial, Abraham. I see by an inner light now, a light which has revealed to me truths I never thought to behold."

"Truth? This isn't truth, John. This is the worst kind of lie. You have been deceived by the power of corruption, the corruption that has infected both of us as it has many others before."

Seward took another step forward and Bram saw that his clothing, though of good fabric and skillfully tailored, was filthy and torn. There were dark stains as well, and he shuddered when he realized the nature of those discolorations. "You are wrong, Abraham. We were all wrong. The truth is greater than any of us. It is a force that can liberate us from the restraints we put upon ourselves. We burden ourselves unwisely protecting the feeble minded, the morally destitute, those who contribute nothing. They should be seen as what they are – a fountain of life for those of us bold enough to drink."

"You are a physician, John. You took an oath to preserve life, not take it."

Seward dismissed this with a gesture. "It was an oath sworn in ignorance. I have seen so much since then, learned so much; I will not be bound by actions taken while my education was so incomplete."

"Then you will be bound otherwise, John. I cannot allow you to continue as you have. This truth you think you perceive is a cruel illusion. It has cost the lives of others, and it may yet cost you your soul."

Seward shook his head and laughed lightly, although there was no sense that he was amused. He moved more confidently and Bram flinched away, but Seward edged slowly to one side, not approaching the two men who blocked the only entrance from the room. Van Helsing had not drawn his pistol, and Bram found himself suddenly wishing that he'd had the foresight to bring one of his own.

"I am not the man I once was, old friend. I am much more now. When I wish to leave here, I will brush you aside without effort. But I confess to feeling lonely at times, and I cannot think of more welcome company. I will show you what I have learned and you can judge for yourself whether or not it is truth."

"We have come for another purpose, John. You must know what we intend. I believe that you have a good soul, but your body and mind are diseased, touched by a plague more terrible than any other."

Seward took a step toward them and it seemed to Bram that he grew in stature, that his body had reshaped itself into a more menacing form. He glanced from side to side, surreptitiously seeking something that might serve as a weapon if they were attacked.

Van Helsing drew his pistol then. Their adversary took another step, then halted, his expression troubled. "You also took an oath to preserve life, Abraham. Would you now steal mine?"

"You have already lost your life, my old friend, and much more." And Van Helsing fired.

The pistol seemed inordinately loud in the confined space and Bram's ears continued to ring even after the echoes had died. Seward stood as before, but there was a dark circle in the center of his forehead that had not been there previously, and with a slightly puzzled expression on his face. Bram wondered what lingering life force might hold the man erect, but even as he thought that, Seward's features changed, his mouth relaxing into a wry smile.

"We're past all that now, Van Helsing. Mortality is just a consequence of ignorance. With knowledge comes the power to transcend such petty limitations."

Bram saw the change in Seward's posture and knew the moment was at hand. From his own pocket, he removed the vial of holy water and twisted the cork to unstopper it, retreating awkwardly when Seward seemed to spring directly toward him. He threw his arm up at the moment of impact, losing his grip on the vial and falling heavily on his back with the smaller man, who seemed impossibly heavy and powerful, perched on his chest. There was a sudden intense pain on the side of his neck and he opened his mouth, perhaps to scream.

Something whistled through the air and there was a heavy, muted thud as though someone had sliced into a melon. In the flickering light, Bram stared directly into the madman's face, saw the look of sudden surprise. Then another whispering rush through the air and the staring face was gone, even though Seward's body still pinned him to the floor.

There was a series of thumps as the severed head rolled to a stop.

Revolted beyond measure, Bram pushed the remains of John Seward away. No blood poured from the body, which was now devoid of animation as well as life. He stood up rather unsteadily, one hand clutched to the burning pain on the side of his neck, his eyes widening with sudden horror as he realized what must have happened.

Van Helsing read his expression and clapped him on the shoulder. "Do not be alarmed. He has not infected you. You fell on the lighted candle."

Relief made him weaker than ever and Bram leaned back against the nearest wall, breathing heavily, refusing to look at Seward's remains. "What do we do now?"

"This present danger is past. We will consign the body to the Thames. I would rather have done better for my old friend, but I believe he will understand. Then I must continue my search for the Harkers."

"Do you think they will change as well?"

Van Helsing's face expressed sudden, deep pain. "The taint cannot be escaped. All who are touched by it will eventually be corrupted." And to prove his point, he lifted his arm, and Bram saw a cluster of blisters on the back of his hand, where the holy water had splashed him.

Van Helsing left London the following evening. He had booked passage to Canada, where he hoped to track down the Harkers, who were rumored to have emigrated there. Stoker saw him off, wishing him luck, concealing the fact that he was glad to see the last of the man. Despite what they'd been through together, he felt a growing antipathy, perhaps because Van Helsing's revelations had shown Bram that the world he lived in was not as he had once believed it to be. He returned home fully intending to destroy the vial of blood which lay in one drawer of his desk, but on the brink of doing so, he relented, sat back in his chair and stared broodingly at the still viscous fluid .

Unobserved, Florence Stoker stood at the door of her husband's study, watching him, understanding his fascination with the unnaturally transformed blood. It was a fascination she shared herself, although for different reasons. She had felt its pull ever since that long ago night when her husband had first brought it home, felt it because the same arcane force coursed through her own veins.

Florence Stoker, previously Florence Bascombe, and before that Mina Harker and Mina Murray, turned away at last, tying her bonnet in place and slipping out into the darkness. Bram had little appetite this evening, but she herself was famished.

IMMORTAL MUSE

"Are you saying Frankenstein was real?" Peter's expression was incredulous.

Connie shook her head. "I don't believe there was a monster

with rivets in its neck. But Victor Frankenstein was an actual person with decidedly macabre interests. Shelley altered the name - he was actually Vittorio Fracatta"

"And she based her book on him?"

"Let's just say she drew inspiration from his life. He had this weird theory that life is inherent in every cell, that just because the brain or heart dies doesn't mean the rest of the body isn't still alive. I have proof that they met in Rome and that he invited her to visit his villa in Pesciadora..."

"...but nothing to indicate she ever took him up on his offer, right?"

"No, except ten days unaccounted for at the right time. C'mon, Peter, this is a chance for me to come up with something really original for my thesis."

He was unhappy, but in the end, he agreed.

The Fracatta villa had been vacant since the war. Connie finally found a local official who was willing to grant her permission to enter, at a reasonable price.

"The boards, they must be replaced when you leave, Signora."

"Don't worry. We'll make sure everything is secured when we're done. Are you certain that the family is extinct, that no one has title to the property?"

"No one, Signora. It has been unclaimed since my grandfather's childhood."

After she'd gone, the magistrate shook his head, wondering if he should have mentioned as well that if any descendants of the Fracattas survived, they were almost certainly unwilling to admit their lineage.

"I gather the family died out?"

Connie nodded. "Vittorio was the last of his line, and when he disappeared, no one ever claimed his estate."

"Disappeared."

"Yup. They found the surgeon he had living with him lying dead in the road one day, heart failure most likely, but Vittorio was never seen again."

"So what do you expect to find?" Peter had removed the

boards covering the main door and had broken the rusting lock with the shaft of a crowbar. "A mad scientist's lab? Body parts?"

Connie refused to allow her spirits to be dampened. "Diaries, letters, something to prove Mary Shelley visited. There might be records of his researches, but that's only important if I can prove a link."

The interior was a disaster. The ceiling was down in several places, the furniture covered with dust and mold. Most of the books and papers they found crumbled to dust or were matted together inseparably. Peter complained occasionally during the course of the day, but Connie ignored him.

It was dusk when they found Fracatta's journal, dusty and stained but well preserved otherwise.

Connie flipped to the appropriate dates, read the scrawled Italian quickly. "Here it is! The Shelleys were both here for four days." She read further. "And yes, he gave her a tour of his laboratory. Peter, this is going to make me famous!"

Peter actually found it in himself to be enthusiastic. "But what laboratory? We haven't seen anything like that and we've already been through the whole house."

"Except the cellars."

"Those doors are pretty solid. I don't think I can break them down."

"We'll take the hinges off."

Easier said than done, since they were rusted in place. It was almost midnight before the door finally sagged free, but Connie refused to wait until morning.

"We have flashlights. I have to know tonight, Peter. Just one quick look and then we'll go."

The laboratory was beyond the wine cellar, an enormous cavern carved from the adjacent hillside. Much of the equipment was unrecognizable. The operating table was marked with dark stains. The walls were covered with shelving filled with glass jars, each bunged shut, each containing a preserved body part, some animal, some plainly human.

"An odd place to search for immortality."

"Is that what he was looking for?"

"Sure," Connie nodded. "All scientists are looking for a way to beat death in one way or another."

"But none of them ever do."

"Not yet anyway. C'mon, let's go back to the hostel. We won't find anything here worth bothering with."

They picked their way through the debris back to the doorway and left, while behind them a pair of eyes followed their movements from within a jar of viscous fluid, and in another a hand clenched with frustration, and in still a set of vocal chords tried to produce a plea for release.

MILITARY DEFERMENT

I was involved in a number of unusual operations during the War, but by far the strangest was a secret mission to Marion Island off the coast of South Africa. I had always been skeptical of the rumors of Hitler's interest in the occult as a source of weapons against our enemies, but after our mission to that small island I knew his efforts to be both real and foolhardy.

Originally I had been a marine serving aboard the *Graf Spee*, a posting which brought with it certain advantages while in port. Young women who would not have given me the time of day if I'd been dressed as a civilian proclaimed their devotion with sometimes annoying persistency. As the war progressed, port calls became less frequent and the truth was that we spent most of our days performing brute labor. Every few weeks, the captain would lay to while we repainted the ship, repositioned the framework of our false superstructure, and did whatever else was possible to disguise our identity. Our purpose was to confuse the British patrols as to our whereabouts and probable path, and also to convince them that there was more than one commerce raider operating in the South Atlantic. At times we would paint the name of the *Admiral Scheer* or another warship across our bow, and then make sure that some of our prisoners saw the lettering before we set them free.

In any case, one morning I woke to excruciating pain, a burst appendix, and as a consequence I don't even remember being transferred to our fuel ship and then to a secret base somewhere on the west coast of Africa. As soon as I recovered I began agitating for reassignment, but no word came for nearly a month, during which period I was of little use at the station, whose primary purpose was to monitor radio transmissions.

I had begun to sink into a lethargic depression when the base commander, Captain Vodelfoeg, summoned me to the cubbyhole that served as his office.

"Your vacation is over at last, Henschler. I have fresh orders for you." He was out of uniform, I noticed, and had not shaved that morning. Since his bearing was so lax, I stood at ease without waiting for permission.

"Is the *Spee* then back in this area?"

"The whereabouts of your former ship is a sensitive matter which I will not share with you." I interpreted this as meaning Vodelfoeg knew no more than I on the subject. "You will be boarding the U466 tomorrow at midnight. Private Speer will bring you to the rendezvous point."

"A U-boat?" I was dumbfounded and a bit troubled by the thought. A mild claustrophobia had troubled me since childhood, when I'd been accidentally locked in a closet for several hours. "There must be some mistake, Captain. I've not been trained for that kind of duty."

He waved a dismissive hand in my general direction, already losing interest. "Yes, yes, I know that. Don't worry, Henschler; you're not joining the crew. They are merely transporting you elsewhere. Your actual duties will be revealed when it is appropriate for you to know them." Which meant he didn't know the nature of my assignment either.

Speer was sullenly uncommunicative as if piloting the launch was a penance he was paying for some past misdeed. There was no questioning his navigation, however, because the conning tower of the U-boat rose up out of the water so close to shore that I could almost have jumped to her deck. Instead I crossed in a rubber dinghy, which was on its way back the moment I stepped out of it. I'd been warned to remain silent and descended uneasily but without speaking into the submersible.

I sat unenlightened in the bunk room for several hours and had actually nodded off once or twice before a civilian wearing khaki approached and brusquely introduced himself. "My name is Kroger and I'm in charge of this operation."

I remained dubious but exerted myself to remain calm and respectful. "I'm unclear about my situation, sir. I have received no written orders and no description of my duties. While I don't doubt your word at all, I don't even know if you do in fact have the authority you claim."

For a moment his face clouded and I thought he would respond angrily, but then he visibly regained control of himself. "Fair enough, although I have neither the time nor the inclination to provide much detail. You are part of a small armed contingent whose sole purpose is to provide security while I and two colleagues make a clandestine visit to a small island. The mission should not take more than a few days, after which you will be released for duty elsewhere. The purpose of this mission is most sensitive, so I can provide no details, but it is essentially to secure a certain artifact from a primitive village, by force if necessary, and return safely to this vessel. My authority comes from Der Fuehrer himself, as the captain of this ship will confirm if you doubt my word. Do you have any further questions?"

I did, and quite a large number of them, but there was something forbidding in the man's eyes and tone, so I ventured only one. "How many total in our party, sir?"

His lips thinned but he provided the information. "Fraulein Brausch, Herr Kurst, and myself. You will be one of six soldiers to accompany us."

I refrained from explaining that I was a sailor, not a soldier. "It seems a small number if we are opposed."

This time Kroger made no effort to hide his annoyance. "This is a primitive, agrarian society that confronts us. It is my understanding that they have nothing more daunting than spears. If this frightens you, perhaps one of the crew could be persuaded to take your place."

"That will not be necessary, sir."

We remained below the surface until we were just north of Marion Island, whose identity I learned only after overhearing Fraulein Brausch mention it to her companions in the cramped mess room. Heidi Brausch was a mildly attractive woman in her late twenties whose bearing was more military than most officers I'd met. She seemed to be on casual, though not warm terms with Rudolf Kroger, though merely polite to the third member, Franz Kurst, an overweight, overbearing, clearly uneducated, and not particularly tidy man who perspired profusely and cursed profanely and constantly.

I believe we broached just north of Cape Davis, then cruised clockwise around the island while Kurst stood on deck, peering at the barren coast. We must have been close to Cape Hooker when he finally turned to the deck officer, who hastened below immediately. We slowed to a near stop while several crewmen broke out two rubber dinghies. Since I'd come up to stretch my legs, I offered to help but they had things well in hand. It was already early in the afternoon and I half expected that we'd lay to until the following morning, but one of the sailors mentioned that there'd been heightened British activity in this area recently and that their captain had no intention of remaining in these waters any longer than was absolutely necessary.

The rest of our party came up on deck. Kroger, Brausch, and Kurst went in the first boat with two of the escort party, a seasoned veteran named Zweig, whom I liked and who was nominally in charge of the marine contingent, and a younger man named Kaiser with whom I'd barely spoken. I joined the other three in the second, and we pushed off toward shore.

At this point I knew very little about our purpose. Zweig had explained Kurst's presence; he had previously visited the island and had apparently seen some artifact which we were to retrieve. Kroger and Brausch were both archaeologists, which puzzled me. What possible value could they contribute to the war effort? We were fighting in the present, not the past. Zweig had simply shrugged, apparently unconcerned and uninterested, but he later mentioned that the two scientists were not entirely happy with the mission either.

It was uncomfortably hot and humid when we landed, pulling the boats up onto shore and concealing them between two rocky outcrops. One of the men was stationed to watch them while the rest of us trekked inland. We had seen no indication that anyone was aware of our presence, but Zweig, who frequently deferred to Kroger for instructions, reminded us to remain alert. We spread out to protect the three civilians as best we could on the uneven ground.

We climbed steadily for the first few minutes, after which the ground leveled out. The forest started here, mostly stunted trees and heavy brush, but the vegetation was soon lush and began to impede our progress. On two occasions we stopped while Kurst and Kroger exchanged words, not entirely amicably, and Brausch stood by disdainfully.

After the second pause we changed direction and soon crossed a narrow but serviceable path which I at first took for a game trail. We followed it for only a very short period, however, before it brought us within sight of a stockaded village. The protective walls were badly in need of repair, and the main gate had stood open long enough that saplings had grown up all around it, so that it could not have been closed without considerable effort. There were clusters of dense shrub growth scattered all about. We could see thatched huts inside the walls as well as a few that had spread beyond. These seemed for the most part to be in good condition, though primitive. Several goats roamed the village, but there was no sign of human habitation.

"Looks deserted," observed Kroger.

"They're about," replied Kurst, who was shading his eyes against the brilliant sun. "They'll have seen us coming and they know about modern weapons and uniforms. We don't look like a trade mission, after all."

The man's certainty convinced me and I held my weapon more tightly, my eyes scanning for any sign of an ambush. Nevertheless, we were inside the stockade a few minutes later, and I still hadn't seen any sign of the local inhabitants.

"It's this one, up here. The witch doctor's hut." Kurst led us to one of the smaller dwelling places. Zweig posted Kaiser and myself outside while he accompanied the three civilians into the hut. They kept their voices inaudibly low but they weren't inside very long. When they emerged, Kroger was holding a small bag made out of animal skin, his expression neutral. Kurst looked pleased with himself, but Fraulein Brausch made no attempt at all to conceal her bored contempt for the entire situation.

When we emerged from the stockade, Kurst suddenly told us all to stop where we were. "Whatever you do, don't fire a weapon unless we're attacked." I looked to Zweig, but his face was impassive and he merely nodded, acknowledgment if not acquiescence.

A lone figure stood waiting for us, dressed in simple cloth garments but with a brilliantly rainbow colored sash. He stood in our path with his arms crossed, remained motionless while Kurst addressed him in what I assumed was the local tongue. After a few sentences, the native responded, and the two spoke for several minutes while the rest of us awaited enlightenment.

"This is Moro, the witch doctor," Kurst explained at last. "He knows why we've come."

"Will he try to stop us?" Kroger seemed perfectly at ease, perhaps reassured by our weapons. Personally, I wasn't so confident. There was something about the situation I didn't like.

"No, apparently not." For the first time, Kurst seemed uncertain. "He hasn't even accused us of theft, although he knows we've taken the shield rings. They were afraid we wanted something else, apparently. I don't understand it, but we're apparently welcome to take them away."

"The man's obviously not a fool," interjected Brausch. "We could wipe out his entire village in seconds."

"I don't believe he's afraid," Kurst replied firmly. "In any case, his people will come out of cover if I tell him that it's safe for them to do so."

"Where are they hiding then?" Kroger swiveled his head, as did I, but there was nothing to be seen.

"All around us, apparently. I assume your men are steady, Zweig."

"We are German soldiers, Herr Kurst."

Our guide spoke to the native once more and then we were all clutching our weapons tightly. The villagers emerged all around us, some having lain concealed within bushes, others in holes in the ground that were covered with thatch. Some were hidden within the roofs of the small huts, and at least two had been crouched among the goats with skins covering their bodies so that we had taken them for members of the herd. Most were armed with knives, a few with spears, and a few more with a mismatched collection of modern firearms. We were better equipped, but I didn't need to be told that we could have been wiped out easily had they been so inclined.

So why were they letting us steal whatever it was that Kroger held in his hand? Was this all a ruse to put us off guard? It seemed not, because after another brief round of conversation, Kurst indicated that we should go, and we returned to the beach without incident.

On the way back to the submarine, I rode in the boat with Kroger's party. Brausch's temper grew steadily more heated. "I interrupted my work simply to retrieve these baubles?"

"It was felt that two experts should accompany the party, to ensure that the artifacts were genuine." Kroger seemed distracted now, and he wouldn't meet her eyes.

"Genuine? Genuine what? Trinkets from a culture about which I know nothing. Objects of questionable historical value surrounded by a quaint but obviously fantastic legend. Someone should be disciplined for authorizing this stupendous waste of valuable time."

Suddenly Kroger became agitated. "Hush, Heidi. Remember that this mission was authorized at the highest level. The very highest level."

She didn't seem at all mollified, but she fell silent for the rest of the trip.

The First Officer was waiting on deck when we arrived. "I trust your mission was a success," was his greeting.

Fraulein Brausch's temper had not improved. "A success?" She turned and abruptly snatched the bag from Kroger's hand and reached inside. Her long, slender fingers emerged holding what was clearly an ornamental ring fashioned as a diminutive shield painted red and white and black. "If you consider a bag of costume jewelry a success, then I suppose it was."

Kurst must have realized what Brausch intended because he lunged toward her, shouting "No, don't", but it was too late. The ring now adorned her left hand.

"Now if it were a diamond..."she began.

"You fool!" Kurst literally stamped his feet with anger. "I warned you about trying it on. According to the legend, it cannot be removed while you live."

"Nonsense," she answered, and immediately tried to slide it off. It resisted her efforts and she frowned. "Stuck on a knuckle. Wait one moment."

But we didn't have one moment. From out of the clouds, a British warplane dropped suddenly, its machine guns strafing the deck with frightening accuracy. I confess that I had been surreptitiously watching Fraulein Brausch's breasts at the time; she was almost the only white woman I had seen for the better part of the previous year. So it was that I saw the bullets strike, and the top of her torso literally burst open with the impact. Then I was leaping for the gangway and rushing below, ignoring the sound of screams behind me.

I remember only snatches of the next few minutes. Zweig, Kaiser, the First Officer, Kurst, and several others died during that first strafing run. Kroger and one deckhand descended before me, and one of the nameless marines came behind, although he died the following day of internal bleeding. We submerged immediately but the British pilot had not been alone. Other planes dropped depth charges, at least a score over the next hour. The bombardment inflicted considerable superficial damage, but no mortal blows, although I have never been so frightened as I was while we lay silent and motionless on the ocean floor waiting for our deaths.

When things fell quiet, we circumnavigated the island while still submerged. The conning tower had been damaged, the periscope was not functioning properly, and the captain decided to surface during the darkness to see if they could be repaired quickly. I was not among the party that went above; in fact, I had been invited to Kroger's cabin for a drink. The man was terrified by the consequences of his failure; the skin bag had been lost in the scramble to get undercover along with its contents and he wanted to explain to me, as the only other surviving member of the shore party, why they had been so important.

"According to Kurst, the rings originated among a small tribe called the Komari on the fringe of the Zulu empire. It was said that even the Zulu feared their warriors because they could not be killed no matter how gravely wounded. Finally, Cetschwayo, the last of the great Zulu kings, decided that their existence was a challenge to his supremacy. He raised an immense army who overcame the Komari by cutting off their hands. Once separated from the shield rings, the warriors became mortal."

"But how did they end up in this remote place?"

"Cetschwayo feared the power of the rings because those who wore them were subject to some unspecified curse. He ordered a group of warriors to carry them to the coast, sail far out to sea, and throw them into the ocean. Unfortunately, a storm drove them ashore on this island and all of them died except one, who tried to convince the village chief to finish the job. The chief liked the idea of becoming invulnerable, murdered the last survivor, and eventually fell prey to the curse, whatever it was. Kurst never found out that little detail."

"And the villagers have guarded the shield rings ever since?"

"Apparently."

"And what do you think this curse might be?" But I didn't receive an answer to this question until later because that's when all hell broke loose.

I could hear shouting and what sounded like a scream. With my sidearm in my hand, I rushed through the narrow corridors of the U-boat and arrived just as Heidi Brausch descended from the deck.

I had seen the woman die. There wasn't the slightest doubt in my mind that her wounds had been almost instantly mortal. But here she stood among us, apparently in excellent health. The bullets had torn away most of the clothing on her upper body, so I was able to see her bare breasts and chest quite clearly just before one of the officers offered her his jacket. There wasn't a mark on them, no sign at all of the destruction I had seen only hours before. That was so shocking in itself that it never occurred to me until later that she had managed to cling to the deck rail for all the time since the initial attack, even though we'd been fully submerged for most of that time. She should have drowned a hundred times over, but she had not.

It appeared that the story of the shield rings was not fantasy after all.

Brausch and Kroger were taken to the captain's cabin and the rest of us were ordered back to our duties. Since I had none, I returned to my bunk in a state of considerable confusion and alarm. Clearly the shield ring did in fact have some supernatural power. I wanted to deny that fact, but I knew there was no rational explanation for what had just happened. I thought about the implications of an army of invincible warriors committed to the defense of the Reich, but despite the obvious advantages, I was troubled by the concept. And I still didn't know the nature of the supposed curse that accompanied the shield ring.

I found out about that on the following day.

Emergency repairs had restored us to seaworthiness, although the engines could not be trusted at full speed and the forward torpedo tubes were all inoperable. There had been considerable hull damage, although we remained watertight, and the radio mast had to be replaced. The sailors aboard were not entirely unhappy, since the extensive repairs required would almost certainly remove them from combat for at least several weeks. All we had to do was reach a safe port, probably somewhere on the French coast.

I had offered to help, but the crew had no time for me, so I was napping on my bunk when the trouble began. Brausch had remained out of sight for the most part since her miraculous reappearance, probably at the captain's request. I had overheard uneasy talk on several occasions, and several members of the crew were openly frightened. The specifics of our mission had never been explained to them, and speculation about her survival encompassed everything from mechanical bodies to vampirism.

For whatever reason, perhaps simple restlessness, Brausch was in the passageway outside the bunkroom when she discovered the downside of her new immortality. Her screams were so loud and prolonged that for the first few seconds I thought they were the sound of tearing metal and that we had breached the hull. I was the first to arrive, closely followed by several sailors, and I had a clear view until the officers arrived. Fraulein Brausch lay in the passageway, her body convulsing like a scalded cat. She arched her back at impossible angles and threw herself back and forth between the walls, her face contorted in agony. Under normal circumstances, I doubt she could have survived the initial seizure, but if anything they intensified with the passage of time, and it required four stout sailors to hold her down while the ship's doctor administered a soporific.

The drug had no effect, nor did the painkiller he used later, after they had somehow managed to move her thrashing body into one of the small cabins. By then the crew was buzzing with new speculations, and I had gone to find Kroger.

I found him sitting by himself. "Have they quieted her yet?" He spoke to me without looking up.

"No." I was surprised at how unsteady my voice was. "What in God's name is happening?"

He sighed. "According to Kurtz, the rings protect the wearer against death or injury, but not against pain. The pain is only…deferred for a while."

The image of Brausch's body as it was struck by the machine gun rounds made my stomach clench. "How long will it last?"

"I have no idea."

In fact, the pain from her wounds lasted for only an hour or so. The screaming stopped abruptly and one of the sailors on duty said she had actually relaxed for a few seconds before the new trouble started, apparently in reaction to the drowning. Mercifully, the walls contained most of the strangled retching that ensued, because that portion of her ordeal lasted for almost a full day, after which the doctors finally managed to sedate her.

"Her mind's gone," one of the sailors confided in me. "She just stares without seeing anything." I couldn't confirm the accuracy of that statement, but Brausch remained in her cabin with an armed guard just outside the door.

The captain was able to raise the periscope, but he could not traverse it across the horizon, so our viewpoint was extremely narrow. For that reason, he was reluctant to surface during the day. The damage we'd sustained made it necessary to rise every forty-eight hours to freshen our air, an act we invariably performed just after midnight. It was on the third such occasion that the British found us.

I was actually asleep when the klaxons went off and the deck began to drop away, spilling me out of my bunk. Almost immediately there was an enormous explosion and the ship literally shivered around me. We'd been hit by either a bomb or a torpedo; I never did find out which one. There were more explosions after that, but they were comparatively muted. The lights flickered and dimmed but did not go out, and I cautiously climbed to my feet. The deck remained canted at a sharp angle and it was difficult to maneuver, but I eventually made my way out into the passageway.

A crewman climbed past me, his face a mask of terror. "We're sinking!" he shouted. "I must get out!"

But he didn't. None of us did.

I'll spare you the details of the next hour. They aren't relevant to the story I have to tell. Suffice it to say that the hull was breached in more than one place, the captain and most of the crew were already dead, and we were sinking to the ocean floor with inoperable engines.

Five of us eventually gathered in the mess area. Kroger, two sailors, myself, and Heidi Brausch. There may have been other survivors trapped elsewhere but the remaining compartments were sealed off and possibly filled with water. One of the sailors sat motionless in a corner, refusing to speak or acknowledge our presence. The other, Hans something-or-other, alternated between calm acceptance of our fate and wild hysteria. Kroger was withdrawn but appeared to be in control of himself. Brausch, on the other hand, sat with her arms crossed, watching us alertly, responding when spoken to but without volunteering anything. There was something about her attitude that disturbed me, but I was too preoccupied by my own imminent death to lend it much thought.

Hans informed us that the batteries would provide light and limited power for at least a few hours. "More than enough time, since we will all have suffocated before the lights are gone." He also deflated every escape plan I suggested. There was no way we could get through the hull, and even if we did, our depth was too great. If we lasted until we reached the surface, we would die painfully of the bends.

The second sailor slashed his wrists with a knife before we could stop him. That meant the oxygen would last a little longer for the rest of us.

Kroger approached Brausch, who barely acknowledged his presence. "I apologize for having brought you to this, Heidi." He touched her arm and I suddenly realized they must have been lovers at one time, although probably no longer.

"No apology is necessary, Rudy. I'll miss you."

At first I thought this confirmed the rumor that she'd lost her mind, but after several minutes I realized she was speaking the simple truth. We were all doomed, but she would survive because of the shield ring. Hans was a little quicker than I.

Angry shouts tore me from my thoughts and I looked up to see the crewman struggling with Kroger. He held one of the galley knives in his hand and was struggling to break free and approach Brausch. Kroger was almost the man's match but not quite, and as I scrambled to my feet, uncertain whether or not to help, his grip faltered and Hans plunged the knife into his chest. The archaeologist stood upright for just a second or two, then closed his eyes and silently collapsed.

I moved to intervene then, but the disabled U-boat chose that moment to shift position and I was thrown violently across the compartment, striking my head against a stanchion. When I recovered my senses, it was nearly done. Brausch pulled the knife out of her throat and plunged it into Hans' abdomen. She barely even bled, but he more than made up for it. I saw that much before losing consciousness, expecting never to open my eyes again.

Obviously, I was wrong. I don't know how long it was before I recovered, but the air was noticeably foul and the lights were fading. I was troubled by a grating noise that I could not identify until I slowly sat up and looked around. At the opposite end of the compartment, Brausch was using a knife to scratch at the hatchway. I laughed silently; it would take years to cut through the metal plating. But then I realized that she might well have years. If the ring protected her until she was out of danger, she'd have all the time she needed.

I thought about that until my head began to swim, not entirely from oxygen deprivation. And then I silently began to creep toward her.

It was relatively merciful. I struck with a cleaver, severing her wrist before she even knew I was there. She died quickly and with comparatively little pain, nothing compared to what she had already experienced. Then I put on the ring, picked up her fallen knife, and resumed the work she'd begun.

I estimate that it took ten years to reach the next compartment. The oxygen ran out first although my chest continues to rise and fall, through reflex I suspect. The lights went next. When I broke through the hatchway, water rushed in. This hampered my movements somewhat but caused no other inconvenience and I soon adapted to it. If there'd been anything to eat, I might have put on considerable muscle mass working under those conditions, but there was none to be had, and I never felt a hunger pang.

The next hatchway took only half as long because it had been damaged and I was able to remove it in one piece.

Getting through the hull was more of a problem. I have no way to measure the passage of time down here, but I wore out every knife, fork, spoon, and tool on the ship scratching my way through the metal. Twenty years, thirty, perhaps even more before I had a hole through which I could extend my hand. Another ten and it was almost large enough. It would have taken even longer if I needed to sleep or rest, but I don't. Nor do I appear to be aging. It seems that during a crisis, all normal physical changes are suspended.

In another few days, I could leave this sunken tomb, but I have stopped work and will not resume. I've scratched this account into the walls as a warning. As the day of my liberation grew close, I suddenly remembered Brausch's ordeal after she was recovered from the sea. She was immersed for almost a day, and later experienced the sensation of drowning for a similar period of time. If I escape this ship and return to the surface, I would face at least thirty years of that same sensation, as well as a like period of starvation, and a shorter case of the bends. It is a fate I will not accept.

Instead, as soon as I have finished these last few words, I will grind my wrist against the rough metal edges I have cut until my hand is severed and I am free of the shield ring. I expect to feel no pain until the act is done, after which I will drown quickly and comparatively easily. I understand now why the natives on Marion Island willingly relinquished these cursed things. As tempting as it may be to hold death and pain at arm's length, all deferments eventually end, and sometimes the ultimate cost is far too great.

www.ingramcontent.com/pod-product-compliance
Lightning Source LLC
Chambersburg PA
CBHW072057170626
46813CB00004B/1395